ICIE

PAMELA LEIGH STARR

Genesis Press, Inc.

Indigo Love Stories

An imprint of Genesis Press, Inc.
Publishing Company

Genesis Press, Inc.
P.O. Box 101
Columbus, MS 39703

ISBN-13: 978-1-58571-275-5
ISBN-10: 1-58571-275-2
Manufactured in the United States of America

First Edition 2002
Second Edition 2008

Visit us at www.genesis-press.com or call at 1-888-Indigo-1

DEDICATION

To my daughter, Tabitha, with a future of limitless opportunities. Become a physical therapist like Icie or ANYTHING that touches your soul and fulfills your Dreams!

CHAPTER 1

Rrrrrr-ing!

"Just ignore it," Icie Ellis commanded slipping her feet into her lucky white tennis shoes.

Rrrrrr-ing!

Walk straight out the door. You're already going to be late for your exam. Nothing's more important than that. But then again—it could be—maybe the hospital—Mr. M. No, he was still hanging in there.

Rrrrrr-ing! Books in one hand. Rrrrrr-ing! Keys in the other. Rrrrrr-ing! It seemed to scream urgent. Icie did an about face at the door to her dorm room, shifted the heavy load of books in her arms and picked up the phone.

"Icie."

"Ray? Something's wrong." It wasn't a question. Somehow, she had known, had even let the phone ring because she didn't want to face her own instinctive feelings. Ray Armstrong, a friend to both her and Mr. M, breathed heavily, his message suddenly too painful to deliver. "Ray?" Icie repeated. "It's that time, isn't it?"

"Yes."

"I'll be there." She threw her books onto a chair and was out the door, down the stairs and inside her relic of a car; a 1988 Nova. She leaned forward and turned the key, her hands steady, her heart fluttering with nerves. Would she make it to the hospital in time to say goodbye forever?

Silence was her answer. She turned the key once again. Nothing. Icie froze. Not a muscle in her body moved. This was not happening. A single tear squeezed out of the corner of her eye, rolled down her cheek to land on her fisted hand surrounding the key and ignition. She sniffed and turned the key once again. A reluctant sputter vibrated throughout the car before the engine came to life.

"Thank you, thank you, thank you!" she muttered, pulling away from the curb and into the busy traffic.

Ten minutes later she was on the elevator, taking her up to the now familiar floor; familiar nurses' station, familiar faces. She maneuvered her way past it all, completely dry eyed—if another tear fell she'd lose what little self control, what little composure, she had.

"Icie." Ray came toward her walking out of the same door she had entered and exited too many times in the last month.

"Ray—is he—?"

"No, not yet. I called Clay."

"The infamous son."

"Icie, you don't know him. He's not—"

A white uniformed nurse came out of the hospital room. One Icie hadn't seen before, and she didn't like the strange look on the woman's face.

"Who's that?" she asked Ray.

"Nurse Helen."

Icie didn't need to ask that question. She didn't need to know that little inconsequential fact. She was stalling. She didn't want to say good-bye, but she didn't want to miss her last moments with Mr. M. either. Ray seemed to understand how she was feeling. He took her hand, clasped it and held it to his solid roughened one.

"Your hands are as cold as your name," he told her.

"Ha!" Icie eked out, a feeble reaction to the ritual name teasing. He was trying to give her courage, trying to make her feel better. They both knew that. They stood close straining their ears to hear what nurse Helen was whispering to her co-worker at the desk.

"The man's dying and he wants ice."

"That's me!" Icie's voice rang out urgently. She gave Ray's hand a soft squeeze of thanks before releasing it to rush for the door. Pausing a second, she slowly entered the room.

He was still as dea—. No, not that—He couldn't be—Not yet! She hadn't told him how much she'd come to love him. How much she had enjoyed talking to him, how his wisdom had kept her going, kept her strong.

"Icie." His voice was loud and firm. Not like someone who was dying. "It's about time."

But her relief was short-lived. The force of his reprimand degenerated into harsh, raspy breaths as he attempted to feed his dying lungs. He sounded so much worse. He looked so exhausted. This was his last day, these were her last moments with him. He coughed. The spasms shook his entire body, bed and all. Icie waited. The sight of Mr. M. so weak and help-less was heartbreaking, almost unendurable. The coughing spell ended. Icie waited once again. He slowly continued.

"…time you got here." A long, heavy breath ended the statement as if a tremendous power had forced the words past his throat.

"Say no more. I'm here now."

She leaned against the silver guardrail of the hospital bed and touched his soft weathered brown cheek staring into his quiet eyes.

"I see that," he said so softly Icie could barely hear. "Come closer. Feed an old man's fantasy. Sit." A deep, long breath later. "Hold my hand. Tell me your dreams."

She did as he asked, sitting on the edge of the bed, taking his hand, forcing hers to remain steady, and gave him the same answer she had over two years ago, not long after she had met him. "I want to be a Physical Therapist. I want to work with kids. I want to help them mend their lives and their bodies."

"What a beautiful dream."

"You always say that, Mr. M."

"True."

They were both quiet, even though there was no more time for quiet. Time was running out. "I wish I could mend your body, Mr. M."

"Cancers got me, girl."

"I know." Icie laid her head upon his shoulder. "I'm going to miss you."

"Same here."

They were silent once again, their mutual loss understood and already being mourned. There was nothing more to say except, "I love you, Old Man."

"Same here," he whispered without a cough or a pause.

"And I'll never forget you."

His eyes smiled at hers. Then, as they shifted upward toward the door, they lit up into the most joyous expression she had ever seen on his face. What was he seeing? Angels? Icie had heard of that kind of thing happening. She was afraid to turn around. Instead she whispered, "Why do you have to leave me now?"

"It's time," he told her. "You know I love you. Now be a good girl and let me say goodbye to my son."

"I'd drag him in here on his butt if I could find him."

"He's here."

Icie quickly turned to discover a huge mountain of a man towering above them.

"Can I have a few words with my dying father. Alone." He bore his deep, dark, angry eyes into hers. The steady gaze seemed to condemn her.

"Icie?" Mr. M. implored softly.

She turned toward the old man who had meant so much to her and whispered, "The angels might take you away, but you'll always be in my heart." Then slowly inching to the edge of the bed, she stood to face this son who had had no time for his dying father. The contempt she felt for him radiated from every cell in her body, shouted at him with each movement she made.

One last caress of Mr. M.'s dear face and she was gone.

As soon as she was out of the hospital room, she searched for Ray. He was at her side before she could scan the hall, the comforting arms of a friend surrounding her.

"So, Clay came," Icie whispered, resentful of the intrusion and relieved at the same time for Mr. M.'s sake.

"I never doubted that he would."

"I did. I'm glad I was wrong." She kept her other feelings, though they were no secret to Ray, unsaid. "Seeing Clay, live and in person, is so odd. There's no doubt he's Mr. M.'s son."

"A younger version of his father. That's Clay."

Icie pushed out a deep frustrated sigh. "He hates me. I'm losing a father in there and his son hates me!"

"No, that can't be."

"And the feeling's mutual!"

"I can tell," Ray told her calmly and without a bit of censorship. Why was she talking about this now! Icie could care less how Clay Mammoth felt about her. It had to be that she was going a little crazy, already grieving for Mr. M. and turning into a selfish fool. Ray was grieving, too. Icie shook herself good, grabbed each one of Ray's strong hands, gave them a big squeeze and tilted her head toward the hospital room. "Why don't you go inside, say your goodbyes."

"I've done that." He turned away releasing her hands. Ray cleared his throat a few times.

"It was right after I called you. We talked."

Now it was Icie's turn to lay comforting hands on Ray's shoulder. "These last few moments should be for them," Ray continued, "father and son."

She nodded her head in understanding if not agreement. Clay Mammoth, had no right to hog the last minutes with the man he had totally ignored, so absent that Icie had never met him. The few times he was in town he was either practicing for a game, playing a game, or leaving for a game, in and out in such a hurry there was no time for a meeting.

Mr. M. would say, "You just missed Clay," or "I tried to get Clay to stay and have dinner with us but he had someplace to go."

Whether it was a game, an endorsement, or just fun, all Icie knew of Clay Mammoth was excuses. Fame, fortune, and an ego longer than the Mississippi River. That was Clay. His life was all about him. It did not matter if he was racing across the field for the New Orleans Crescents, being interviewed after a win or making a commercial. It was always the same.

Oh, he was good, a superb athlete, and an asset to the Crescents. A superb athlete, yes! A heart, no!

"Uncle Ray" a deep sorrowful voice interrupted her thoughts.

Icie stared at Clay Mammoth, his dark eyes red-rimmed. He sniffed. The sound was strange coming from such a big man. He swallowed. The muscles in his neck contracted. He raised his hands, palms flat out staring at them, then folded his arms as if he didn't know what to do with them. It was obvious that he was hurting. "He's gone. My dad's gone" His chin rested on his solid chest.

"I know, son." Ray released her and hugged the huge man, his arms barely meeting around the football player.

"He was hurting," Clay confided. "He was in pain—"

Standing only a few steps away, Icie strained to hear about Mr. M.'s last moments. She needed to know.

"—but he had a lot to say," Clay whispered to Ray. I know. He told me."

"I had a lot to say to him myself."

There was anger on Clay's face that Icie couldn't begin to understand. She unashamedly listened to the conversation. She felt she had a right. She was family. Almost. How many times had Mr. M. called her daughter'?

"Did you tell him everything you wanted to say?" Ray was asking. "Yeah." Clay nodded, his eyes suddenly turning hard. "He talked about this woman. The young, fat one I saw in the picture last Christmas when I stopped to give dad his present."

The muscles in Icie's face tensed. He talked as if she weren't standing right there beside them.

"Icie?" Ray turned to her. So did Clay.

Fat? She wasn't fat. Big boned, voluptuous, not fat. Clay's hard eyes were still boring into her.

"What are you still doing here gold-digger?"

"Gold digger?"

"Clay." One of Ray's hand rested on a muscled arm the size of a small tree trunk.

"What did you do? Tell him lies? Seduce an old dying man to get your hands on my money? That was your game, wasn't it?"

Icie was stunned. Money? Clay Mammoth thought she was after his money? She stared at him, her eyes unwavering, almost frozen.

"I see that it was. The game is over. You lost, and know now that you will never get a dent of my money. Never."

Icie was outraged, but said nothing.

Nurse Helen was suddenly between them breaking the standoff. "Can you please take this outside? There are sick people in here."

"Don't worry, it's over;" Icie answered the nurse, and then in a voice that would freeze Lake Pontchartrain in the heat of a New Orleans summer; she finally spoke to Clay. "Think what you like. I have already gotten everything I ever wanted or needed from Mr. M."

"You fat tramp—"

"Stop it boy!" Ray had somehow wrapped his arms around Clay from behind, and although his hands did not meet, the pressure against his chest seemed to be enough to hold him back.

"I'll talk to you later; Ray" Icie said, as she hurried out of the hospital just before a waterfall of silent tears fell down her face.

Those were the first, and last, tears Icie cried. She went back to her dorm and, pushing aside the pain and outrage throbbing inside of her; consoled herself with the memory of a man she'd come to love. She moved through her tiny apartment, cleaning every crack and crevice as her mind rolled back to her first encounter with Ray and Mr. M.

As always, she had been working the night shift at the toll plaza for the Crescent City Connection, the bridge that crossed the Mighty Mississippi connecting downtown New Orleans to the west bank of the river. The traffic was slow, as usual. Most late night drivers used the toll tag booth that didn't require an attendant. Icie forced herself to concentrate on the notes scribbled in the margins of the book, worried about her first exam. It was hard enough to get accepted into LSU Medical School to study physical therapy, she had to make sure that she made it through the two and a half years of training. She had been questioning her ability to do just that. The book before her seemed to be too thick, holding too much knowledge that was too extensive and much too hard for her to hold inside her head.

In despair and uncertainty, Icie glanced around staring at the few cars driving by in the lanes beside her. She didn't want to do this for the rest of her life. She didn't want to be this. So she went back to the process of forcing important facts into her head before a car decided to pass through her lane.

"Skeletal muscles work by performing isometric, isotonic, or eccentric contractions. Rehabilitation of many injuries in physical therapy will often focus on the many different ways a muscle can contract." She closed her eyes and mumbled over and over again. When she opened her eyes, she found herself staring at a very attractive middle-aged man with serious light brown eyes staring back at her.

"Muscles? Some interesting studying, I bet." He handed her a five dollar bill and told her to keep the change before driving away.

That was when she met Ray and the first of many tips and frequent predawn visits to her toll booth. She didn't know it at the time, but Mr. M. had been in the back seat of the PT Cruiser; that new old-fashioned modem type car that had become so popular. She would never be able to look at one without thinking of Mr. M.

Icie found herself standing in the middle of her sparkling clean dorm room. What to do now?

"Live your dreams," Mr. M.'s voice sounded in her head. "Build your character."

Spotting the books she had left on the chair earlier; Icie scooped them up and went to take an exam, better late than never.

The funeral was beautiful. A local vocalist sang Mr. M.'s favorite song, a gospel rendition of Wade in the Water. Lying in his hospital bed, Mr. M. had hummed along with her many times as she sang this song to him.

The priest honored his memory with few but powerful words that described Mr. M. to a T. Ray's eulogy reflected on the life of his employer; and friend. He held up steady and strong as ever. Clay Mammoth appeared next. That's when the beauty died. His barely coherent blubbering turned her stomach. Even though every other soul in the church seemed to think his act was sincere, Icie couldn't believe that it was. Clay turned Mr. M.'s funeral into a self-absorbed discourse revolving completely around him. He spoke of his loss, his misery. Not one word was uttered about the man he called father. Icie left the church before he was through. She sat in her little Nova perspiring in the heat of May, her air-conditioning having died ages ago.

The pall-bearers carefully carried Mr. M. to the waiting hearse. Clay stopped performing long enough to help carry his father's casket along with Ray and an

awesome representative of the Crescent defensive line.
Icie smiled sadly at the sight. Mr. M. would have
loved this. Her smile faded. What he wouldn't have
liked was the gathering of newspaper reporters,
cameramen and sports personalities outside of the
church, all waiting to catch a glimpse of the grieving
son.

Icie was the last to join the long line of cars in the
solemn procession heading to the graveyard. There
were so many people. So many people she didn't
know. For the last two years it had always been Mr.
M, Ray and herself. Everyone else here today had to
be friends of Clay's.

She parked but did not step out of the hot car. She
could not tolerate another of Clay Mammoth's
performances. Witnessing his theatrics would make
her scream, rant and rave at the unfairness of death
and the unfairness of Mr. M. having had such a lousy
son. So she sat and perspired in her black skirt and
white blouse, quietly mourning until every car
departed. Only then did she get out herself.

Icie walked up the graveled road and turned at its
end coming around a large tombstone unique to New
Orleans. They were designed so that loved ones could
be buried above the soggy, swampy ground found in
southern Louisiana. Her view of the grave site clear;
Icie felt a sudden urge to run. The dark condemning
eyes of Clay Mammoth landed on her.

"What the hell are you doing here?" The upper half of his body twisted her way.

Icie stood where she was, staring up, but not too far, having been blessed with more than average height. As before, when she saw him her tongue seemed to have trouble finding words. She wasn't sure how to respond to his rudeness—what to say—if she should say anything at all. In the silence between them, Clay turned completely toward her; his attention focused on her. Icie could have sworn she saw a glimpse of deep sorrow but then his face turned as dark as before, once again commanding. "Go away!"

He waved a huge arm at her. His other hand hung above his shoulder; a dark custom made suit jacket draped across it. Still Icie said nothing. She stared at the wide shoulders turned away from her once again wondering if the pain she thought she saw was simply wishful thinking. She wanted to believe that Clay Mammoth actually cared for and loved his father.

"You must realize that you're not going to get anything from him. No one is, he's gone now."

"I don't want anything." The outrage she'd felt at their last meeting surfaced once again squelching any hopeful feelings she had regarding Mr. M.'s son. "I came to say goodbye."

"Do it and go!" he growled without sparing another glance in her direction, his entire six-three two-hundred fifty pound frame stiff as a board.

More theatrics. What else should she have expected? Obviously an audience of one was still an audience. Icie took a deep breath and spoke directly to Mr. M, but only loud enough for her to hear. I will honor you by fulfilling my dream and living my life truthfully. I love you." Icie turned and left without another word.

Ray intercepted her before she could reach her car. "Icie, don't go away mad. Clay didn't mean what he said."

"So you heard?" At Ray's nod, Icie contradicted. "He does."

"You caught him at a bad time. He'd just asked everyone to leave him alone to say goodbye, then you showed up. That must have thrown him. You haven't met the real Clay. He hasn't seen the real you either."

"And he won't, Ray. Not now, not ever I'm gone."

"You're not coming to the repast?"

"Who would I know there but you, Ray? Who would Mr. M. have known?"

Ray sadly shrugged his shoulders seeing the truth in her words.

Icie left with a sadness in her heart, but a determination that would have lit Mr. M.'s eyes with pride. The next few months weren't easy. She spent her days at school, her evenings and her nights divided into intervals of sleep and work in the toll booth, without the respite and comfort of time spent with Mr. M.

Ray tried to fill in, and in their shared grief, their friendship grew deeper.

Icie graduated, not with honors but far from the last in her class. Ray had come to her graduation, and they kept in touch over the years. He had even attempted to drag her to the reading of Mr. M.'s will. The same will Clay Mammoth had contested. Unsuccessful in that dispute, he next tried to prove his father incompetent. The man was beyond selfish. Icie wanted nothing to do with Clay Mammoth and his money. She had enough of her own and even when she didn't, survived without it.

Helping children deal with overcoming near crippling injuries, that was her life. She took pride in her work. Mr. M. would have been proud to see her dream come true.

CHAPTER 2

"You will!" Icie Ellis demanded of her patient.

"I can't." Little Antonia Lopez grimaced with a distinct twist to her lips as she stood between the parallel bars. Beads of perspiration on her brow attested to the pain the ten-year-old must endure to merely lift her foot off the floor.

"You will!"

"I can't!" A note of despair; the first Icie had heard during today's session, laced her tiny voice.

Icie moved to stand before her motioning for her assistant Steve to take over behind her. She knew that simply holding the weight of her body on her legs was a strain for Antonia, but she should have moved beyond that milestone two sessions ago. Fear was stopping her. Now was the time to push. Laying the palm of her hand on each side of the frightened, panic filled face, Icie forced the child to focus. "You will, Antonia. Not just because I want you to, not just because Mr. Steve wants you to, not even for your parents, but because you want to. You will!"

"How do you know?" the little girl asked, tears gathering in her eyes. "I just know." And it was true,

Icie just knew when to push, when to pull back, when her patient could truly do no more. Now wasn't the time to coddle even if she wanted to coddle. She would stop the session after this last try but she would not let Antonia know that. Part of her success with her patients was a show of being pushy and relentless without revealing the deep sympathy she actually felt for them all. If Icie listened to her heart she'd have grabbed Antonia in her arms, hugged her tight and told her she wouldn't have to do these painful exercises ever again. But then she would never walk, never retrain her muscles to move the way they were meant to move. And so, Icie the therapist hardened her heart, stared into the little girl's eyes despite the pain, willed her the strength and the power to raise her foot an inch off the floor.

"You did it!" Steve suddenly yelled. "You did it, Toni!"

It took a second for Icie to comprehend the words coming out of her assistant's mouth. But when she did, Icie pulled Antonia into her arms, hugging the child with so much joy and relief she was shaking with it. She could stop the pain, at least until next session.

"I did it, Princess! I did it!" Trapped inside Icie's shirt Toni's voice rang out, muffled though proud.

Icie leaned back allowing the child to breathe. "I knew you could do it."

Steve came beside them with the wheelchair helping Antonia to sit.

"You always know what I can do. You make me know." She swiped at the sweat on her brow. Icie handed her the small pack of tissues she kept in her pocket.

"That's my job. I'm here to make sure you do yours, and you know what?"

"What?"

"You did a wonderful job today, Toni. I'm proud of you."

"Thanks, Princess." Antonia was full of smiles. If she could have stretched her lips any further they would cover her entire face.

"Now go with Mr. Steve for your cool down. You've got to let your muscles know this session is over. Besides your parents will be here soon and—"

"Let me tell them! Pleassse!"

Icie caught Steve's eye. She was sure that hers were sparkling with as much happiness as his. 'We wouldn't have it any other way. Right, Steve?"

"Right," her assistant agreed.

"Go on and get those muscles relaxed. They had a good workout today. I have some papers to fill out for your parents."

"Come with me, please, Princess Ice. Fill them out while you tell me a story."

Icie smiled at the nickname Steve had given her after their first day working together. "As sweet as a princess and as unyielding as a block of solid ice," he explained that day long ago.

"I can't do two things at one time," Icie hedged, wanting to grant the request but knowing how little time she had before her next patient was due.

"Yes, you can! You can do anything!"

That declaration of complete faith did it. "Well, then maybe I will. . ." Icie began, but was stopped by the sound of a familiar; though unfamiliar; voice.

"That was impressive."

Icie watched as the tall man purposefully strode towards her as if he had every right to intrude on her patient's privacy. Icie's offense at his rudeness immediately turned to fury at the man's placating smile. The expression he wore was far removed from the man she'd seen pacing on the sidelines, threatening both players and referees with loud words and even louder body language. His smile widened as he came closer. His pleasant demeanor did not fool her. He wanted something. What, Icie had no idea. Though she was curious about why a famous NFL coach, the head coach of the New Orleans Crescents, would be in her office. His place to reign was the football field where he ranted and raved at the least infraction made by one of his players. Well, none of them were here now. This was her domain, and no matter how famous he was,

her patients had a right to privacy as they went
through the painful road to recovery.

"Sir, I don't know where you came from or why
you're here, but you have to leave."

The older man stood before her; stunned.

"Leaving now would be a good time," she
suggested.

"That's not very friendly, especially considering the
monster traffic I drove through to get here from
training camp."

I don't believe you have a scheduled appointment."

"No I don't." He didn't hesitate at the admission,
but instead reached out his hand to hers. "But I need
to see you. The name's Coach Barnes, Greg Barnes."

"I know exactly who you are." Icie let the statement
hang in the air watching a flicker of doubt flash across
his face. "It would not matter if you were the President
of the United States himself, you are taking up my
patient's time." She stared directly into his eyes. "I
suggest you apologize to her."

The tall man's eyes narrowed, focusing on her for
several seconds as he made up his mind. "Sorry there,
little girl," he finally threw over his shoulder at
Antonia.

Icie gave a single nod of dismissal once again
directing her attention on where it should be, her
patient. She was interrupted by a heavy hand on her
shoulder.

"Miss Ellis, we need to talk."

"Is that a request or a demand?"

Again that same look, his eyes narrowing before he spoke. "If it's not too much to ask," he began rather sarcastically, but Icie let it slide. "I request a moment of your time, between patients, of course."

She nodded once again not trusting herself to speak. She was nearly finished for the day. Her next patient was her last, but she lingered with Antonia when a phone call informed her that her next patient had to reschedule. She didn't actually do it on purpose, but the excitement of such a major accomplishment deserved celebration, and when Antonia asked for a second story she couldn't deny her brave little patient. So Icie weaved stories of a little girl who slew dragons and sailed around the world seeking adventures. Then her post conference with Antonia's parents lasted longer than usual, extended by the cries of joy and excitement when Antonia proudly announced her newest accomplishment. Icie waved as the family left nearly a half hour after the end of the session. Steve came up behind her laying a hand on her shoulder.

"Amazing, isn't it?"

"Each and every time." Icie tilted her head toward his hand appreciating the comfort her assistant and friend was always there to give.

"From your glowing reputation, I understand that you have great success with any patient who comes

under your care." Coach Barnes' voice jabbed at her
from behind. Icie lifted a corner of her shirt to dry her
eyes. She had forgotten that the rude man was still
waiting.

"I could get rid of him for you," Steve whispered.

Icie looked up at her assistant knowing that if she
gave him a nod, Coach Barnes would be good and
gone in a matter of seconds, ruining the chances of
getting the autograph she knew Steve was dying for.
But Steve's protective nature would let her decide. He
was a man of restraint but he could use brain, brawn
and his impressive height when necessary. "That's
okay, he'll only come back, but stick around. You
might as well get that autograph you're dying for."
Steve grinned; then switching on his computer; he
settled down to wrap up the day's business.

"So Coach, you've done some homework on me,"
Icie declared. "Yes, it's true, I can admit to being good
at what I do. Although, it's not so much what I do, but
what I convince my patients to do and the talented
skills of the surgeons whose success I ride on."

"Yeah, yeah I know about all that. We've dealt with
the surgeons already. You're what I need."

"I don't see how. I'm not a specialist in sports medicine. I work with kids. But there must me something
you need from me. Let's get it over with. What is it?"

Coach Barnes' immediate answer was a narrow-
eyed stare. Then, suddenly, he strode to the other side

of the room and pulled the rolling chair she had been sitting in earlier toward them and silently offered it to her. After she accepted the offer; he faced her straddling a straight back chair Icie had available for parent consultations.

"You're aware of the foolish actions of one of my star players."

"Isn't everyone."

"Up to a point. It's out and about that he may have re-injured the knee that kept him from finishing the second half of the Super Bowl last January, which most loyal Crescent fans believe gave the other team's offensive players the extra umph to slaughter us in the second half."

"Is that what happened?"

"The magic was gone. The defensive line failed. We won't fail again. I'm not going to bore you with all the details just yet—"

Icie could not control the snort that momentarily stopped the coach's speech. Details. She'd need details if 'the who' she was thinking about was 'the who' coach was talking about.

"What it all boils down to is that Clay Mammoth needs you."

Clay Mammoth needs you! Although she suspected 'the who' to be him, the words spun through her at a dizzying speed throwing all her senses off balance.

Needs me! Needs me!

This was impossible. Impossible! Anger; strong and deep, shot up her spine spreading to her arm and legs, reaching her fingers and toes, instantly fortifying her. Just as quickly, she rose, springing from the chair; sending it rolling across the room, the far wall the only thing stopping its progression. "Clay Mammoth needs me!" she shouted, her throat raw from the words that ripped through her vocal cords.

Coach Barnes stopped talking mid-sentence, a hand held up in self-defense, as if she were about to attack him. Steve was across the room and beside her.

To look at her now, no one could tell that a second ago she was on the verge of a panic attack. Calm and cool is how she appeared now. Calm and cool is how she would project herself to this man who had no idea what the words 'Clay Mammoth needs you' had momentarily done to her.

Quietly, almost delicately, she cleared her throat. "For what?" Her voice was quiet. "For what does he need me?"

"I believe I was in the middle of explaining that, Ms. Ellis."

"You are telling me that the Hiesman-winning, two time Most Valuable Player of the year; Clay Mammoth, the Crescents' all star; needs me."

A bit confused but pulling the mask of coach-in-control-and-in-charge firmly into place he agreed, "Exactly!"

"Impossible," she finally said out loud. "For what could he possibly need me?" Icie asked coldly.

His hands waving before him Coach Barnes finally blew. "Damn it, woman! Have you listened to a word I said?"

"Now there's no call for that," Steve was saying.

"I didn't hear a single word," Icie readily admitted. "As soon as you implied that Clay Mammoth needed anything from me, my mind completely shut down."

Coach Barnes, the toughest coach of the NFL, who had led the Crescents on a unprecedented winning streak, not including last years fluke, for five straight years, threw his hands up in the air, spun around in a complete circle muttering loudly, "This can't be happening! This can't be happening!" Then, his fit over; he continued matter-of-factly.

"What did he do? Break your heart? Throw you on the side? That's it, isn't it?"

"Break my—no—I would never have been that stupid. Clay Mammoth is known for his love-'em-and-leave-'em ways. He didn't break any heart of mine," Icie answered him, her contempt for the famous football player clearly evident.

"A sister? A friend then? Maybe they were stupid."

"No, and I warn you, your rudeness is about to cut this conversation short."

The coach's frustrations seemed to mount. "Then what the hell is it!"

"He broke the heart of someone much more important."

"More important! What could be more important than supporting a legend, aiding a man of glory and fame so that he can rise again to the place where he belongs. For his fans, the kids who look up to him, the men who want to be like him, the women who adore him."

He was very entertaining.

The coach quickly sensed that she found him ridiculous. He got up, walked around his chair; sat down again, then cleared his throat. "This isn't working, is it?" Coach Barnes asked.

"No."

"I understand why you have a one hundred percent success rate. You're cool and persistent. Tough. If it wasn't for that one time you yelled out, I'd think you weren't human."

"I've heard it said before."

"I needed a quality person to do a quality job. You were my last hope."

"I don't know how that could be possible. There are physical therapists all over the world. I don't even work with athletes. I work with children. Last I remember; Clay Mammoth wasn't a child."

"That doesn't stop him from behaving like one—" he stopped as if he had said too much. "Look," a weary expression crept over his face, the gray in his eyes highlighting the gray streaks in his jet black hair. "No one else will work with him. He's gotten resentful and won't do what the therapists demand."

"Therapists?" Icie put an emphasis on the plural.

"I'll level with you, show you how much we need you. He's seen fifty."

"He's gone through fifty therapists?"

With a sharp nod the coach continued. "That includes the first twenty he went through with the first injury, but if he finds the right one the doc said that he'll be as good as new. He could play by mid-season, maybe Thanksgiving Day. If he had the right therapist…"

Coach let that statement hang in the air. Another ploy. He was good. First the here's-an-opportunity-for-you, then the think-of-the-fans, and now the sympathy ploy. No wonder the man got what he wanted.

"By right, you mean?" Icie asked, not that she was even considering changing her mind. She was curious to know the bits of information he was leaving out. Curious to know more about Clay Mammoth's childish behavior. Did he throw temper tantrums, threaten to hold his breath, lock himself in a room?

"A therapist who not only knows her job but who is strong-willed." Definitely temper tantrums.

"Determined."

Locks himself in his room, Icie mentally nodded. 'Who will go all out for her patient."

Stubborn, Icie concluded, but she already knew that.

"Exactly what I witnessed today. You're the one for the job. You come highly recommended. He really does need you."

"You're very good at flattery but you've got it wrong, Coach Barnes. You need me. You also need another Super Bowl win to prove that you haven't lost it. Do you really believe Clay Mammoth holds some kind of magic to insure that?" Icie went on without waiting for him to answer. "Whatever the case, it's not my problem. Football is not the be all and end all of everything. As I said before, the idea that he needs me is impossible."

"I'll ignore everything you've said, young lady."

"Because it's true."

"Because I'm a nice guy You seem like a decent person yourself, which is why I find it hard to believe that you would refuse to help a man when he's down. A role model to young kids just like the ones you help. He could almost be a poster child. Do you know what kind of inspiration he could generate?"

Icie stiffened. Easy now, she warned herself, no more outbursts.

"Don't get all worked up. He's trying every game in the play book, Princess." Steve was at her side. "I think you had better leave," he advised the coach. "Now."

"Ever play football?" Coach had the nerve to ask.

"No."

"You got the build for it."

"Leave now."

"Can't do. If the lady has something more to say then I have to hear it," he stubbornly insisted.

Icie had quietly watched and listened to the short conversation as she pulled herself together. She now moved closer to the man who had just spoken, her body still stiff with, indignation, as inflexible as a robot. "Role model?" she softly spoke. "You dare to present this man as a role model?" Her voice was a frigid wind whirling across the room. "A man who uses women for playthings, callously disregards the feelings of others, judges people by his own immoral behavior. This childish, immature football player; a role model? Thurgood Marshall, the first black supreme court judge; Martin Luther King, Jr., civil rights leader; Garret Morgan, creator of great inventions; those were leaders, role models."

"Hey?" The coach held his hands up helplessly. "When did this turn into a black thing?"

"A black thing? It isn't. You want more examples of role models? Here we go: Ghandi, leader of peaceful resistance; Mother Theresa, savior to the poor; Saint

Katherine Drexel, heiress to a fortune spent on minorities."

"Now you're getting religious on me! Enough. I get you. You don't like sports. You're one of them anti-athletic people."

"Untrue. I love football. I never miss a home game. I'm a Crescent fan through and through."

"Then, why?"

"I ha—, I have a strong dislike for Clay Mammoth," she stated coldly. Although the words were softly stated they bounced off the smooth walls, echoing across the room, shaming her with the hollow feeling the admission left inside. It wasn't enough to make her change her mind though. Her feelings were real. They were her own. She had only said them out loud for the first time in her life. They had the desired effect. Coach Barnes finally realized that his mission was a useless one.

Icie watched the famous coach leave, glancing once more at her as if he were trying to figure her out. Steve was looking at her with a similar expression.

"Guess I won't get that autograph now. You okay? Wanna tell me about it?"

Icie shrugged, then shook her head. She had made right decision. She understood why.

That was all that mattered.

CHAPTER 3

"I don't understand," the older man murmured, after Icie refused, once again, to have anything to do with aiding Clay Mammoth's miserable self-centered hide.

"You understand just as well as Coach Barnes. That's why you took me out instead of letting me make you a good home cooked meal like I've done every Monday for the last two years." Icie took in her surroundings allowing the soft Jazz melody to flow around her. She loved this restaurant. It brought back wonderful memories. She hadn't been to the House of Blues in a long, long time. The spicy N'awlin's cuisine, the atmosphere, and a chance to admire the beautiful folk art covering the walls were a nostalgic treat.

"I just thought you would like to do something different."

She had to admit, she was enjoying herself. Icie didn't get out too often ,but she wasn't going to let the relaxed atmosphere of the restaurant lull her into compliance. "I hope your sacrifice of missing out on a good home-cooked meal was worth it. I don't know how you thought you could butter me up enough to give in to helping Clay Mammoth."

"What's so wrong about that, Icie?"

I can't believe you even asked me that, Ray."

"Easy now. I know you to be a giving person, not someone who holds a grudge."

"In this instance, I do."

"Because of that one meeting—"

"Two."

"He was hurting."

"So was I."

"His father was dying."

"I felt as if mine was too." Tears moistened her eyes at the memory of her loss. Ray laid a large brown wrinkled hand on hers. Since when had his hands become wrinkled?

"I know, but Icie—"

"But what, Ray? Clay Mammoth brought this on himself. It was stupid of him to do what he did."

"Yes, it was."

"It was idiotic of him to jeopardize the team's reputation."

"I agree."

"Why would he goof around with a bunch of his friends and play football against his doctor's orders, only to re-injure himself worse than before?"

"Answers the same as when I explained it all to you half an hour ago. I have no idea."

"If he wanted to take that kind of risk it should have been on the field defending the Crescents' winning streak."

"I agree."

"Stop agreeing with me, Ray."

He shrugged his shoulders nonchalantly. "All of what you're saying is true." Ray's eyes bore into hers, not as uncaring as that casual shrug would suggest. "This injury was his own fault. He's let the Crescents, the coach, and his fans down."

"Then he deserves what he's got."

"No, I can't go with that."

"Then we have to agree to disagree."

Ray nodded slowly, sadness welling in his eyes; his nod, faltering halfway, turned into an agonized shake. "Icie, I never thought you would allow your dislike for Clay—"

"Dislike? Ray, you can't possibly think this is simple dislike." She turned on the cold act. Ray ignored it continuing as if she hadn't interrupted.

"—your dislike for Clay to fester and outgrow all the love you ever felt for Manuel."

"It hasn't. I loved Mr. M. like a father. I took care of him. I grieved for him. I—still—miss—him," she slowly ended.

"Then in honor of his memory, help his son."

"But I—"

"Icie…"

Icie swallowed carefully, the only sign that Ray's words had gotten to her. "Clay Mammoth called me a tramp. He actually thought Mr. M. and I had something going on, and he accused me of being a gold digger."

"We both know that none of that's true." Ray paused then pressed on. "Because you loved Manuel, help his son."

Icie couldn't resist any longer remembering hours spent with Mr. M, the wisdom he shared, the solid and sometimes comical advice he gave. The honesty and love between them had meant so much to her at a time in her life when she felt so alone in the world.

"Before I agree to anything, tell me why, precisely, that he needs me to help him."

"It's because he hates himself. He hates the choices he made. Clay knows he put himself in this predicament and has not been too receptive to help. He's also suffering from a lack of patience. The healing process has been slow."

"Where's the me in there, Ray?"

"He tends to blame everything on the therapist," Ray quickly got out.

"And that's why they quit?

"None of them quit. Clay fired them."

"All fifty?"

"Each and every one." Ray finally released her hand and sat back. "Word's gotten out. I'm surprised every step of his recovery never made it to the papers. Coach Barnes is handling that end, but who knows, it probably will anyway. He needs someone to work with him who won't blab to the media. He needs you, Icie."

There go those words again.

"He needs someone who won't take any sh—, um, excuse me, mess from him. Who can set him straight at the very beginning."

"What if he fires me?"

"He's desperate. Coach has forced Clay to sign a contract binding him to the next qualified therapist we could find willing to work with him."

"Suckered into working with Clay Mammoth you mean, better yet, guilted into taking the job."

"You'd be doing this out of love, not guilt."

"Sure feels like guilt."

"But you'll take the job anyway?"

Icie peered into his gentle face. "Clay Mammoth's lucky to have someone like you on his side. I'll take the job," she said, knowing she only did so for the love of two good men. One gone three years past, the other sitting across from her. Clay Mammoth had no idea how lucky he was.

"I know this woman, you say?" Clay paused between sets, his leg in a brace stretched out before him, the other on the floor keeping him steady. He took a few deep breaths, counting as he waited for an answer from his lifelong friend.

"The new, unfireable physical therapist?" Ray answered.

"Yeah," he agreed, grudgingly accepting the quiet reminder of the contract he'd signed with coach just a few days ago. He continued counting, lifting the weights on the end of the cable, feeling good to be able to at least exercise the upper half of his body. He had to keep in some kind of shape.

"You met her a time or two," Ray hedged.

"Will I remember her?

"Who knows?" the older man shrugged.

Clay got it. Ray wasn't too keen on answering questions about this woman. Which probably meant she wasn't much to look at.

Good.

Clay didn't think he could handle some beautiful woman fawning all over him, watching him sweat out a few baby exercises that were so damn easy once, but now, a living nightmare. A homely woman, he could handle that. She'd be too impressed with his fame and looks to make a proposition he'd have to refuse. Although he loved women, at this depressing time in his life, Clay had no time for that kind of a distraction. He needed to concentrate on his career. This stupid injury, which had started out as a minor problem, had deprived him of finishing an amazing Super Bowl game, which could escalate into a drastic turning point in his life. What happened in the next few months would determine his future as a football player.

A simple tear in the cartilage of his knee, called the meniscus, which had been the cause of his knee locking on him in the middle of the game, is what started it all.

"A small tear along the edge of the meniscus," is what the doctor had said.

"A repair; a few weeks of rest and physical therapy and he would be as good as new," is what the man had told him.

And that's how it should have been. That's what should have happened. But he'd messed that up big time.

Clay pumped harder and faster as the thoughts flew by. He didn't want to be forced into early retirement. He was too young for that. His professional career couldn't end at the age of twenty-nine.

"Slow down, son." Clay heard the calming voice behind him. "Overworking the muscle in your arms won't make the one in your leg heal any faster."

Clay relaxed allowing the weights to land on the other end of the cable. His hands were raised about his head still gripping the handle. "I realize that."

"And rantin' and ravin' and acting like a fool is not gonna make that knee of yours work again either."

Clay grinned at the quiet, but firm put down. Uncle Ray was so much like his father. That was probably why the two men had been such good friends. They were as close as brothers. Uncle Ray was all he had left after his father passed, so Clay had worked hard to strengthen their relationship ever since, even going as far as inviting Ray to live with him in his home. He would some nights, but he kept his own place. "I think I realize that too," Clay finally answered.

"It's about time. Too bad you had to run through fifty specialists to finally come to that realization."

The grin still in place Clay quipped, "You know, fifty-one is my lucky number."

"I pray to God that's true, Number-Fifty-one-Out-For-Fun-Mammoth," Ray muttered just loud enough for him to hear the often chanted nickname, before moving to answer the ringing doorbell echoing throughout the house. He jogged down two flights of stairs in a matter of seconds. Ray never used the elevator unless Clay was riding with him up to his own personal gym on the third floor of his Eastover Mansion. This fairly new gated community for the wealthy is where he had settled himself after his father died. His house was a beauty, a showcase with high ceilings, a spiral staircase he couldn't climb now, ceiling to floor sparkling glass windows, a covered pool, and five huge bedrooms, each with a complete bath. Whoever the new therapist was, she had the privilege of enjoying his luxurious home.

Clay thought about grabbing his crutches and hopping over to the elevator to go down to meet his new miracle worker; as Ray called her. No—that would appear too—eager. He was paying her salary, let her come up to see him. A single ding announced the arrival of the elevator car. The door opened and Clay got a quick view of Ray, his arms wrapped around a woman, gently, but familiarly patting her back. She was almost as tall as Ray, which was tall because Ray stood only a few inches under his own six feet two inch frame. She had long, solid legs, and a nice round behind, (a little rounder than he usually preferred but firm, definitely eye-catching, an I'd-love-to-caress-you kind of firm), which filled out her blue jeans to a T. The door slid closed. What the hell was all that about? Whatever it was, they hadn't seemed to notice him or the fact that the elevator doors had opened revealing the cozy little scene.

Clay reached for his crutches and hobbled over to the elevator; impatiently banging on the down button. Uncle Ray, the old sly dog. That old, old sly dog. Clay didn't think Uncle Ray had it in him. He must, by the look of things. Wasn't he just recently amazed at the man's stamina? "Still rivers run deep and young." Clay chuckled at his own corny joke and banged on the button again trying to force the reluctant elevator to return. It didn't budge. What were they doing? Ray looked like he was trying to cheer up the mysterious visitor. She probably wasn't that new therapist they were waiting for. He glanced at his watch. If that were the case, she was late. Then who was the woman in the elevator and why wouldn't it come up. Then it dawned. "Not in the elevator. Uncle Ray, you sly, sly old dog."

The doors opened two seconds later. Uncle Ray stood there, alone, which was strange in itself because he usually took the stairs. Too nosy to contain his curiosity Clay blurted, "Who was that?"

"Your therapist." Ray walked right past him without another word.

"For me or for you?"

Ray took a while to answer but Clay was clued into a few things before he did. The stiffening of his back a sure indication that he had made the wrong assumption. The grimace of disgust another crystal clear clue. "Get your immature, dirty mind out of the gutter." Uncle Ray's tone was harsh, not quietly firm as usual.

At the reprimand, Clay felt like a kid again and fell back on what usually worked, his charm. "Hey, Uncle Ray, what did I say?"

"Nothing more, I hope. Not one more crude word about her."

An innocent wide-eyed expression spread across his face before denying, "But I wasn't—"

A rare narrowed-eyed stare from the only family he had left turned Clay speechless. A rare thing for him. This whole mess was making him feel raw and uncertain. The charm was obviously not working, and Uncle Ray had already been witness to too many of his angry, foolish outbursts for him to resort to that. Time to grow up and act like the man he claimed to be.

"She's your therapist, your last hope. The media would eat you alive if they got wind of the way you've been behaving."

Clay nodded sharply, irritated by the reminder. "Tell me what I don't know. What's wrong with her anyway? She didn't look up to performing any miracles from what I could see."

"She suffered a loss."

Clay instantly became sympathetic remembering the pain from his fathers death. "Somebody in her family?"

"You can say that."

"Not blood then, close friends, just like family," at Uncle Ray's nod, Clay added.

"Exactly like you then."

"That's something else you can say." Ray was staring at him again, his expression less stern. "Clay, right when I think you have reached a new low, you turn around and show me your good side."

"Got to keep you on your toes, old man."

"I just can't wait for you to get back on yours. Defending the Crescents!"

"—and blocking the foe!" Clay's voice rang out ending the often heard phrase on the football field as the defense took the field. The cheer usually lifted his spirits but as the last word slipped from his mouth a small lingering bit of depression picked at the determination, the drive, the desperation to be whole again. He hopped to the closest chair and sat, extending his leg on a footstool.

"Defending the Crescents!" Uncle Ray's voice boomed again. But he got no response.

Clay's answer was a frustrated grunt. He couldn't defend the Crescents! He couldn't run across the field. He was not preparing himself for training camp where he would practice with his fellow football players. He pounded his upper thighs once, twice, despite the pain shooting down to his knee.

For the last week he'd worked on controlling his temper; having resigned himself to working on what he could fix instead of reacting to what he couldn't. Now here he was reverting back to his old ways suddenly. He stopped himself. He gripped the soft sides of the leather chair; grabbed his crutches, balanced himself on them and moved toward the elevator. The large blue and white door bearing the Crescent emblem opened and there stood the most greedy, self-absorbed woman he knew. The only person in the world he had immediately disliked with a passion. "What the hell are you doing here?"

She stood still and cool as ever, staring at him no more than two seconds before ignoring him and his question. Without a blink she turned to Uncle Ray and said, "—blocking the foe it appears. I thought he knew."

Uncle Ray shrugged his shoulders innocently.

"Thought I knew what?" An icy dread froze Clay's spine as he looked her up and down, absently taking in her cool, hazel eyes the steady stare, the solid expression that held no warmth, but a deep beauty he couldn't deny. A beauty he had somehow ignored, been too hurt and angry to see when he first met her three years ago, the day his father died.

She had smooth, deep brown skin, and a wide mouth, luscious lips. How could he have ignored such a beautiful woman? Despite the dread spreading through him, Clay's eyes moved down to the shapely breast, more than enough to satisfy and then some. Her hands were folded across her waist, a bit wider than he liked but definitely holding his attention. Now the back. He'd like to view that but paused deciding to wait until he kicked her out of his house—"Uncle Ray?" he yelled, hopping across the room toward the man he thought he could trust. "That woman is not my miracle worker! She is not my physical therapist! She is not going to lay a hand on me or my money!"

A chilling laugh, completely without humor rang out behind him. Clay spun around. She was standing so close he could feel a draft of frozen air from her stare alone. Her light colored eyes connected with his, transmitting anger and disbelief. Exactly what he was feeling. She didn't have a right to those feelings.

"From what I understand, I'm you're last hope. I thought you knew that. I suppose I could go tip off to the media."

"Icie," Uncle Ray said in a quiet reprimand.

"You do that you greedy little—"

"Clay!" Ray yelled.

The loud outburst so foreign to his usual soft spoken tone stunned them

"—calm down. Work out your anger on the weights."

Anger? He was furious. So furious he thought it best to take Uncle Ray's advice. He had learned the hard way what the instant release of anger and frustration brought. Fifty times he remembered. The face of each therapist he'd fired because they had ticked him off in one way or another began to flash through his mind.

Clay was now across the room settling himself on the workout bench, but he still heard her voice. It was soft, but cold. "I can't do it."

"Can't keep your mouth shut, huh? Offer her some money, Uncle Ray," Clay called out.

"Cold, hard cash, that's what she wants." He strained his ears to hear more.

"Okay," he heard her say. It was low, but had reached his ears.

"Finally offered her enough?" Clay knew he was pushing it. He wanted a reaction. He needed one. She made him want to goad her; show something besides that cold, solid, rock-hard expression.

At his last crack her eyes trained on him and held him frozen in place. She slowly walked over to him and leaned forward to peer at him like a spectator staring at a dangerous creature through a glass wall. He felt pinned to his chair; mesmerized, 'What is this woman doing to me?' he wondered. Then she spoke.

"You're stuck with me. Get used to it, brat. I want to be here even less than you want me here."

Her voice was soft, but frigid. What game was she playing? Suddenly his anger turned to fascination. He was intrigued by the whole situation, even somewhat amused. Those eyes resembling hazel icicles, could he defrost them a bit?

Warm them?

Melt them?

Maybe even, her?

'What a wonderful idea,' Clay decided. He could take that luscious mouth and use it as a heating tool to light her fire. He'd play her game. His way of course. As he rebuilt his body, he'd teach her gold digging soul a lesson. A lesson he would take great pleasure in.

"I hear what ye' saying," he finally told her. "And don't worry, this will be the fastest recovery in history," he assured her as he thought to himself, "And the fastest melt-down, too."

The smile he gave her held all the Clay Mammoth charm and style he could throw her way.

CHAPTER 4

"One more. That's right. Take it slow."

Her eyes shifted to his. Only then did his leg slowly lift from the bench. Her voice commanded; her eyes demanded; somehow, he couldn't refuse. Clay focused on the lift trying to ignore the stiffness as his leg rose with the slow speed of a drawbridge. What else was behind the demand she flashed at him? Was she laughing inside, waiting for him to give up? Damn, this was harder than he thought it would be. None of his other therapists forced this much on him in one session.

"One more. You're doing fine. Keep it steady."

She flashed those cold eyes at him again. Yeah, he'd do one more.

She had already run him through what seemed like dozens of exercises. She'd checked his range of motion with a little instrument that looked like some kind of ruler and compass combined. He'd tightened his thigh muscles as he concentrated on lifting his knee while the rest of his leg lay flat. They worked on a floor mat where she pushed him to do one exercise after another before demanding that they do even more on the bench.

No big deal.

He was tough.

He could take it.

Beads of perspiration flowed down the sides of his face. He swiped at his eyes, gripped the sides of the bench and, once again, forced his leg to rise up, up, up, a whole two inches to touch her hand. He squeezed his stomach muscles and focused on safely landing his leg back onto the bench instead of letting it collapse like he wanted it to.

"One more. That's—"

That did it. "Woman!" Clay pushed the word out through his tightly clenched teeth. "Do you know what one more means? One!" Clay held up a finger. "It's singular. That means it happens once not over and over again!"

He was suppose to keep it cool. He didn't mean to say all that, but the words had just flown out of his mouth. His only consolation was that he didn't fly off as long, and as loud, as he usually did when he got fed up with a therapist. And Icie Ellis didn't react like any of his other therapists male or female.

She didn't apologize.

She didn't go into any long explanations for why she was doing what she was doing.

She didn't ask if she was pushing him too fast.

She said nothing.

Icie Ellis stood staring at him. Clay didn't think she so much as flinched at his outburst. Her arms were folded across her chest. Her stance firm. Her eyes were as hard and cold as ever.

"You finished?" she asked.

Sweat was falling into his eyes but Clay couldn't be bothered with wiping it away. Her gaze held him.

"I thought you could do better than that," she told him.

"Humph." Clay gave in and wiped an agitated hand across his forehead. "I'm holding back."

"Good. Keep that temper in check, focus your energy on what's important, and give me one more."

"One more?"

"One more as in singular. O-N-E," she slowly spelled.

Clay gladly followed the command wanting this frustrating session to be over. Wanting to show her that he could do it. That he was a man, not a brat. The drawbridge rose and fell, steady but with a twinge of pain he hadn't felt with the other exercises. Before he could hold it back Clay felt his facial muscles twist into a flinch. That outward show from such a tiny bit of pain added to the annoyance he already felt.

"That's it. We'll do a little cool down and muscle relaxation. That is if you will allow me to put my hands on you."

"Fine, just do what I'm paying you to do."

"Maybe you should check your pockets before I start, possibly put away any money you might have on you. I don't want to accidently touch any of it."

She said all this in a cold, dry voice, not a bit of laughter in her tone but Clay decided to pretend to take it as a joke. "Ha, Ha. Get on with the cool down. I deserve a gentle touch after the torture you put me through." He could be just as cool as she. Clay inched down until he lay flat on his back relaxing the elbows he had been resting on and folding his arms across his chest.

She didn't say another word. All was quiet for such a a long time Clay started to get nervous, wondering if the silence was a sign of warning. Would she retaliate by taking out her anger with him on his injured knee?

Probably.

She was an unscrupulous, cold, heartless gold digger. He wouldn't put it past her to lay her ice cold hands on him and somehow make matters worse. He couldn't afford that. A friend of Uncle Ray's or not, this woman needed to be watched. Clay casually eased back up into a semi-reclining position resting on his elbows once again. Her back was to him. She stood as still as a block of ice. The slight movement of her elbows the only indication that she was a living, breathing person. She turned in one motion standing before him with a tube of something in her hand. Her eyes caught his a second before looking down to his leg, his injured leg. She was really making him nervous. Clay had begun to sweat again and all he'd been doing was lying on the floor for the last five minutes. Yeah, he was good and nervous, his whole career literally lay in her hands, but he wasn't gonna let her know it.

"What's that?" he demanded. "Something—."

"What kind of something?" He was so nervous he cut off her answer.

"Don't worry about it." Her eyes narrowed his way "I'm the professional here. I know what I'm doing."

"But I don't. What in the hell are you about to put on my body?"

"My hands of course. I'll be doing a patellar motion giving your knee that gentle touch you requested," she told him as if she could care less about any request he'd issued. "Unless you want stiffness and excess scar tissue around your kneecap." She paused giving him a second to let her words sink in. "The lotion is for me."

"Then use it and get started." Clay nodded as if he approved, her answer a relief to his anxiety.

He watched as she squeezed a bit of the lotion onto her hands rubbing them together in smooth, soft movements, one hand caressed the other—palm to outer hand over and over as if they couldn't get enough of each other. Then her palms brushed against each other; rubbing together in an unhurried meeting, up and down, up and down. He could hear the friction of skin grazing skin. Her fingers entwined, closing together tightly, perfectly fitting as one. They flexed, still melded together. Slowly, they parted as if it was the last thing they wanted to do. Clay's eyes followed them as her hands dropped to her sides.

Immediately, he felt that he had lost something. The sight of those fingers, beautiful, long , brown, clasped together as one—had been so erotic. Never in his life had the meeting of two hands and lotion ever done that to him—Clay was almost too embarrassed to admit it to himself. Her hands had turned him on. He was hard and ready and hoped she wouldn't notice.

Hey, why should he care if she noticed? He had been without a woman for far too long. She had to have seen a man excited before. She could see or not see. It didn't matter. She was here to do a job and nothing else mattered—"Ahhhhhh!" Clay sighed deep and long. Those hands. They were nothing like her name. Icie, weird name, but it fit, so different from her hands. Those hands. They were warm, soft, firm, molding his muscles, touching his skin. Touching. Man, her touch was taking him to another level. He was fast moving past excited. Clay lay completely on his back savoring the feeling, enjoying the slow build up of pleasure until—they were gone.

Her hands were gone!

Clay opened one eye. She was flinging a bag on her shoulder.

He opened both eyes. She was at the elevator door pressing the down button.

"Hey, where are you going?

"The session is over, you can finish the rest all by yourself."

What did that mean? Did she notice what her hands had done to him or was she just being her regular frosty self. Either way, didn't matter; Clay reminded himself. She was here to do a job and she was going to do it. "You can't go."

"The session is over Mr. Mammoth."

"I realize that, but you can't leave."

"And why is that?" she asked, cold exasperation flowing toward him.

"You're my therapist."

"And."

"My therapist in residence. You have to live here for the next few months." Clay sat up completely.

"I don't think so."

"I know so. It's a fact. You and me together for the next few months." Clay carefully leaned onto the side of the bench, pulled himself up and reached for his crutches.

"Impossible."

Icie, the woman with the cold eyes, frosty voice, and soft, warm hands stood staring at him as he hopped across the room.

"It's in that little contract you signed. You must have been smart enough to read it all. Or is manipulating old men your only talent?"

"Good bye, Mr. Mammoth."

"You can't go. You'll be in violation of the contract you signed."

"Where's Ray?"

"Need a shoulder to cry on?"

Her eyes bore into him. The look she gave him sent a warm chill down his spine. How a woman could make him feel hot and cold at the same time was a mystery to him.

"No I don't, and I don't need to stand here talking to a professional brat who thinks the world revolves around him."

"That's a professional football playing brat, Miss Icie."

"If that title makes you feel more important, use it. Just tell Ray I need to talk to him."

The elevator doors swished opened and she stepped inside. Clay leaned forward to hold the doors. The crutch on his good leg fell.

"Be careful, you might hurt yourself," she told him issuing the warning without emotion.

"I know what I'm doing."

She shrugged her shoulders, a stiff, slow movement. He wanted to step inside with her.

He wanted to take her hands one by one and thank them for their gentle pleasurable touch. He had an irresistible urge to lay his lips across them, to nibble and caress her smooth brown fingers with his tongue and breath. Instead he said, "You can't go."

"I can and I will, to a world where there are other people, to a place without self-centered ego maniacs. I could not possibly stay in the same house with you twenty four hours a day. This last hour has tested my limits. Now, move your hand, so that I can be on my way"

"You move it." She didn't hesitate and reached over to remove his hand. His fingers closed around hers gently squeezing as he replaced the hand that had been holding the door with his good leg leaning his weight against it, the crutch still under his other arm. Clay slowly brought her hand toward his lips. "Beautiful hand," he whispered before she snatched it away. The movement caught him off balance. He stumbled back a step using his good leg to catch himself and looked up just as the elevator doors. Closed. "I'll have to dock your pay!" he shouted through the closed doors, the Crescent emblem staring at him, reminding him of his goal, of his pride and dignity as a football player. He was Clay Mammoth. Clay Mammoth didn't run after anybody.

"Alright Tonia!" Icie watched as Antonia lifted her right leg once, twice, and a third time before resting. "That's one step closer to walking out of here."

"I can't wait! I just can't wait!" Antonia's face was full of hope and joy, reminding Icie of why she had picked this career to begin with. A reminder she needed after an hour spent in Clay Mammoth's presence.

"I can't wait either;" Icie agreed with her.

"But then," Antonia's face turned suddenly sad, "I'll miss seeing you and Mr. Steve."

"You can always visit."

"That's a good idea!" Her face brightened just as fast.

"Cool down," Icie announced. Those two words brought Clay Mammoth to the front of her mind. Dealing with him had forced her to rethink her usual method of ending a session with her patient. Her combination of a standard cool down combined with a massage that focused on relaxation never brought about the kind of response she had gotten from Clay today.

At the start, this first session with him had gone smoother than she had thought possible. Tension and anger—she expected to deal with that. Attraction and flirtation—that was unexpected. The sexual tension in the air during Clay's cool down was much too much for her. It had caught her off guard. The session itself had been professional. She was a professional. The rest was unexpected, uncomfortable, and left her feeling completely off balance. And she wasn't going to stand for it.

"Princess Ice, don't forget my story!" Antonia called from across the room where Steve had already rolled her wheelchair.

A story. Icie was glad to delve into creating one. Maybe it would shove Clay Mammoth out of her mind.

Fifteen minutes later Antonia and her parents waved a goodbye as Icie made a few notations on the little girl's chart.

"That was some story," Steve commented as Icie stood to file the chart.

"Mmmm, yeah, I guess."

"Never heard you tell one about a football player before."

"I'm sure I must have."

"And a mean, nasty one at that."

"Oh, he was the villain. There's always a bad guy in a good fairy tale."

"A dragon villain named Clammoth, who put a curse on his doctor and tried to take over the world and change it into a giant football field."

"What can I say? I have a great imagination."

"You also have a great heart, a wonderful spirit, and a special talent, and I'm starting to think that you might not be doing the right thing by working with Clay Mammoth."

"Could be," Icie sighed. "Saw right through me, huh?"

"Yeah. Let me guess. Ego too big? Mouth too loose?"

"That's only part of it."

"What else about him would bother you?"

"It's complicated. We sort of have a history."

"Not romantic, like the coach implied."

"No, more like antagonistic."

"So you clash? Quit. You're not the therapist for him."

"Steve, I'm not sure there is a therapist for him. Besides, I'm obligated."

"That contract you signed. I thought that was strange but contracts can be dissolved, voided. Tell me about the session, I'll find a loop hole."

"The session itself was fine and I can deal with his ego. It's…" Steve stood beside her patiently waiting, elbow resting on top of the file cabinet that stood between them before finally asking, "It's what, Icie?"

Icie looked around at her well equipped office. She had everything she needed for her patients and more. Prolonging her response, Icie mentally compared her office to Clay's own private physical therapist heaven. He had everything he needed and more. Most of the equipment he was far from able to use yet. There was an elliptical trainer that limits impact on the knee, a treadmill, stair climber, trampoline, weights and even an electrical stimulation unit.

"Icie."

She could tell Steve anything, Icie reminded herself, but she didn't want to admit this aloud. Maybe he could help. But maybe she should be having this conversation with Ray. No, Ray was too close to both her and Clay Mammoth. Having concentrated so much on school and then work, Icie didn't have any girlfriends to talk with about this sort of thing. There was Tim Long, an old class mate who'd painted the mural on her back wall, but she hadn't seen him in a while and would feel funny contacting him to talk about this. Steve was it. So she might as well... . "A sort of sexual tension," she said in a rush.

Steve's hand banged against the metal cabinet. "Did he make a pass at you?"

"Not exactly."

"What do you mean, not exactly? That's sexual harassment. Want me to beat him up for you?" Icie watched Steve's fist clench and unclench. "I can make him sorry. I can persuade him to apologize and think twice about ever doing something like that again."

"No...I mean he didn't exactly make a pass, Steve."

"Well, then what?"

How much to say? Icie knew how protective Steve was toward her; but she hadn't expected him to get this upset.

"Icie?"

"It was a feeling."

"A feeling? You're attracted to him?"

"I don't know. I don't want to be."

"Oh, Princess Icie, the bug has finally bit you."

"What bug?"

"The love bug."

"I don't love Clay Mammoth."

"Not yet, but this is how it starts."

"Please," she denied.

"Please what?"

"Please come help me. I don't want to be attracted to him. I don't want any Clay Mammoth bug infecting me."

"What do you want me to do?"

Icie thought a minute carefully analyzing the best way Steve could help her.

"Out with it. Tell me what's going on behind that hard stare."

"Come work with me."

"I already do."

"With Clay Mammoth. You're my assistant. You can assist me. I'll handle the workout. You handle the cool downs. "Yeah," she slowly nodded, "you can cool him down." Cool downs that she normally tailored to the needs of each of her patients. Cool downs that were so much a part of her relaxing her patient and ending the session on a good note.

"Me doing the cool down? That's important to you?"

"Oh yeah. You do it often enough here."

"True." He shrugged his wide shoulders. "Okay, no problem, I'll do it."

"Good."

"But you have to know he's not gonna like this."

"Who cares? But I have to know why you're avoiding the cool down."

"Because…"

"Go on. In all the years I've known you I haven't heard this much excitement in your voice unless you were talking about one of our patients. Besides I need to know what I'm getting myself in to."

"You're going to make me say it all , aren't you?"

"Yep."

"Okay. I'll tell you. That's when the tension…"

He waited for her to continue. When Icie tried to tell him but only succeeded in opening and closing her mouth, Steve demanded. "Go on, just say it."

"That's when the tension…"

"The tension, the sexual tension?"

Icie nodded feeling the heat of embarrassment wash across her skin. "…surfaced."

"Mmmmm." Steve was quiet for a minute. "Was there any visual evidence?"

Icie nodded.

"He's gonna love me then."

Icie nodded once again. "Thanks, Steve."

"You know I'll do almost anything for you, Icie."

"I know, but this is asking a lot."

"No, it's not."

"Then would you consider living there in his Eastover mansion with me until this is over?"

"That would be too much."

"I thought so."

"Will you have to do that?" Steve asked his brow wrinkling.

"I think so. A bit of fine print I didn't notice before signing that little agreement confirmed it."

"But you have other patients."

"A little something Clay Mammoth will have to compromise on"

"Compromise? Doesn't quite fit the image of the Clay Mammoth I've seen."

"It's something we all have to learn to do. This is a lesson he'll have to learn."

"And you're the one to teach him."

"That's right!"

Steve gave her a hug. "Call and give me the low down."

Icie nodded.

"I've got a date so I'm heading out unless you need me to do something."

"No, I'll pick up in here. You go on."

Icie straightened things that didn't need to be straightened, looked over files she knew almost by heart, her case load a confirmation of her inability to be only Clay Mammoth's therapist. She had a commitment to

Antonia, Corey, Neisha, and Roy. Although, the last three would soon have no need for her services. She had four other new clients that she had been scheduled to see but had now been referred to other therapists. What more did he want? Her entire life for the next four months? "Mr. M. you're asking for too much," she said aloud to the empty room, hoping to somehow communicate with him.

Icie replaced the files she'd been studying and turned to answer the ringing phone.

"Hello."

"Icie Ellis."

"This is Icie Ellis. How can I help you?"

"By returning to your place of employment immediately."

"Clay Mammoth," Icie said loudly into the phone.

"Your employer; but not for long at this rate."

"That could change. There are situations that can nullify a contract."

"Such as…"

"Should we go over this on the phone Mr. Mammoth?"

"Why not? Tell me what you were going to say. Situations can nullify a contract, such as…"

"Unnecessary handling."

"You were the one doing all the handling."

"The elevator; my hand."

"Fine. I won't touch you again."

"And your own physical reaction—"

"Not something I can help. You'll have to grow up Miss Ice. Maybe sprinkle a bit more of that icy charm around to help prevent a repeat occurrence. I'm a man, one who hasn't been with a woman-"

"I've heard enough. I get the idea, and don't worry, I'm old enough to handle it." His laughter in her ear as deep and as sexy as his voice resurrected a bit of that sexual tension she had been feeling earlier. And that was just from hearing him. How was she going to deal with hearing and seeing him over and over again everyday for the next four months?

"Good, so when should I expect you back at your post? I've been keeping a record and have already docked you for the last four hours. Not good news for somebody so in love with money. But," he continued, not giving her a chance to say a word, "you'll be happy to know this. Uncle Ray has been worried about you." He paused a second before asking. "Is that why you left to begin with? Trying to keep the old man's attention, aren't you?"

"Tell Ray," Icie spoke carefully, concealing her emotions, "that I will be there to discuss this situation. As for you, Mr. Mammoth, I advise, you to think along the lines of a compromise."

"Compromise?"

"Goodbye Mr. Mammoth." Icie laid the receiver onto the phone's base, her thoughts, his voice and foolish words swirling inside her head despite her resolve not to let them bother her.

She took a calming breath and sat. Clay Mammoth would not get the best of her. She would be calm, cool and determined as always. "Mr. M," Icie sat on a nearby rolling stool, "Ray, you don't know what you're doing to me," she called out to the empty room.

She locked the door to the therapy clinic and drove back to the Eastover mansion. Live with Clay Mammoth twenty-four seven? No way.

As soon as the beautiful carved door was opened in response to her knock, Icie realized two things. Ray knew about the little addition to the contract she'd signed. It was all over the guilty, relieved face staring at her expectedly.

Her other realization?

Clay Mammoth was enjoying himself immensely. The two men stood in the doorway waiting quietly. But not for long.

"Four and a half hours late? You know you can't make a habit of this." Clay Mammoth filled the quiet moment with the worst possible comment.

"Icie, come inside so we can talk about this," Ray said, knowing without having to ask that she was far from happy.

"Ray, Mr. Mammoth," she shot them each a frosty look. "I have a life. I have patients that I cannot simply drop."

"There must be some other therapist who can take over," Clay said, as if it were a simple matter of changing a pair of shoes.

"My patients work with me. Once I start a relationship, I follow through."

"Good to know you'll be sticking with me then, Miss Ice."

"Clay, you're not helping things any" Ray hissed at him.

"You can't blame me for trying to clarify a few points, Uncle Ray. Now if Miss Ice will come inside we can talk about these compromises I was supposed to think about."

Miss Ice? Now he was giving her a nickname? Icie had had about all she was going to take off Clay Mammoth for one night. "We can handle them right here. I will continue to see the patients already under my care. I will not live here twenty-four hours a day"

"But what about the media?" Ray interjected somberly.

"I will not reveal anything I know about Mr. Mammoth's situation. I know how to keep a tight lip."

"More like a frozen one," Clay muttered loud enough for her to hear. Icie went on. "We will have two sessions a day five days a week, morning and evening."

"You're the professional," Clay muttered between clenched teeth. "But Icie, what if Clay needs you at night? The other therapists were here in residence. Just in case there were complications."

"Will you be staying, Ray?"

"I can."

Icie reconsidered the possibility of staying overnight. Ray's presence would make a difference; she would be honoring the contract, but she would not even consider being stuck with Clay seven days a week. "My weekends would be my own."

"We can deal with that, right Clay?"

"Whatever. See you tomorrow, Miss Ice."

"Make that Monday, tomorrow's Saturday" Icie watched a sullen Clay Mammoth turn away from the door.

"Everything okay then?" Ray asked, an enormous look of relief overtaking his face giving it a comical expression.

"Yeah," Icie answered satisfied, but then, "Oh no!"

"What?" Ray asked immediately concerned. Even Clay turned back in her direction.

"I've forgotten all about Michelle. She's gone. I've got a funeral to handle."

"Want me to come with you. Maybe I could help."

"No, this is something I have to do on my own."

Icie left forgetting Clay Mammoth and even Ray's omission of the contract, thinking only of the pet she'd found at the bottom of the bird cage just this morning. She was a beautiful African Gray parrot, a gift from Mr.

M. four years ago. How could she forget? Her reluctant relationship with Clay Mammoth was marked by another loss. That's why she had been so upset this morning. But Ray had helped her see that it was just Michelle's time to go. She was an old parrot and had lived well past her expected lifetime.

Icie was home in less than twenty minutes. The shoe box she'd placed Michelle inside still rested on top of the end table near the cage. The empty cage. The silent house. Never had she entered her home without the welcoming call of her favorite pet. Her only pet. Suddenly Icie felt very lonely and cold inside. She lifted the box without opening the lid knowing she wouldn't be able to take seeing the once beautiful white feathers limp and lifeless.

She went to her small yard and concentrated on doing nothing more than digging a hole so that she could bury her companion. "Good-bye my talkative friend," were the only words she spoke. Then she went inside and took a warm shower to revive. As the water poured over her another element of heat, a natural element, a male element, flashed through her mind.

"Wash that vision away," she demanded of herself. There will be no more. Besides, she remembered smiling directly into the spray letting the water land and spread where it may, Steve was now her cool down man. She had nothing to worry about.

CHAPTER 5

"Who the hell are you?" were Clay Mammoth's first words of welcome. "And can you believe that I've been dying to meet you?" Steve coolly answered the famous football player as he exited the elevator. "Guess I shouldn't have expected you to feel the same about meeting me."

Clay put his crutches in full throttle, moving past Steve and effectively blocking Icie's progress across the room with his huge, firm body. "Who the hell is that? My compromise?"

"Partly" Icie answered. "You two ready to get started?"

"Us two? Getting started on what?" Clay's eyes shifted from one to the other.

"On the session. Steve, my PTA, will be assisting me from now on."

"Your P what?"

"My physical therapist assistant."

"You never said anything about this. You didn't have an assistant last week." Clay did that twisted thing with his upper lip again but this time she watched long enough to see his face spring back into place like a rubber band.

"I couldn't make it," Steve interjected, "but I'm here now."

"For what, man? None of my other physical therapists had assistants."

"But I do," Icie stated, a distinct nip blowing into the room with her words. "Steve," Icie turned to her assistant, "could you get my bag from out of the car? I left the chart I started on Mr. Mammoth in it." She threw him her keys as well as an I-can-handle-this-much-on-my-own look of reassurance.

"The compromise," Clay said in a confident tone after the elevator doors closed. "You had no plans to use an assistant when you started this job. Admit it."

"I admit to nothing but the fact that I work with an assistant, always have. Get used to it."

"This guy? Is he really an assistant? What's that? Like a nurse's aide or something? Is this Steve guy someone you hired to throw me off?"

"Would you like to see his credentials?"

"No, I can play this your way. You are the professional. It's too bad you didn't give me a chance to issue some of these compromises I'm forced to deal with."

"There aren't many and they are not too demanding," Icie told him, careful to keep her voice cool and firm. His sudden friendly tone was a bit suspicious to her.

"You're right, Miss Ice. It's just that I was looking forward to having my say. It's my body, my busted knee, my career. Doesn't seem fair; now does it?"

"Maybe, maybe not. Whatever the case you got the better end of the deal. Not one, but two professionals working hard to get you back on your feet."

Before he could respond to that the elevator returned a smiling Steve, bag in hand. "Ready to start?"

"Compromise," Clay Mammoth whispered into her ear then hopped over to Steve. "Where do we start, Steve?" he asked, then in a loud whisper; "Tell me, exactly what it is a PTA does."

"I spot you. Like in gymnastics, make sure you don't re-injure yourself during the session. And whatever Princess Ice tells me I need to do."

"Princess Ice?"

"A nickname." Icie gave both men a frosty stare. "On the floor; legs extended, we'll be working on the bench later."

Clay obeyed. Very uncharacteristic for him, but still he obeyed and continued to obey throughout the session as she demanded one type of exercise after another. Steve filled the session with talk of football. Real football talk, not just the noise of a fan. The man really knew the sport and the Crescents. It felt good to talk man to man. Clay hadn't had that in awhile. His buddies on the team, he couldn't talk to them. He wanted to, had tried a few times, but somehow they'd get on the subject of his busted knee, then talk about everything he was missing. Their visits would leave him frustrated and annoyed. Having Steve around might not be so bad.

"Steve, man, you can't tell me you never played the game. The way you know football, you're more than a spectator."

"Yeah, I played, a long time ago."

"High School?"

"Saint Aug."

"That's my alma mater."

"Yeah, Fifty-one, but I came through after you."

"No college football? Didn't think about turning pro?"

"Done," Icie's voice breezed toward him. "Time for your cool down."

"Done?" The conversation had taken his mind off the painful exercises. It had even taken his mind off of his beautiful, cool-faced physical therapist. But the best was yet to come.

Clay was looking forward to Miss Ice laying her warm hands on him again. "You might want to get started Steve," Icie prompted from across the room. We've got a ten o'clock coming in at the clinic."

"Get started with what?

"Your cool down, Fifty-one," Steve told him with a dead serious expression on his face.

"From you?"

"Hey, it's my job."

"Can't be! Won't be! Miss Ice, you had better get over here and do your job."

"That's exactly what I'm doing Mr. Mammoth," she answered, writing in that stupid chart with cold concentration.

Clay stared at her a long minute. He would not lose his temper; but this wasn't going to happen. He looked over at Steve. He was leaning against the wall arms folded, waiting. "I've got nothing against you man, but this ain't right."

"I'm just here to do a job."

"It's her job!"

"And she's the boss." Steve shrugged his shoulders.

"This is not compromise, Miss Ice. This is sabotage," Clay called across the room his voice rising with each word.

"Sabotage? I don't follow Mr. Mammoth."

With a tremendous effort Clay gulped down an outrageous, angry response. She didn't follow? Of course she followed. She knew what she was doing when she brought her assistant here today. And now she gave him this cold little answer, keeping her chilly eyes on him, waiting for him to explode. Waiting for him to fire her. Waiting for his last chance to play again get crushed by his own temper. If she could be cool, then he could be cool. "I am a man. You are sabotaging my ability to be a man."

"Mmmmm. I had no idea I was capable of such a thing."

"There will be no cool down today. Not unless you, the therapist named in my contract, give me the cool down. I won't accept it from anyone else."

"I'm in charge, you will do as you're told."

"No, I have compromised enough. It's your turn."

"Then I quit."

"You can't. So make your way across this room and come promise me something for being such a good patient."

"Come promise?"

"Same as compromising, right, Steve?"

"No comment," was all Icie's assistant would say, hand raised in innocence. "It's your call Icie."

"Yes, Miss Ice, come promise."

Icie didn't know what to do. Her patient was challenging her, but was he asking for something unreasonable? Was it any different from Antonia asking her for a story? Choose your battles, Icie advised herself. She hadn't wanted to touch Clay Mammoth if she could help it, but at least Steve was still here.

"Miss Ice, I need your expert care," Clay cajoled from across the room.

"Alright!" Icie all but shouted. "I'll compromise. I'll do the cool down, Steve stand by in case I need you."

"Need him for what?"

For what? For support, to run interference, a buffer zone. Any one of those would do.

Steve's face asked the same question, but Icie turned away from them both to find the lotion which she had used to rub on her hands before touching Clay's warm, brown skin. Be quick and professional, this was her job. As Icie's hand landed on his hard thigh she tried to lose herself in the routine but instead found herself lost in the man. The feel of solid muscle, in no way deteriorated because of his injury, the warmth of his breath, as he leaned closer to watch the movement of her hands, the sound of air pushing in and out of his system, a soft lulling tune that excited her. His scent rousing more of those dreaded sexual urges that were beginning to feel so good.

"Icie, you about done?" Steve asked from across the room.

"Mmmm." Steve? What was he doing here?

"We got a ten o'clock remember?"

"Oh, we do." Icie mentally shook herself. "Yes—you're right we have to go." Icie lifted her hands from Clay's thigh and clasped them together. "We'll be seeing you this afternoon. You did a good job with those assistive range-of-motion exercises," she said coolly. "We'll be doing more of the same."

"I'll be looking forward to it. I enjoy and appreciate your assistance," Clay said with a meaningful expres-

sion, then to her assistant, "Catch you then, Steve."
Almost as if he meant it. As if he didn't mind Steve's
presence after all.

Icie and Steve rode down the elevator together in
silence, even waved a good bye to Ray who was outside
washing his car as they each hopped in their own.
They walked into the clinic together fifteen minutes
early for their appointment and went about preparing
the room for Antonia's session before Icie could stand
no more. "Sorry, Steve."

He was across the room and at her side in a second.
"Nothing to be sorry for. You can't help who you fall
for."

"Fall? I haven't done any falling. There's no love
between me and that mountain of lust."

"Oh yeah, but there's that sexual tension you told
me about."

Icie could feel her face heat up with Steve's
reminder. She felt as if her skin had easily toasted a
darker shade of brown. She couldn't believe she was
having this discussion with Steve.

But then again, who else? "Lust and sex is not the
same as love."

"I agree, but for a lot of us guys out there it's pretty
much the same thing—at first," he added at her frosty
stare. "And besides, I'm not so sure lust is all I'm seeing
there Princess." Steve rolled up a chair and waited for
her to sit before pulling one up for himself. "I felt like

a third wheel up in that workout room most of the time today."

"Not totally. You and Fifty-one were having a good ol' time with all that football talk. I didn't think you noticed me much today."

"We knew you were there. He knew you were there, especially during the longest cool down session in history. Something's happening, Princess, and that something started the minute we walked out of that elevator this morning."

"I'm in trouble. This isn't how it was supposed to work."

"Something's in the air."

"But I don't want to catch it. That's why I need you there. You're not gonna skip out on me, Steve, are you?" Icie felt a panic chill run down her spine.

"Of course not. Overall I had a good time, got to talk to a real live football player in person, and had a little fun threatening his manhood. Did you see the look on his face when you told me to get on with the cool down. Princess, I could have died laughing."

"Yeah, it was kind of funny" Icie admitted, although at the time the dread of putting her hands on Clay had overpowered any urge she had had to laugh.

Antonia and her parents came in to find them both laughing. The session went well and was over before she knew it. They waved their good-byes, and had a final session at the clinic with Kyle, a little boy who had injured his hand so severely, he had to relearn how to use the muscles in them once again.

"When you get back to class you'll be ready for all that Reading, 'Riting, and 'Rithmatic," Icie told the little boy.

"Don't forget marbles!" Kyle reminded her.

"And you'll be the number one marble champ in the school."

"Thanks for the tip," the happy mom whispered to Icie. "Marbles were not only a good at-home-therapy but the game also worked wonders for his self-esteem."

"And that's just as important, right Steve?" Icie turned to her assistant.

"Princess Icie knows all."

They both left the clinic for lunch, Steve promising to meet her back at the Eastover Mansion at three that afternoon. Icie went home. The silence that greeted her a sharp reminder that Michelle was gone. Maybe it was a good thing she was staying with Clay Mammoth, and Ray. It would keep her mind off of Michelle. Losing her seemed to bring fresh in her mind her loss of Mr. M. all over again.

Icie checked her nearly bare fridge and made herself a quick sandwich with the lone slice of smoked turkey she'd found. A little bit of mustard, a few dill chips from the bottom of the jar, the last two slices of honey wheat bread and she had herself a quick lunch. She desperately needed to make a run to the grocery.

What should she cook for herself and Ray today? Icie leaned against the fridge and went over ideas in her head as she ate. She still felt funny about cooking in Clay Mammoth's kitchen, but hey, she wasn't gonna let that stop tradition. Monday nights she cooked. Monday nights she enjoyed Ray's company. Things would go on as they should.

The huge carved door opened.

"Groceries? I have food in the house," Clay announced, surprising Icie by sounding a bit insulted.

"I'm sure."

"Room and board's part of the deal."

"I understand." Icie barely squeezed past his massive, tension arousing bulk blocking the doorway. He reached out to a grab a bag from her loaded arms halting Icie in her tracks. "I've got it," she assured him.

"No, I think I should help—be a gentleman."

"Gentle?"

"—man," he finished emphasizing the word.

"Man." She shrugged stiffly intending to let it go at that when two other words slipped past her lips. "But gentle?" Having added that much more, Icie found herself unable to stop the flow of questions breezing through her head. "But gentle?" she repeated pausing a second before rushing on. "Gentle when? Gentle how? With words? With manners? With demands?

With a football?" She didn't know what had gotten into her. Why was she doing this?

Seeing all of him blocking the door; having all that was Clay Mammoth slam into her at once, had to have loosened her tongue—no her brain. She hadn't meant to have a discussion with him that had nothing to do with his therapy. Icie glanced down at the strong brown hand that still held the plastic grocery bag and then up at him once again. Why had she done that? Steve was so right. She was attracted to the handsome football player. He stood tall and sure resting his weight on his good leg, the crutch under his arm staring at her.

"Gentle? Oh, Miss Ice. There are many times when gentle is the only way to be. Don't ask when, ask how. Ask me how gentle my voice gets when it softens to a quiet whisper just before I describe the way—"

"—you'll let go of my bag." Icie's attempt to change his train of thought was unsuccessful. Stubborn man that he was, Clay Mammoth continued without pause.

"—the way smooth, moist, hot, kisses can melt the coldest, iciest, layer of resistance," he teased. Then the slamming of a car door grabbed his attention long enough for her to pull the bag out his grasp, putting him off balance, but not enough to make him fall. Icie heard him stumble slightly then Steve's voice behind her.

"Hey man, you never gonna get back to defending the Crescents if you're stumbling around ready to fall on your face."

"I'm alright. Miss Ice's got me wondering if she wants to stay in my house longer than we anticipated. She moved by me so fast she almost made me fall."

"I'm sure it wasn't intentional."

"Yep, I'm sure." Clay looked at his watch. "See you guys upstairs in ten, right?"

Icie vaguely heard the short conversation between Steve and the football player as she made her way to the enormous kitchen. It was a stainless paradise that Icie barely noticed. She paid little attention to the silvery gleam of the fridge, stove and freezer; the sparkling sink in the center of the island, the brand new pots and pans. All she noticed was her frustration, her total preoccupation with the way Clay Mammoth made her feel. Icie dug into a bag she had laid on the counter.

"What was he up to with all that?" She asked the head of lettuce, some carrots and a bunch of green onions in her hand. He'd already told her there wouldn't be anymore of that funny stuff. Funny? Oh no, it wasn't funny What it was was almost believable. She could almost believe that Clay actually wanted to kiss her; and that indeed he could melt her. That they could have something, and she had been so far gone she couldn't pin this last stumble out of bounds all on him. She couldn't, so she wouldn't. She'd let this one slide. He got the message. She would just have to harden her resolve and remain cold and aloof from him, keep Steve or Ray nearby at all times and constantly remind herself of his true nature.

"Clay Mammoth is a selfish brat," Icie muttered as she opened the shiny fridge to deposit the vegetables that were still in her hands, taking a mental note of its full contents. "He was a horrible son," she told the packages of crawfish tails before laying them next to the vegetables. She placed the package of frozen pie shells in the freezer before announcing to the kitchen, "and a player with a history of using women." The freezer door slammed shut.

"So, getting along with Clay a little better?" Ray asked behind her.

"As best as I can by reminding myself of his many endearing qualities."

"He's got quite a few."

"Don't I know it." Icie grabbed the empty shopping bags and turned to find a place to save them until she could drop them off at the store or her house for recycling.

"Don't think you do." At Icie's incredulous expression, Ray pointed to the opposite side of the room. "Recycling containers are over there." Icie moved to a small alcove. "Got something delicious planned for tonight, right?" Ray asked.

"Huh- huh," Icie answered preoccupied with the sight of the mini-recycling center just outside the kitchen. There was a place for newspapers, a separate container for plastic bottles, and aluminum cans. All were lined up nice and neat in stainless steel containers labeled for each recyclable. Did Clay Mammoth actually care about the environment? Naw, whoever designed this big beautiful mansion was an earth-conscious person and Clay simply bought it the way he found it. He couldn't have had anything to do with it.

A buzzer type noise interrupted her thoughts as she stuffed the bags into the almost full container. "Miss Ice," Clay Mammoth's smooth, deep voice came at her from somewhere in the kitchen.

"The intercom," Ray pointed much like he'd done earlier.

"Calling for; Miss Ice. Your patient is patiently waiting for you to attend him."

"Attend?" Icie tuned to Ray

"Kind of endearing, don't you think?"

"To whom, a herd of Crescentettes?"

"Miss—"

Icie pressed the talk button on the intercom before he could go on. "On my way" she blew into the speaker then headed for the stairs, dreading the coming session, dreading the physical contact with Clay Mammoth, dreading and craving it at the same time.

CHAPTER 6

Clay laughed out loud only because Steve had stopped talking and was laughing so hard himself. Actually Clay had no idea what the man had just said. He had other things on his mind.

"When you finish laughing and the entire bench stops shaking I want you to try that exercise again."

"Of course." Clay obeyed catching her hard hazel-eyed look.

"Sorry princess, my fault," Steve apologized.

"Not a problem," Icie indulged her assistant. Then to Clay "Once more." Clay glanced at her; then his knee. "Once," he reminded, "means the same as one."

"One," she nodded.

Naw, Clay thought to himself. It was all his imagination. But no! For a second, as he stood next to her; forcing his help on her; pulling from those icy eyes a response to him, they seemed to connect. For just a moment they were on the same level. He didn't want a relationship with a woman all out for what she could get. And she didn't want one with him.

Some fun?

Now that was different. He could go for that. Clay was wide open for some mutual enjoyment. He just needed to make her see that a little fun was what she wanted too. After all, the melting had already begun. A few degrees at a time would get her to the end zone where she'd find number fifty-one-out-for-fun, willing and waiting.

Steve pulled the stool he had been sitting on a little closer to Clay and was going on about the coming season. Clay didn't mind talking about football with Steve. Steve had the insight of a player but didn't raise an ounce of resentment in him as his teammates sometimes did when they were over. Listening earnestly, because he felt a little bad about ignoring his story earlier; Clay realized he had missed Miss Ice's erotic lotion caress because her warm hands had already landed on his thigh right above the knee. So soft, so soothing. Below the knee, so gentle. Clay almost laughed. More like exciting. Miss Ice was some contradiction.

"Done, for now, Mr. Mammoth." She was gathering her things, putting stuff away hanging on to that chart of hers. "See you tomorrow morning."

"How about a consultation?" he asked not wanting her to stop, not wanting her to leave his side. If she was gone, how could he use his charm to continue the melting process. "Don't I get a post session conference."

"When necessary."

"Are you implying that now it's not necessary?"

"Exactly. This is just your second day of therapy"

"There must be something you can tell me. Tell me more about those range-of-motion exercises." Clay turned to Steve who had gone quiet. "Isn't a therapist normally there for her client? Shouldn't she answer questions and review his progress."

"Well?" Clay almost shouted.

"Normally" Steve stood suddenly anxious to leave.

"So what's the problem."

"No problem, Mr. Mammoth," Icie replied. "I have your chart right here. We can go over it together as I fill it in. I'll even tell you a story if you like."

Steve laughed at that.

Story? What was that all about? Clay frowned as another one of those we-know-but-you-don't-know-currents passed through the air. "Only if you know one about an Ice Princess who has a problem compromising," Clay shot back at her.

"I wouldn't know where to begin," she answered. "Give me a second I'll be right over."

"No, I'll get up. Feel free to make yourself comfortable at that desk over there. I need to stand for a while. I'm coming. I promise." Clay reached for his crutches. "No more melting today" Clay whispered to himself.

Steve hung in the background while Miss Ice explained the purpose of certain exercises using the most professional terms she could dig up. Terms Clay was very familiar with from the surgeon who had operated on his knee, and the extensive research he'd done before the surgery.

After standing over her as close as he dared for a good ten minutes, Clay leaned in even closer to whisper in her ear. "Thank you for your time, Miss Ice. I almost think you care about your new patient."

"Of course I care," she answered loudly. "I care about all my patients. Especially you. I want you to be as good as new as soon as possible."

"I want the same thing. That's why I figure we'd be good with that compromising thing you introduced but never fully committed to."

When he got no response but still had her attention, Clay continued, "Come on Miss Ice. Come promise me something."

"Promises. What's this about promises?" Steve stood behind them.

"Nothing worth repeating. Besides no one around here is making any" Icie answered.

"Good," Steve said looking directly at Miss Ice. "Need any help settling in before I leave? Suitcases to bring up? Furniture to move?"

"No, I've just got an overnight bag. I'm not moving in permanently"

"Alright then. See ya' tomorrow, Clay," Steve threw at him heading to the elevator.

"Walk me out, Princess." Steve's look was asking for a whole lot more. She quickly followed Steve into the elevator; the chart still in her hand.

What was she in a hurry for? Disgusted, Clay got busy working on his abs, the only six-pack he'd be having anything to do with tonight. The evening loomed long and boring. The possibility of Miss Ice making it more interesting was as good as dead. After a half hour of training, Clay hopped to the elevator. The doors closed and opened once again on the second floor. He went to his room, took a shower, and had just finished the struggle of pulling a pair of shorts up his leg when his bedroom door burst open.

"Hey man, what cha' doing? Playing with yourself in here?" Randy the Crescents' star quarter back asked as he hummed a football at Clay.

"Me, myself and your mama." Clay gave the usual locker room comeback catching the ball instinctively, its texture and hardness pressing into his hands. He hummed it back at Randy, a choked feeling rising in his throat.

"Good reflexes. Shows you're not losing it all." Larry the running back commented.

"Can't lose what comes naturally" Clay answered, his cocky attitude rising to the surface, covering the uncomfortable feelings that had almost taken over.

"Losing it? Fifty- one. No way man." Joe, a defensive lineman chimed in. "Never; never; never. Did you see that hot number downstairs? Don't think he's losing it in any way, shape or form." Larry swiped a hand at Randy's head.

"Number fifty-one-out-for-fun!" the trio chorused together. Back slapping and high-fives usually followed the chant, but for some reason Clay couldn't bring himself to participate. His three friends and teammate noticed. Barely.

"Hey Clay man, where's the enthusiasm?"

"Deep inside."

"Come on and dig it up!," Joe shouted strutting across the room doing something that looked like a chicken walk, his blond hair flying all over his head.

"I would if I could, but it's not like that with the lady downstairs."

"It's not? Real funny there, Clay." Randy popped him on the back.

"It's the truth. She's my therapist."

"The new one? What's this, number five? How many more are you going to go through before you get that knee back in business?" Joe asked.

"This is the last one, man," Clay assured them, thankful they had no idea exactly how many therapists he had gone through already. Princess Icie's cracks about him being a brat had begun to make him feel worse about the way he had treated the others.

"Cause she's so fine…" Larry started to sing with the other two joining in. There was a time when Clay would be right along with them. But not this time, not when the 'she' in 'She's so fine,' was Miss Ice.

"Clay's not singing." Joe stated the obvious.

"Come on Clay-man. Let's get out of here. Find a club, meet some women, have some fun," Randy suggested.

"Yeah, we're entitled. Coach gave us an extra day of rest," Joe announced.

"An extra day of chick hunting you mean," Clay clarified.

"And what's wrong with that?" Larry wanted to know.

Yeah, Clay asked himself, blocking out a pair of cold hazel eyes. What was wrong with that?

"You coming or you staying in this miserable little room to rot because of that little boo-boo on your knee?" Randy asked.

"I'm coming," Clay laughed, reaching for his crutches and hopping around the miserable little room that was easily twice the size of their locker room in the Superdome. What was there to do here besides freeze in the presence of his new therapist anyway?

They rode down the elevator bringing with them the sounds of loud men acting like rowdy little boys.

Clay stopped them at the front door. "Let me holler at Uncle Ray."

Clay hopped to the kitchen, stunned to walk in on the cozy little scene before him. Ray and Miss Ice stood near the breakfast table talking and smiling at each other in the far corner of the kitchen. A delicious smell filled the air. Seafood? Shrimp? Crawfish? Two place settings laid on the table. Two bowls of some kind of salad. A buzzer sounded.

"The crawfish pie's ready" Miss Ice announced in the sweetest, warmest voice he had ever heard her use.

"So am I," Ray said as he rubbed his hands together.

"It has to set. You can have your salad while it does that." She placed the hot pie on the table.

"Crawfish pie," Clay heard himself say as he moved toward them. "I can't remember the last time I had crawfish pie." He peered over Ray's shoulder at the well seasoned dish.

"Neither can I. Icie made it especially for me."

"Especially for us—" Icie emphasized.

"—You can have a slice if you want some," Ray offered, cutting off whatever else Miss Ice was about to say.

"I don't think so."

"Come on, Clay, have a taste. Icie doesn't mind, do you?"

She paused just long enough to show that she did mind. "If he would like," she finally answered.

Clay Mammoth didn't stay where he wasn't welcome. "No thanks. The guys are here. I'm off."

Then he left his own kitchen, his own house feeling out of place, feeling that indeed he wasn't welcome.

The loud music, the semi-darkness, the gyrating bodies. Clay felt out of place, unwelcome, almost like a broken toy cast to the side while everyone played with the shiny new ones, new and in perfect shape. The new ones being his teammates, of course. This bar that Joe, Larry and Randy had dragged him to was a huge part of what his life used to be. This bar, on the edge of the French Quarter, was pretty much the Crescents' hang out when they were in town.

They.

Not we.

Not us.

Now it was they.

It sucked. Clay lifted the bottle to his mouth and made a face. Root beer. A cold one was what he needed right now, not a bunch of fizz.

Clay looked around at his fellow teammates, if he could still call them that. They were all high on an extra day to party. The guys who were married brought their wives, some were here with girlfriends and some were here to find a girlfriend, or just a girl.

Clay was miserable. Not that anybody had done anything to make him feel left out. He just did. He had gotten pounced, nudged with elbows and ribbed about his injury endlessly when he first walked in, but now not a soul was around. No one hung around his little table in the corner of the dark room too long. It was his table. Had been for the last three years. He'd never felt lonely there before. But then he could leave when he wanted, move and dance around the floor; get his own drink, meet his own woman. A few did come over; like the fine young thing making her way to his lonely little corner right now. Things could be looking up for him tonight.

"Hey fifty-one," the shapely young thing said in a soft sultry whisper.

"Hello, yourself."

"Too bad about your knee."

"Comes with the territory."

Her head moved in a slow up and down movement. "I hope you get better."

"I'm working on it. Want to sit down and join me for a drink."

"No, I'm with—I gotta get back to—"

"Okay then." Clay raised a hand in understanding stopping her from stumbling through an excuse. "Thanks for stopping by."

And that's how it went all night long. No dancing, no women, and he couldn't even sit at the bar because of his stupid knee. A beer? Clay couldn't even have that comfort. He had been prohibited from drinking after the surgery and decided to stay off alcohol until he got well. He felt the rumbling growl of frustration travel up his throat.

He had had enough. Clay dug into his pocket for his cell phone and called a cab. He couldn't even drive yet. He spotted Randy on the outer edges of the dance floor and hopped over to reach him before he was swallowed up by the crowd again.

"I'm on my way out, Randy"

"Leaving? Already?"

"Gotta rest, work on getting back in the game."

"I understand. Wanna ride?"

"Keep dancing. I called a cab."

Randy nodded and moved across the dance floor following behind his partner.

Clay leaned against the outside wall of the old building on Esplanade Avenue. He didn't have long to wait. A yellow cab pulled to the curb. Despite the darkness Clay put on a pair of sunglasses hoping the driver wouldn't recognize him. He didn't, and the ride passed as an empty blur. He paid the driver and went into his house.

Clay was tired. Tired of using these stupid crutches, tired of waiting for his knee to heal. Tired of being angry.

At his teammates.

At himself.

He wanted to smash something. He felt the fire of his temper beginning to rise like a slow flame in his gut. He threw his crutches down to the floor. They landed with a loud crash on the marble tile, the sound echoing in his ears. Knowing it was probably the most stupid thing he could do, knowing that the doctor warned him more times than could remember; Clay lifted the leg of his injured knee, moved it forward and began to rest all two-hundred twenty-five pounds of weight on his leg.

He closed his eyes as pain shot straight to his knee, then it stopped almost as quickly as it started. There was a sudden pressure, a weight, pressed against him, a warm, soft, pressure. Clay knew what it was, who it was. His Ice Princess had come to save him from himself.

"No you don't Clay Mammoth. There is no way in hell I'm going to allow you to make your recovery drag by any longer than necessary."

The sound of her cool, steady voice telling him what to do, bossing him around as usual, stopped any more thoughts of Miss Ice being his. Clay actually smiled. The anger inside began to slowly drain away.

He kept his eyes shut tight enjoying the feel of her against him, holding him up. He lifted some of his weight from her; shifted it to his good leg, trying not to be obvious about it.

"Just because you decided to go drinking with the boys does not mean you come back here and tear apart what we've just started putting together. We.

Clay smiled even wider. He'd found a we.

"Look at me when I'm talking to you, Fifty-one!"

"Fifty-one,' Clay slowly nodded to himself. Not Clay Mammoth, not Mr. Mammoth, but Fifty-one. He liked that. Clay liked it so much he opened his eyes. "I'm not drunk. I only had root beer."

"Oh," she said looking up at him, her raised eyebrows the only indication that maybe she had spoken too soon. "Lean against the rail, I'll get your crutches."

"If you aren't drunk then what was all of that about?" she calmly asked, handing him the crutches.

"I was feeling sorry for myself." Clay surprised himself by answering honestly. For some reason he wanted to tell her the truth. He almost laughed. Tell the lying gold digger the truth?

Gold digger?

Clay studied her up and down. Her round curves, full breast and frosty expression. She was a cold one. On the outside anyway but somehow—Clay wasn't so sure his Ice Princess fit the mold anymore.

"Oh," she said again. Then, "Do you still want a piece of crawfish pie? We have some left over."

"Feeling a little bad about being rude earlier or is this some sort of compromise, Miss Ice?"

She didn't answer.

"No, thank you. I'd rather make arrangements for you to come promise me something—else."

"What else?"

Clay didn't know himself. He found that he enjoyed playing with her this way. "Don't worry. It's strictly professional, therapist and patient."

"Of course, I was only making sure you remembered that."

"It's always on my mind." Clay placed the crutches under his arms and turned toward the elevator. "Good night," he threw over his shoulder.

"Good night."

She answered him. Clay had almost expected her not to. He stopped at the doors. "Want to ride up with me?"

"Only to make sure you don't pull another crazy act."

Miss Ice crossed in front of him, pressed the button to open the doors and even held them open as he entered. She smelled good. Like crawfish, spicy seasonings and woman. Not a perfumed, made up woman. Natural. Clay had a mild mental shake. That was not the summation of a cold calculating woman.

No, not at all. That tiny observation slipped inside his head without much conscious thought. Maybe he was wrong about her.

The elevator doors opened. Clay's eyes shifted left toward his bedroom. He stared down the empty hallway. "Thanks," he whispered as she turned right, making her way toward her own room.

"You're welcome," she turned to wave at him.

Clay felt the mild disturbance her wave had created in the air around them. A small tremor passed through him. It scared the hell out of him.

And it scared the hell out of her. Icie closed the door to her room, telling herself that the sight of Clay Mammoth intending to abuse his knee, potentially causing more damage and possibly prolonging her stay in his company was a huge scare. That's what she kept telling herself. Nothing else could have left her feeling this shaky. An admission to sexual tension was one thing. Feeling as if she was about to pass out from such close body contact was another. Ridiculous!

She wouldn't give it another thought. But something she should consider was the reason behind his actions tonight. On the outside his outburst looked like another temper tantrum. Instinct told her there was more to it than the rantings of a spoiled football star.

She sat on the edge of the queen-sized bed not bothering to turn on the lights and thought about Clay Mammoth. With great difficulty she tried to block out what she knew about him, her experiences and her feelings. A deep breath pushed past her lips. It wasn't working. She had been able to see him as merely a patient during that five minute encounter in the foyer and elevator. With their history, anything more was asking too much of herself. He deserved to be treated the same as any one of her patients. Icie knew this. She would simply have to look past his selfish chauvinistic side to do that.

"There must be more inside him. Right, Mr. M?" She turned to peer out of her window and look up at the night sky. The stars were bright, the moon full. Icie felt as if Mr. M. was listening as the moonlight shone on her directly though the panes. "Some of your good qualities must have rubbed off on him." For her own sanity she hoped that was true. Icie was dealing with something more than a bout of sexual tension; her professional ethics were being tested

Icie had always liked her patients, so it had always been a joy to help them both physically and emotionally. How could she be there for Clay Mammoth both physically and emotionally if she couldn't stand the man? "You gotta help me with this one, Mr. M," she pleaded to the night sky.

She stood and went to her overnight bag, found her toiletries and laid her clothes out for the next day. She usually wore casual clothes with a decorative lab coat that was lively and colorful; comics, cartoons, anything cute and entertaining for her young patients. For Clay, her causal clothes would have to do, though a white lab coat might present a more professional image, hopefully stopping that "come promise" nonsense he kept throwing at her.

Come promise in place of compromise? Ha. She certainly wasn't going to promise him anything, and he certainly did not have a way with words. Icie laughed to herself as she reached inside a zippered pocket for her undies. It wasn't until she was halfway to her own personal bathroom, quite a distance in this huge bedroom, that she realized that she had laughed at something connected with Clay Mammoth. Not good. But then again, maybe it was. Laughter was certainly better then anger.

She showered, dressed in her nightshirt and finally snuggled herself between the cool satiny sheets. A perk for suffering nights here she thought. Icie wouldn't find satin sheets on her bed. The practical plain cotton kind was all she'd ever bought. She could get used to this, a little something to soften the edges of her frazzled nerves after trying to figure how to handle Clay Mammoth. A little something to soothe her heart when she thought about her pet. Michelle always called out goodnight when Icie turned off the TV, leaving the house in darkness and silence as she settled between her plain cotton sheets.

She stretched. Yes, somehow satin was good for the soul. She drifted off and slept soundly until morning when a bang and muffled curses woke her. Not completely awake, Icie ran to her bedroom door flinging it open without a second thought to anything beyond stopping her patient from doing any more damage to his knee.

There Clay Mammoth stood, crutches under both his arms, exactly where they belonged. "What was that?" she asked holding back a yawn.

"Nothing, at least, nothing I can't handle." He was staring at her; but in her sleepy state Icie couldn't begin to even figure out why.

"Good." She lifted her shoulders rolling them back a few times as he went on explaining almost babbling.

"I opened my window this morning." He stopped, shook his head once and went on.

"Big mistake. I let in one of those New Orleans bred cockroaches." He waved a crutch in the air. "I was trying to kill it."

"Yeah, I hate those things." Icie shook all over just thinking about one of those creepy insects crawling around. "They're pests." She stretched, raising her hands high pulling her muscles from the tips of her fingers to her toes as she did every morning. "There are too many of those things around. They should be the city's mascot." She yawned unable to keep it in.

"Oh-h-h-h, I agree-e-e-e," he slowly dragged out sounding as if that was the best idea she had ever had.

Now she was wide awake. That's when she realized that she was standing in front of Clay Mammoth half naked, her cotton nightie lifting well past her thighs. Her regular morning stretch emphasizing certain parts of her body

"Excuse me." She slammed the door in his face.

Half an hour later Icie walked into the gym turned therapy room vowing to forget that Clay Mammoth had seen her wearing the least amount of clothes any man had ever seen her in. Steve was already here. Good. "Just act professional," she softly reminded herself. As soon as she said those words she wanted to erase the thought. She didn't have to act. She never had to act. Icie was a professional.

"Okay gentlemen, let's get started." Icie was standing before the pair. Clay was talking to Steve as he stood beside some weights. His deep voice paused at the sound of her own. It seemed as if a soothing vibration, an energy in the air had suddenly disappeared.

Ridiculous!

"No good morning to me, Princess?" Steve said giving her a peck on the cheek.

"I thought I said that. Good morning."

"We've already said our good mornings, Miss Ice. You don't owe me one."

Icie bit her bottom lip, a sure sign that she was still embarrassed. "Right. Let's get this session started. If you keep up and do as well as yesterday, you could be completely off those crutches by the end of the week." She moved away from the men going to the other side of the room.

Was she babbling? She felt like she was babbling.

"Princess, you okay?"

Icie almost jumped. Steve was standing right behind her. Clay was still across the room adjusting the crutches under his arms.

"Yeah, I'm fine," she answered coolly. "Why?"

"Thought you might have had trouble sleeping in a strange place."

"No, I'm fine." She was repeating herself. Think of something else. We've got a ten o'clock, right?" she asked Steve, already knowing the answer.

Steve nodded. Clay was standing behind him. "Miss Ice, do you mind repeating what you just said a minute ago? I was way across the room, and I must have gotten it wrong."

Repeat what she said? A new wave of energy had disturbed the particles of air around her; shifting it as Clay lifted himself to the bench. What did she say? Her mind was a blank.

"The crutches, Icie," Steve hinted.

"Oh, that." Icie pulled at the lapels of her lab coat. "Keep doing what you're doing and soon you'll be walking without the crutches."

"There was more."

"More?" Icie wished there was more to her outfit this morning. She wished she had put on the set Ray had bought for her birthday. They were long, covered every inch of her body and were much too hot for a New Orleans summer night, even with air conditioning and satin sheets.

"I think I heard something about me doing good."

"Yes, I guess I said that."

"A compliment. Steve did you hear that? I got my first compliment from my therapist."

"They're rare. Only deserving patients receive them."

Steve knew all her patients received tons of compliments. The reinforcement was critical for their recovery...Praise. Had she really not given him any. He was a grown man. Did he really need the kind of encouragement she gave the kids she serviced?

"Well, I've got a compliment for you today, Miss Ice."

Icie stood frozen in place and held her breath. There was no telling what he might say All she had gotten from Clay Mammoth were insults and innuendo.

"I like what your wearing."

He was looking at her lab coat.

Steve was looking at her lab coat.

Icie looked down at her lab coat. She didn't have a white one, but felt the need to put one on anyway. After this morning's encounter Icie felt that she needed it as an extra layer of protection.

"Castles and dragons seem to fit."

"Thanks." Icie moved to stand beside the bench, Clay's large frame was relaxed as he inched back resting on his elbows.

"But I liked what you had on earlier even better."

Icie knew she had been getting off too easy. It wasn't in Clay Mammoth to let something like this morning's encounter go without comment. "Thanks," was all she said as she looked him straight in the eye, hoping the direct cold approach would squelch any more comments. At the same time, Icie avoided any visual contact with Steve. He was full of questions already. Her assistant, her right hand man, her all important buffer for all the sexual tension pulsating in the air was dying to know what was going on.

"As I said before, let's get started."

The routine began. Clay was already in tune to what she wanted and started with the usual warm up. The men talked football as Icie threw in instructions, and even reminded herself to add in a few compliments now and then. She soon noticed a fine layer of perspiration forming on the firm body stretched out before her. Clay had thrown off his t-shirt mid-session causing Icie to lose her breath for a moment before resuming a professional demeanor. She silently thanked Steve for launching into some football trivia at that precise moment.

"Good session, Fifty-one," Icie said after the last round of exercises, relieved yet full of dread as she anticipated the cool down.

"You're just full of compliments today aren't you, Miss Ice."

Icie nodded as she rubbed lotion on her hands. "Simply part of the job." She avoided laying her eyes on his solid chest and muscular arms. Instead she focused on massaging his leg muscles as the men continued to talk. Their conversation, initiated by Steve, was meant to distract Clay, but also worked to distract her. Icie didn't want to let herself melt into the heat and texture of the smooth, brown skin beneath her hands. Steve was doing a wonderful job. Icie didn't know what she'd do without him. "Done!" she said out loud. "Keep this up and you'll be out on the field before you know it."

"And still another compliment?" Clay smiled at her. I mean, he really smiled at her. It was as if a compliment from her meant something to him. How could it, she thought, when he only saw her as a gold digging good for nothing parasite? She left for her next session, with Steve right behind her; deciding not to even bother reading anything into that.

And so it went for the rest of the week. The three of them fell into a routine. Icie was the professional she prided herself on being. She focused a tremendous amount of energy on viewing Clay Mammoth as a patient, complimented him to boost his performance, and daily thanked Steve for his presence. Any other part of the day she spent in Clay Mammoth's house she was sure to make herself scarce, still uncomfortable about spending the night there at all. But she had already been reminded once more by Coach Barnes of how crucial it was to keep any negative publicity about Clay out of the media. His voice replayed in her head, "If I have to put so much into busting my balls to keep this news out of the news, then you can get used to spending a few nights in sweet luxury."

Icie wouldn't have put it that way. Sweet torture was a better description. At least she got to spend more time with Ray. Sometimes they would play checkers in Ray's room, maybe a card game or two, or she'd curl up with a good book in her own luxurious room. Even though Icie found it ridiculous for her to have to spend the night here she was trying her best to deal with it.

The end of the week arrived at last and her Friday evening session with Clay was almost over. Icie could go back to her own house for the weekend.

"Look at her, Steve Miss Ice can't wait to leave me. Must be planning to spend the weekend having some fun."

"I've got plans," she answered knowing the best way to shut him up was by answering.

"Mind sharing them with us?"

"Yes."

"How about you Steve, you got plans?"

"As a matter fact I do. Big plans."

"Hear that, Miss Ice, Steve's got big plans. Tell us about them. Open up. Share. Then maybe we could get Miss Ice to do the same," Clay insisted.

"Later. I'd rather tell Princess in private."

"Oh, it's personal," Clay went on. "Just you and the Ice Princess, none of it involves me then."

"In an off-hand sort of way."

"Then you have to let it out, man. I'm all ears." Clay twisted his head to lay a pointed look on both of them. "How about you, Ice Princess? Ready to hear Steve's big plans?"

Barely registering Clay's interpretation of her nick-name, the cool down forgotten, Icie looked from his taunting face to Steve's guilty one. Something was wrong. "What is it?"

"I'd rather tell you later."

Icie didn't think she could wait for later. She had to know what was making Steve nervous. "Tell me now."

"Don't look so worried. It's actually good news."

"For you or for me?"

"For me mostly. But I know you'll be happy for me."

"Go on."

"I'm going back to school to get a license to become a physical therapist."

"That's great news!" Icie rounded the bench to grab Steve around the neck and squeeze him with all her might. "You had me so scared. I thought you were leaving me."

"Actually" he said in her ear as he gently pulled her arms down. "I am."

"What? Why?"

"You know there aren't any schools here that cater to Physical Therapist Assistants attempting to get a license."

"You're right. I forgot." She stood before her assistant, her friend, feeling a misery that reached straight down to her toes. It was selfish of her she knew, but she didn't want him to go.

"Congratulations, man! You're gonna make a hell of a physical therapist, but I still think you belong on the football field."

Icie turned to stare at Clay. Why had he opened his mouth? She was supposed to tell Steve that. She hadn't gotten it out yet because she didn't want him to go, but she did want to wish him well. A friend could do nothing less.

"You okay with this, Princess?" Steve asked.

"How can I not be? Fifty-one's right," Icie admitted, then promptly tried to ignore Clay. "You're going to be one great therapist. Don't worry about me, I'm just trying to deal with how much I'm going to miss you."

"I understand."

"Where will you go?"

"Loma Linda University in Loma Linda, California."

"California's beautiful, Steve, the ocean, the waves, the women. You're gonna love it!" The Ice Princess was shooting frozen daggers at Clay.

"We'll talk more later," she said to Steve before turning to Clay. "I believe we're done." She turned her back on him and began packing things into her shoulder bag.

"Don't I get a, 'Keep this up and you'll be back on the field before you know it,' today?"

"Exactly as you said it," she told him without turning around. "Can I take you out to dinner?" she asked Steve.

"A farewell celebration. I can be ready in ten. No make that twenty," Clay interjected. He didn't know what was wrong with him but the idea of Icie and Steve sitting together in some dark quiet restaurant saying tearful goodbyes tore at his gut. A threesome with him as the third wheel was more to his liking. More daggers from the Ice Princess. No surprise.

"Not tonight," Steve said, "I've got some packing to do."

Clay lay propped up on his elbows taking no shame in openly eavesdropping. They were having this discussion right in front of him, and he needed to know what was what. Steve and Miss Ice? Could they have something going on? The thought bothered him.

A lot.

A whole lot.

"So soon? When exactly are you leaving."

Steve mumbled something that he couldn't hear, then Miss Icie blurted, "Sunday!"

That was the first time he had heard so much emotion in her voice, but then the droop of her shoulders, and a sadness in the tilt of her head were the only other signs of what she was feeling.

"Can we talk about this downstairs?" Steve asked nodding in Clay's direction. Miss Ice turned to look at him too. The misery reflected there almost knocked him off the bench.

"Yeah, I'll meet you down by your car. Goodbye, Mr. Mammoth," she said as she waved goodbye.

Clay sat up. "Until Monday, right! I'll see you Monday!" Clay almost in a panic, yelled at the closing elevator door. He was relieved to see a slight nod before the doors closed completely. Turning, he found Steve standing beside the bench, in the same place he'd stood for the last week and a half. "Sorry to see you go, man."

"No, you're not."

He was right, but then again, he wasn't. Clay had come to really like the man, the only guy he could probably call a friend who wasn't a professional football player.

"Now, why do you say that?"

"You've got some ideas about Icie—"

"Don't you mean, Princess?" Clay asked his tone dripping with sarcasm. He didn't like the idea that Steve knew anything about what he thought of Miss Ice. Clay wasn't sure what he thought of her anymore. All he knew was that he felt good about Steve not being around her anymore. No more of him touching her shoulders or her hands. No more smiling with her. And not one more silent message to her from across the room.

"She is a Princess. Don't you forget it."

"I'll handle her with kid gloves."

"Don't handle her at all if you know what I mean."

Clay knew what he meant. "I like you, Steve. You're an okay guy but what makes you think you can tell me what to do."

"I'm not telling you what to do. I'm warning you. Don't hurt her in any way"

Clay was offended, yet amused. This was his first warning and it couldn't have been more ironic. Remembering Miss Ice's past, and her unsuccessful attempt to get close to his father so she could get close to his money, Clay thought that he was the one that needed protection.

"Understood," Clay finally told the impatient man before him. "Believe it or not," he found himself saying, "I'm going to miss our conversations. Good luck."

"Same here."

Steve shook his hand and was gone.

Clay was glad. One obstacle out of his way. He felt good about that. There were some other feelings bouncing around inside of him, but he wasn't paying attention to any of them. He was going to be the dragon that stole the princess using the fire and heat of his charm to melt her to his side.

CHAPTER 7

Monday morning Icie sat in her CR-V Honda jeep on top the high rise bridge spanning across the Industrial Canal. There had to be an accident causing the backup. She was heading east, away from the city. Mostly everyone else was going into the city, a normal cause of congestion, to begin their work day. The last thing she wanted to do was begin her workday without Steve. Icie was missing him already.

After leaving Clay Mammoth's mansion Friday she had been so upset that she had thrown question after question at her now former assistant. Why didn't he tell her before? Why was he leaving her so soon? What was she going to do without him? He had thrown out the answers just as fast, Icie remembered.

"I couldn't tell you because l just found out today. I'm leaving so soon because I'm taking an extra course on Human Anatomy before the semester begins this fall. And you will survive without me because you're one strong woman who can handle anything, even a bout of sexual tension."

Icie laughed as she drove a few inches forward. She hoped Steve was right because there was something about Clay Mammoth that brought out wild feelings in her. Her anger at him for the way he treated his father; that was a wild emotion she had trouble taming. The unsteady pounding of her heart, the desire to touch more than was necessary, the thoughts of lips, tongues and breath mingling wildly and insanely when she knew what she knew about him, was another wild emotion.

Suddenly the highway was clear and the cars were moving, which was strange because there was nothing there that would have caused the congestion to begin with. Maybe this little traffic jam was a clue to how she should handle this situation with Clay Mammoth. Her anger could be feeding the sexual tension making it grow for no good reason. If she forgot the past, maybe a sort of friendship could evolve knocking out all these sexual feelings. Like a cold, it needed to run its course with the help of a few doses of vitamin C.

Friendliness.

Yeah, friendship would be her vitamin C. She'd overcome the Clay Mammoth bug. Icie slammed her hand on the steering wheel.

It was all so logical.

Clay was the only man she had had this problem with and he was also the only man she had so much anger toward. Ray and Mr. M.? Two completely platonic relationships no matter what Clay Mammoth thought. Both men were her friends. Steve? They had gotten along from the moment they met, no tension

there. It all made perfect sense to her. Treat Clay
Mammoth like a friend and he would become one,
effectively doing away with all those frustrating feelings.
She would have to push aside the justifiable anger she
felt toward him. After all, wouldn't Mr. M. have wanted
her to?

Her mind made up, Icie entered his house fifteen
minutes later without the dread that had hung over her
head less than a quarter of an hour before. The relief she
felt was so energizing she practically bounced into the
elevator; fortified with friendliness.

"Good morning, Fifty-one! Let's get this session
started."

"What did you say?" The words were similar to what
he was used to hearing but the tone was something new
altogether.

"I'm always ready" he told the cheery, pleasant faced
woman who looked like his therapist.

"That's what I like to hear. Make your way across
this room and let's get to it. The sooner you work these
muscles the sooner you get back on the field."

Clay moved forward with an inward caution he had
never felt before. She sounded a little more like the Ice
Princess he knew but not completely. "You'd like that,
wouldn't you?" He was standing in front of her. Her
hazel eyes were less frosty. If he was not mistaken they
actually held a trace of warmth. Nervous warmth is
what it looked like to him.

"I want all my patients to heal and move on with life as they once knew it," she told him moving to the other side of the bench where she normally stood.

"You got me there." Clay rested the crutches on the floor and eased onto the bench not sure what to make of this new Ice Princess. Was she playing one of her little games? Did she act like this with his father? Was that why he had spoken so much of her every time Clay called or visited? Is that how she drew him to her? Maybe she was trying to sucker him in too. That's what he figured she'd do to begin with. That had to be why she was playing nice now.

Her assistant was gone. If that's what Steve really was. Her boyfriend, more likely, who was now out of the way. Now she could try her hand on him. That didn't make sense, he realized as soon as the thought was complete. She was the one who wanted Steve here to begin with, so she would have no reason to be happy now that he was gone.

Then exactly why was she cheerful now? Clay leaned back on his elbows studying her as he waited for her next cheery comment.

She smiled at him. And what a smile.

Oh yeah, the Ice Princess was a beauty with smooth skin the shade of—a football? Perfect! He grinned to himself as his eyes traveled downward. Her build, now that was closer to an oak than a football. Sturdy, firm, but built to admire. He chuckled at the way his mind was working.

She smiled back at him.

Her smile held something more than relief. It was spread wider and sparkled deeper within her eyes. She was nothing like those skinny sapling women he was used to hanging around with.

Funny, thinking about all those woman now, Clay couldn't remember wanting them to hang around much after they'd spent time in bed together. He hadn't thought of it before, but seeing the Ice Princess smiling at him somehow brought this realization to light. He wouldn't want her to go anywhere after spending a few hours in bed. A few days, weeks even, was more like it.

"Warm up's done."

The warm up was done? Clay glanced up at her trying to keep the look of surprise off his face.

"How about we try some new exercises?"

When had they even begun the warm-up exercises? Clay wondered to himself.

"Let's see if that knee is strong enough to take on a little more," her voice sang with an even more pleasant ring.

'While you were grinning up at the Ice Princess and letting weird ideas float in your head. That's when.' Clay answered his own question. His eyes zoned in on her curves. She had full breasts he wanted to claim, a waist he wished he could wrap his arms around, and hips that promised him something he hadn't experienced before. A football? Oh yeah, one he wanted to grab and not let go of even after he made a touchdown.

"Are you listening? Pay attention, Fifty-one, I'm only going to tell you how this is done one time."

Clay looked up. What he saw was the perfect mix of who he'd come to know as the Ice Princess and the friendly woman who had walked into his home this morning.

Clay suddenly realized that he liked her. He wanted to keep her this way. But if he found that she was up to something...Well then he'd deal with that when the time came.

"What's going on here today?"

"Nothing beyond a woman doing a job."

"Without your assistant."

"Without my assistant."

"I have to tell you, you seem happier without him," Clay told her, hoping it was true.

"Not happier; resigned. I'm resigned to work hard, to help you reach your goal."

"That's always been your goal, right? How has that changed?"

"I have declared a truce."

"A one-sided truce? Without telling me?"

"I'm telling you now. No more snide remarks or put downs. We build a pleasant, professional relationship and when it's done, go our separate ways."

"Sounds—boring."

"Probably will be, but I'm not here to entertain you."

That was true, but he wanted entertainment from her. He wanted her attention, her smiles. And not just the nervous ones she gave him today. He wanted the kind she gave Steve and Uncle Ray. Whoa man, that sounded pathetic.

"Truce," he said out loud before he revealed some of what he had really been thinking.

They exercised in almost complete silence now that Steve was gone. No more football talk, no more banter to take his mind off of the Ice Princess standing so close to him, emitting some strange vibration that severely tested his ability to persevere in their new truce.

But he withstood the test. Even through the excitement called the cool down. He survived.

The session was over.

But as Clay returned the cheerful wave goodbye, he couldn't help feeling deprived.

Physically deprived.

He wanted more from the Ice Princess than a happy disposition and a cheerful session. Something was going to give.

Hours later at the end of their second session Clay thought it would be his sanity.

"You okay there, Clay?" Ray asked after the Ice Princess left the room. He had come into the gym not long after the session had begun, which was unusual. Clay hadn't seen much of his uncle in the last week.

"I'm fine, Uncle Ray" He reached for the crutches he hoped to be able to toss by the end of the week.

"Fine is good. You and Icie seem to be getting along.., fine."

"Yeah."

"Without Steve around, even."

"Yeah." Clay hopped toward the elevator with Ray following behind. "I never wanted him around to begin with."

"Sort of kept you from seeing the real Icie."

"I'm not sure who, or what, the real Icie is, Uncle Ray"

"The sweet woman that invited you to join us for a home cooked meal."

"That was your idea, old man. You pushed her hand because you could tell she was trying to be nice to me. It's all part of this truce thing she came up with." Clay hopped into the elevator.

"A truce sounds good to me, but what's this about my idea?"

"It was your idea to invite me, admit it." When his uncle's only response was a quiet stare, Clay asked. "Coming down?"

He shook his head. "The steps are my friend. They keep me fit."

"I'll race you when I'm off of these bad boys." Clay eyed the crutches with disgust. The only reason he'd used them so long was because he was determined to follow every rule the doctors gave. He'd never forgiven himself for the stupidity of playing around and hurting himself worse than he had on the field, even after the doctors advised him against it.

Strange.

That twisting, frustrating self-loathing he felt for the part of himself he once believed to be invincible, for once didn't explode inside his head spreading through his brain and irritating every nerve ending. The elevator stopped on the second floor. The anger was still there but not the fist flying rage that consumed him whenever he thought about what he'd done to get himself into this predicament.

Stranger still, he now felt a satisfying sense of relief ease through every joint and muscle. He took a step out of the elevator and stood there unmoving. It took a minute for it to sink in, but Clay realized that he was finally starting to forgive himself. He tilted his head in amazement before walking down the hall to his room. If forgiving himself left him with such a satisfying feeling, then what could happen if he allowed himself to forgive the Ice Princess?

Both the morning and evening sessions with Clay Mammoth had gone so well. Icie went straight into her bathroom wanting to shower before making dinner tonight. She had been right, friendliness was the key. The sessions went smoothly and were trouble-free.

'Except,' a voice at the back of her head intruded on her self-praise.

"Except for that small amount of lingering tension in the air;" she admitted as she stared into the bathroom mirror above the sink.

"Lingering?"

"Not a thing to worry about," she told herself. Why else would she have invited Clay to join in on the Monday night dinner she and Ray shared every week.

"It was Ray's idea."

"The tension simply had to be worked out of my system," she said out loud. "That was all." Then clamped her mouth shut. Since when did she begin talking to herself?

Since she'd lost Michelle and had no one to talk to.

A refreshing shower later; Icie was in Clay Mammoth's kitchen cooking a meal for him. Well, not exactly. She was following her normal routine, cooking a nice meal for Ray and herself, and Clay Mammoth was joining them. It was that simple. Icie never thought this would happen. She was inviting the enemy to dinner. "Better than sleeping with the enemy," she muttered to herself as she dug into the fridge for the ingredients she'd packed there earlier. Which is where all the sexual tension had been heading.

"What's that about sleeping? You plan on taking a nap?" Ray said behind her.

Icie almost threw a bag of raw shrimp into the air.

"I don't think you have time for that Icie, girl."

"Ray, don't scare me like that."

"Didn't mean to," he grinned, proving that he had meant to. "Mind if I sit while you cook? Unless you really plan on taking a nap."

"No, I was just thinking aloud about something else."

"Hump," was all Ray said as she filled a large pot with water to boil some fresh mirlitons. Icie had expected to hear more and was relieved when that was all she got for an answer.

They talked and joked as they peeled shrimp, saving the heads to make shrimp stock. She scooped the light green pulp from the cooked mirliton to mix for a stuffing, placing the skins on a baking pan as Ray chopped the celery, onions, and bell peppers, the trinity that is the beginning of any authentic New Orleans dish.

Icie basted her pot roast that had been slow roasting since her last session with Clay, and popped the stuffed mirliton and macaroni into the oven to bake when Ray surprised her by saying, "Thanks for forgiving Clay, Icie girl."

She turned to face her dear friend. She could simply acknowledge his thanks and move on to talk about something else. But that wouldn't be honest; it wouldn't be her. She moved to the counter and leaned across to hold both his hands within her own. "I'd like to say no problem, Ray, it was easy. Of course, I'd be lying. You haven't witnessed forgiveness Ray. What you saw upstairs today was self-preservation."

"Call it what you want. What I saw today—let's just say Manuel would have been proud."

At the mention of Mr. M, Icie forgot the words of protest that begun to form and asked, "Do you really think so?"

"I know so."

"That has to be stuffed mirliton I'm smelling," Clay said as he hopped into the kitchen, pronouncing the dish the same as all natives of the area did. "Oooh man, it sure is!" he said before anyone could confirm it. "I can't remember the last time I had stuffed mirliton."

"You said that about the crawfish pie, too," Ray reminded him.

"True, but I only got to smell it. This time around I've been invited. Right, Ice Princess? And you can't take it back, not with my taste buds dancing around inside my mouth."

"I won't," she smiled, wondering if inviting Clay to dinner had been pushing friendly too far. "I don't say or do something I don't mean." What she didn't mean to do was invite such a good-smelling, smooth-dressing, handsome man to her table. Or should she say his table?

Icie had expected the sweat pants wearing, t-shirt hugging man she had been working with to show up. It was bad enough being around him when he dressed that way, but now...

"You're dressed mighty sharp for somebody having dinner at home." Ray stated exactly what Icie had been thinking.

"It's not everyday a beautiful woman cooks dinner for me."

"Thanks for the compliment, but I cooked dinner for us, Ray, myself and you of course."

"Of course." He laid the crutches against the counter and leaned across it to ask, "Anything left to do?"

Icie turned away from the smooth, clean shaven face and went to the sink to wash an already clean serving spoon. "Not much. You and Ray can set out the dishes. The food will be ready soon." She hadn't turned back around to answer but felt his eyes linger. Finally relieved to hear movement, she guessed he'd turned to the large breakfast table on the other side of the kitchen where she and Ray had eaten the week before. There was too much lingering going on around here.

"I've got the plates," Ray said from the other side of the room. From the corner of her eye she watched as Ray grabbed a stack of plates getting another peek at Clay. The tense coil of her intestines relaxed bit by bit as she made a show of checking on the food in the oven. Now why should she be so worked up? Clay wasn't wearing anything abnormal, a pair of dress slacks that hugged his bottom but fell loosely, hiding the firm muscles she knew lay beneath. A white collarless shirt hugged every muscle in his upper body.

And she was watching him move.

Icie stood before the open oven door; her corner-eyed gaze trapped on the smooth even movements Clay made as he placed glasses on the table.

"Icie girl, have you got something else to add to that oven we don't know about?"

"Dessert?" Clay asked hopefully.

Icie shook her head.

"Then close the door and let what's in there finish cooking." Embarrassed, Icie lifted the door shut. She was embarrassed in more ways than one. How many times had she seen Clay in a t-shirt, without a shirt even? Somehow the more civilized version of Clay Mammoth twisted the tension to the extreme. She glanced over at the men setting out utensils and glasses. The food had another half hour to cook. Icie was not making small talk with Clay Mammoth for almost half an hour. Besides, she felt hot and annoyed that she wasn't controlling this situation as well as she thought she would. A shower; she could use another shower. She had time.

"Be right back. Listen for the timer;" Icie called out to the men.

"And then what?" she heard Clay yell back.

"Then you take the food out," was the chuckling response Icie heard from Ray as she headed to the stairs and straight to her room, pulling off clothes and throwing herself into the shower faster than she'd ever done before.

She ran the water hot, then cold, then lukewarm, trying anything to relax. Icie had no idea which temperature was the most beneficial, but by the time she rejoined the men, the food was set on the table pipin' hot and ready to be eaten, and she herself was as cool and prepared as she could possibly be.

Icie held herself well and made small talk even including Clay in the conversation. She tried her best not to look at him too often. His sexy bottom half was easy to ignore since it wasn't in view. She was thankful that eating was a sit down acitivty. On the other hand, a stretch for an extra stuffed mirliton or a reach for the gravy she'd made for the pork roast coiled her stomach once again. She was fine, Icie lied to herself as the lingering sexual tension intensified.

She was managing, actually surviving, the evening pretty well, until after cleaning his plate twice Ray stood and announced, "That was as delicious as always, Icie girl, but I've got to cut it short. I have an appointment to keep."

"A what?" She stood with him almost shouting.

"An appointment. Some place I'm scheduled to be."

"But it's Monday our day to talk, catch up with each other."

"And we did. We had a good talk while we were cooking, didn't we?" They had, but Ray was changing things and Icie didn't like it, especially since it was happening in front of Clay Mammoth.

"I'm sorry Icie. I thought I told you. I guess that's why I came down early so we could still have time together."

"No, you didn't tell me." Icie looked from Ray to Clay. Her friend who made her feel comfortable and a man who twisted her up inside. "I tell you what. I'll go with you."

"I don't think so."

"Why?"

Ray looked directly into her eyes. "It's personal."

"Uncle Ray, you've got a date." Clay smirked at his uncle.

"Something like that."

"Why didn't you tell me?" Icie asked, a bit disgusted with herself because she heard accusation in her voice.

But she was a little hurt. Ray should have shared this with her. They were friends, right?

"No wonder I haven't seen much of you lately" Clay said, the smirk turning into a grin that reached ear to ear making his too good-looking face even more handsome.

That handsome face irritated her. Icie should have known that he would grin that way. A female conquest was right up his alley.

"It's not even like that," Ray was saying, "so stop looking at me with eyes as cold as that name of yours, Icie girl."

Icie smiled at that. Ray still made corny jokes about her name. It reminded her of how close they were. So what if he didn't tell her about the first woman he had dated in over a year. He would have gotten around to mentioning it. And maybe it wasn't much to mention. She'd find out, starting now. "What is it like then?"

"One of my friends from church isn't feeling too well. I was going to visit and I sort of promised to see what was wrong with her VCR. She can't watch her favorite tape because she got another one stuck inside."

Immediately, Icie felt selfish and ashamed though she noticed that Ray's eyes shifted a little as he explained. So there was probably more to it than simply helping a fellow church-goer. "Let me fix her a plate," Icie offered.

"Now that would be nice."

Shortly thereafter she handed Ray the full plate and sent him on his way, forging him but still feeling a bit let down.

"So, there's no dessert?"

Icie turned to find Clay Mammoth still sitting at the table, his empty plate a definite sign that he had enjoyed the meal, the methodical patting of his stomach another; and the satisfied grin still another. Yet the intense stare he directed her way was not something she wanted to interpret.

"No, dessert," Icie shook her head, "but I'm glad you enjoyed the meal." She removed the leftovers from the table and stored them in the fridge. The entire time, she felt Clay's eyes on her.

"I wish I had known that. I would have made one."

"Oh?" Icie answered trying to sound as disinterested with her interest as possible.

"My famous peach cobbler."

"Aw, too bad." Icie cleared the table keeping herself busy, keeping herself from looking at Clay from acknowledging the intense stare that had yet to leave her. She didn't want to go back to being rude. They had a truce. To honor it, he needed to leave. Why didn't he leave?

"The best dessert I ever made. Hey the only dessert I've ever made."

"Sounds good," Icie said, her back to him as she began to rinse the dishes and stack them in the dishwasher. Leave, leave, she begged him in her head. Icie couldn't believe herself. Where was the tough girl? Where was the woman that told this two-hundred forty pound man what to do for two hours straight every day? Tell him to leave.

"You don't have to do that, you know." Icie could hear him stand. "A cleaning lady comes in a few times a week. She could handle that. It's what I pay her to do." He was moving toward her.

"I don't mind. I made the mess. I'll clean it up."

"Leave." Her own voice pleaded inside her head.

"Just, go." It said once again.

"You don't have to stay and entertain me," was what she said out loud. "Go on up to bed. Get yourself rested for tomorrow's grueling session." That was good. It sounded nice and truce-like.

"I'm not tired." He was still moving toward her; the thump of the crutches telling her he was right behind her. "I feel like some coffee. How about a cup?"

"No, thanks."

"To toast the truce we made this morning?"

"With coffee?" Icie turned, the suggestion was a surprise, the movement a mistake. She should never have stared into the eyes of a man who activated some dormant sensor in her brain. It threw her body into a vibrating string of warmth.

"I've got beer; wine, scotch, bourbon, and a bar full of every liqueur you could probably name, but I'm staying way from that stuff. I'm in training, remember. The football field's where I need to be. So coffee's what I'm offering."

Beer, wine, liqueurs, and something about coffee mingled in her brain as he Looked at her expectedly. His eyes, they were like coffee. A deep, dark roast. "Coffee," she whispered.

"Coffee it is." He was holding a mug in his hand, and his arms brushed against hers. It was a slight touch, a second's connection, a mere fraction of the time she spent touching or guiding Clay through a tough exercise or administering the dreaded cool down. But that was work, this was…

Icie didn't want to think about what this was. She hadn't meant to agree to having coffee with him, but now she was. She forced herself not to react to the contact, but she could not ignore the instantaneous increase of heated vibrations on the spot where their arms met. She stared at the offending arm as he reached inside the cabinet for another mug. If his eyes were a deep, dark roast then the skin covering the strong arms stretched above her a fine, medium? No, more like a medium to light roast. Icie almost laughed out loud. If she didn't feel so nervous about being around Clay Mammoth, she would have. "Of all things coffee?" she muttered to herself, not meaning to say the words out loud. Clay Mammoth and coffee? No one else would compare the two.

"You don't have to have coffee. I can open a bottle of wine, or do you want a beer?"

Alcohol was not what she needed. "Coffee's fine," she assured him, meaning to drink a quick cup and take herself off to her room.

Clay Mammoth turned away from her then, and she slowly rinsed and placed the last dish into the dishwasher and started the machine. The hum and spray of the dishwasher mixed with the sounds of Clay rummaging through cabinets.

It all seemed so homey, cozy even. Clay Mammoth homey and cozy? She needed to leave, but pride in her word and her commitment to the truce they had agreed on made her stay. She just wouldn't look at him. She shouldn't have taken even one look into his eyes tonight. A blindfold or one of those pirate patches would have been nice. Naw, it wouldn't have worked. There still would have been one eye irresistibly drawn to him. Do not look at him, she commanded herself. Sip coffee for a few minutes and avoid direct eye contact. That was all she had to do.

In no time the rousing aroma of the fresh brew filled the room. The smell put Icie into action. She brought the creamer and sugar that Clay had laid on the counter to the table and then carried the two full mugs of coffee he poured to the table.

"I'd have been a gentleman and done that myself but I need my arms to get around."

"You'll be free of that problem soon," Icie answered as she sat down.

"I'm glad to hear it. I can find a dozen more uses for them." He sat across from her. He raised his hands high above his head stretching, entwining them in a gradual melding before pushing out straight towards her then slowly down, down, down. The entire stretch included an intense bone melting, pleasure making groan, that called out to that hidden sensor she'd newly discovered, sending a flash of heat throughout her body. Even the slight sound of his knuckles cracking seem to translate to her body a signal of—Nope she wasn't even going to think it.

Icie continued to watch as Clay slowly released his long athletic fingers from the grip they had on each other. Capable, firm fingers, that rolled into careless fists and now rested on each thigh. Icie was a mesmerized one-person audience to the Clay Mammoth stretch show right next to her. Legs open, fists resting on each firm muscled leg he leaned in closer as if he wanted to say something else, or as if he was waiting for her to reply.

Trying to pull the heat inside, Icie said the first thing that came to mind. "I bet you can." Needing something to do besides look at the completely masculine way he claimed the chair next to her; she added creamer to her coffee wishing it was a sno-ball, a slurpee, anything cold.

"That sounded like a put-down, breaking the truce already?"

"Not at all, I'm simply applying universal knowledge and drawing a conclusion." That was a cool collected answer. Icie was proud of herself

"Universal knowledge? About me?"

Icie nodded not believing that they were actually conversing without a go-between. There was no Steve, no Ray just the two of them. A few moments of uncomfortable silence, a few sips of coffee, comments about the weather and then a short good-bye was what she had expected.

"You can't leave it like that. Be more specific. Tell me exactly, what do you mean?" he demanded. "Could it be universal knowledge about my injury?' He paused in thought. "No, that's not information that's widely known."

"Which is why I'm stuck here." She was feeling better; more normal. The heat was not as intense, more like a gentle hum, almost as soothing as the sound of the dishwasher. Which was easier to deal with than the lighting flash of heat she'd felt a few minutes before. Sexual tension can be diminished, knocked out even. Icie was sure of it now.

Without pause, he ignored her flip answer. "Universal knowledge about my career? My stats? Awards?" he asked without a break for an answer; then pausing to answer his own question. "No, that tone wasn't a dig at my professional career."

He trained his eyes on her. Icie trained her eyes below his. She was determined not to make direct eye contact with him again. His nose, that's where she'd focus. He had a regular nose. Naw, there was nothing too special about it, which shifted her interest to his mouth.

"Women," he stated. "My love life?" he asked.

As his lips moved to shape the words that formed her exact thoughts, Icie's brain took a trip to Wonderland.

I wonder…how a kiss from those perfect Clay Mammoth lips would feel. A deep sigh built inside of her which she released as tiny puffs hopping it went unnoticed. But that attempt at controlling her outer reaction did nothing to stop her mind from traveling.

It went on wondering. Wondering…how he would initiate a kiss, a first kiss, the first contact between a man and a woman. Would he make a quick grab, ease into a slow lean, or wait for her eyes to say yes as he nibbled at her lips until she took his on her own?

Wondering…how his lips would feel pressed against hers?

Hard?

Soft?

Wondering how he would taste? Like a fine medium roast or—"Well?" His smooth, deep voice pulled her out of Wonderland.

Icie's eyes lowered, but other than that she didn't move a muscle. What was she doing? Could he tell what she was thinking? She hoped her expression didn't reveal any of her thoughts.

"That's it! I know it. I can tell exactly what you're thinking."

"You can?" she asked, a touch of real fear running through her. If he could tell, then he knew about all the sexual tension she was fighting and then he would somehow—.

"It was a dig at my love life."

Relief. A flood of it went through her. Icie looked up but kept her focus away from his lips. She couldn't meet his eyes, and his lips were an invitation to a place she didn't want to visit. His nose was all she had left. Staring at his very ordinary nose and without revealing any of the panic she felt a moment ago Icie asked, "Why would you say that?"

"I have ways of reading people."

"I didn't say anything. I didn't do anything."

"You did."

"What? What did I do?" Icie wanted to know. She had always been so good at hiding what she felt, or what she thought. Few people knew how to read her.

"That's my secret," Clay told her.

Icie didn't like that. "Fine then." She lifted her mug of coffee and took a sip. Three sips, that was all she was going to give him. The coffee had cooled a bit but still sent a warm trail of liquid down her already heated body. Maybe three was too many. She'd give one more sip and be gone.

"Now you're mad at me."

"Of course not." She lifted the mug again, took her second sip. She stood before swallowing and carried the mug across the room to the stainless sink and poured out what was left of the dark liquid. "Thanks for the coffee," she said, her back to him as she rinsed the mug. "I'll talk to you—"

"Now."

He was standing right behind her. Close enough that she could feel him there but far enough that she was able to turn without touching him. He was using only one crutch supporting his weight on his good leg. But that still didn't explain how he had moved so quickly without her hearing him?

That question must have been all over her face because he told her; "I can move quietly when I need to."

"And am I to assume that you needed to just now?" Icie said slowly and carefully, not sure where this was going.

"Of course. You were about to run off without telling me what you meant earlier."

"About what?" Icie could not remember what they had been talking about. Her need to get away from the feelings that had been building since he came into the kitchen created a chaotic jumble in her head.

"The use of my hands in relation to my love life."

"I don't want to talk about your love life."

"You started it, Ice Princess."

The misuse of her nickname normally irritated her but not this time. Icie didn't know why. Maybe it was because he was standing so close. Maybe it was the— whatever it was Icie had not meant to start this. "No," she said and once again more firmly, "no, I didn't."

"Oh, but you did." He shifted the crutch from under his arms and laid it against the sink in one smooth move. "That's one good thing my hands are good for," he nodded at the crutch lying against the counter; "moving obstacles out of my way." The obstacle was the solitary support Icie wished he was still relying on. Instead he gripped the counter with both hands, each one landing much to close to her own. "I won't leave you wondering about my skills. I'll give it to you straight from the source."

"You don't have to, I know all about them," Icie told him, knowing she sounded anything but convincing as her mind busily projected images of what those skills would include. She shook her head trying to erase the sight of arms doing things and going places they had no business going.

"I insist. You see," he leaned in a little closer; "arms are not the only body part playing a specific role in a situation involving the women in my life."

"I wouldn't think so." That was not what she should have said. 'Good night. I don't wish to discuss this. See you in the morning,' were the words she should have been saying.

"Hands play an even larger role in a man/woman encounter."

"Hands," she said softly, knowing this discussion had nothing to do with maintaining a truce, and everything to do with appeasing the heated vibrations, perhaps stroking the tension that was beginning to be so much a part of her since her connection with Clay Mammoth.

"They're attached to the arms, so they're important."

"That's true," was all she could manage to answer.

"Let me demonstrate."

Which is exactly what he did. Clay Mammoth slipped a hand around her waist and somehow shifted so that they had switched places. If she were asked to explain how, Icie would not be able to do so. His back was now to the sink, and he was holding her closer, oh so much closer, than before. She should do something. Icie raised her head and met his direct, uncensored gaze That was the something she should not have done. That vibrating sting of heat, the hum of sexual tension in the air instantly expanded. Feelings of want filled her;

pouring out of her skin, reaching into the air; filling the room with what she didn't want Clay to know, what she didn't want to feel. But it was there.

"Feel that. You can't hide it now, can you?"

Her head nodded in agreement in a sort of half shake. It was foolish of her to even attempt to pretend that she couldn't.

"That was pretty much how I felt that first day. Reacting to being near you. I couldn't help it either."

She understood. Icie couldn't stop the warm tingle of anticipation taking over every inch of her skin. She took a deep breath releasing the sigh that had been stuck inside her all evening long. Was that her breath catching at the end? This was so new but—she wanted it. She wanted Clay Mammoth to show her how he used his hands.

And his eyes told her he understood. Through the soft fabric of her t-shirt, long, firm fingers moved one by one creating little pressure points. An enticement? With her body tingling, and desire spinning inside of her, Icie didn't need much enticement. At this moment she couldn't think of any reason why Clay shouldn't demonstrate. What could it hurt?

"Yeah." His smooth voice lowered to a deep hum that only the two of them could hear. "I think it's about time we did something about it, too."

The finger of one hand traveled across her lips, back and forth, inviting them to part. As her desires intensified, Icie did something she had never done before. She closed her eyes and with the tip of her tongue tasted the hard warmth of his finger. The texture and feel of that one part of him electrified her and had her wondering about the rest of him. But not for long. Slowly he removed that last finger, tracing her lips, her chin, creating a moist zigzag trail along the way.

Beyond the arm holding her side there was no other contact. Her skin craved his touch, the tingling there almost a song calling out to him.

"Open."

What did he mean? Icie wondered as he slowly lifted her face, her chin captured by his thumb and forefinger. That finger that had tasted so, so much like him.

"Open them for me," he said this time, a warm whiff of air touching each eyelid. Each closed eyelid. She hadn't realized that her eyes were closed. Simply feeling Clay had been almost too much for her senses. But she obeyed, and he saw reflected there a desire equal to his.

The tingling of her skin became a throb as he engulfed her; nibbling at her lips but only for the fraction of time it took her to invite him inside. Oh, and she loved having him there.

The heat of him there.

The hard pressure of his mouth pressed against hers.

The soft, gentle caress of his tongue finding pleasure points inside her mouth and inviting her to do the same for his.

And the textures, soft, rough, smooth, so much more than that tiny taste she'd had of him.

That single thrilling finger that wasn't so lonely now, Icie realized as she felt a spiral of sensation move toward her hips. Fingers that were connected to the hands and the arms of Clay Mammoth.

They held her to him as he caressed her bottom, his fingers not an invasion, not a grappling desperate touch but an extension of the kiss that had melded them together. Icie liked it that way. She wanted him to do more with his hand, to demonstrate what satisfaction he could give to every other part of her body.

"Fifty-one! Damn it man! Couldn't you keep your hands off the damn therapist!"

The sound of Coach Barnes' voice landed Icie on her feet. She hadn't known that she'd been standing on her toes trying to get closer to him. His hands left her bottom, his lips pulled away from hers but came back for one last touch, a gentle press, a soft ending.

"No, I couldn't," he said looking into her eyes.

"Fifty-one, there you go again always out for some damn fun. Damn it, man!"

"You said that already coach," Clay answered, his eyes leaving hers to look at the man who had interrupted them.

Icie took a step back moving away from the hand that rested on her lower back. What was she doing? How could she have forgotten? Clay was fifty-one, out for fun. That's what she was to him. Some fun. Icie was nobody's plaything. Her skin, which a moment before held the tingling warmth of his touch, chilled with offense. Her lips froze into a grim line of regret.

"And I'm going to say it again. Damn it man, we don't need this kind of interference. This therapist has to stay," Coach Barnes shouted over her head, his hand waving in her direction

"We?" Clay asked.

"This therapist?" Icie said taking another step back coolly assessing each man.

"Yeah, Miss Frozen, what's your name?"

"Icie Ellis," she told him as Clay snickered behind her. That did it. This was nothing but a moment of fun for him. She threw her hardest, coldest stare his way. The snickering noises coming from his mouth stopped when their eyes met.

"Ice Princess, don't."

"No, Fifty-one, don't you." She moved toward him taking the three steps that brought them face to face once again. "Don't you ever demonstrate any other moves on me. I am not interested in what your hands can do." Icie headed out of the kitchen but stopped at the door. She turned to Coach Barnes. "Thanks for the splash," she told him before leaving the room.

"Icie," she heard Clay say.

"What splash? What's she talking about, Mammoth?" she heard the coach bellow. Then, "You're not leaving! Remember you're still Clay's therapist."

"She didn't say anything about leaving coach, don't be ridiculous. Hand me my crutch."

"For what?"

"I need to talk to her."

"You need to leave her alone. Leave this one alone, Clay"

"As if you can tell me what to do."

The conversation between player and coach followed her down the hall and to the bottom of the stairs where Clay caught up with her.

"Icie, wait."

She didn't want to wait. She wanted to run up the stairs away from him. How could she have forgotten the player he was? She was the only woman around, so of course he made the play for her and she had let him, let that sexual tension rule her judgment. She stood as still as a frozen statue waiting for him to speak.

"It wasn't just for fun," was all he said before turning back toward the kitchen.

"What were you thinking, damn it?" Icie heard the coach howl a moment later. A string of "damn its" and other colorful words followed her up the stairs.

What was she thinking, damn it?

CHAPTER 8

Clay sat in his gym waiting for Icie. It was after three and she was late for his evening session. On purpose he was sure. Clay had had enough of this. For the last four days she had lived up to her name. He couldn't stand another minute of it.

She was cold.

She was unresponsive to anything he did.

He tried to talk, to joke with her even, but every word he uttered slid down the frozen, jagged glacier she had placed between them. It was a solid, though transparent, block making it so easy to see right through her.

They had kissed.

So what.

She had enjoyed him just as much as he had enjoyed her. A quick blink of her eyes, just before plastering on the frozen face whenever she was uncomfortable with a situation was proof enough. And she had done quite a bit of blinking that evening. Then there was the feel of her. Clay knew when an excited, hot woman was in his arms. He was in no doubt that they were together on what they were feeling.

Damn Coach Barnes. What made the man think he had to check up on him?

Damn Uncle Ray for leaving the door unlocked. Coach claimed he'd knocked. Clay understood why he hadn't heard it. He wouldn't have heard a crowd of Crescent fans roaring and cheering an interception and touchdown in the last minute of a game for the win. All he could hear were the soft breathy sighs coming from his Ice Princess, a sure sign that he had begun the melting process. But more than that, he found himself wanting to blend, to merge with the part of her that he had softened with his touch, to get inside, to be a part of her.

It was a mind blowing experience, a head-on rush he hadn't expected. Oh, but it felt so good. And Clay, he knew, just knew, that she felt it too. He was hard with remembrance now.

So what was the problem? If he could look past her shady dealings with his father; why couldn't they get together? Though he no longer believed that she had any romantic involvements with his dad, Clay still wasn't too sure about the money end of the deal. They would talk today. He'd make her talk.

Clay walked to the bench without the aid of his crutches. This morning she had told him to put them away for good. His knee was stiff, a little uncomfortable but not as uncomfortable as the ache between his legs. All this tension couldn't be good for his recovery. At least it kept his focus off the soreness in his knee. The new exercises she pushed on him were a challenge. Was it his imagination or was she being more brutal than before? He sat on the bench just as she came up the stairs.

"No elevator'?" he asked. She was wearing a plain white lab coat over jeans and a silky looking white blouse that invited him to touch it just to see if it was as soft as it looked. He wondered how different it would feel from the t-shirt she wore Monday night. Would the material allow her heat to penetrate to his fingers? The silkiness would be different. With his hand pressed against her breast he could make her—

"Start," she said, a raspy quality to her Voice. "What was that?" he asked.

"Warm up, let's go."

"Sorry, I was daydreaming."

"Hmm," was her non-committal response. "About you."

"Hmm," was all she said again.

He was getting nowhere. "Look we've got to talk about this."

"There's nothing to talk about. I'm the therapist, you're the patient. There's nothing more to say"

"There could be." Clay finished the first round of warm-up exercises. He might as well say what was on his mind. "Look at what you do to me."

They both looked down. "I'm sure a magazine full of explicit photographs or a music video could provide the same results."

"You think so?"

"I know so. That is why I choose to ignore it."

"It will only get worse."

"For whom?"

Clay laughed at that. This was the most he had gotten out of her since Monday when she had been so friendly so full of life. She had even smiled at him then. Clay had liked that. He wanted that Icie back. And unable to lie to himself Clay desperately wanted her the way she had been later that same evening.

Hot.

In his arms.

Hot.

Willing.

But he needed the friendly Icie back even more. "For me, I guess. This could become permanent."

"God forbid, Fifty-one. I know as well as you do that there are enough women out there to help you with that kind of problem. I, myself, have no plans to help you in that area."

"But there's only one woman here I want to help me solve this particular problem."

She blinked twice before answering. "You mean there's only one woman here. Period. I'm convenient, so you're interested."

"Ouch." That hurt worse than the hit he took two years ago that threw him into a flip and knocked the wind out of him. The wind hadn't been knocked out of him just now, but the comment hurt just as much. When had he started to care what she thought of him? "You don't think much of me, do you?" he found himself asking out loud.

"True, so we might as well get this all straight and out in the open."

"It's what I've been trying to do all week."

"Attempting to get me to go to bed with you is what you have been trying to do all week."

"Not true," he told her, although it was partially true. Getting her to bed had been on his mind ever since she pressed her body into his without signs of backing away. She was backing away now, good and fast.

"I don't go to bed with people I have such a low opinion of."

"Okay."

She blinked again looking beautifully confused. "That's it?"

"That's it," Clay told her.

"So we understand each other."

"Absolutely"

She blinked again but didn't say a word.

The session continued in almost complete silence. The only sounds were the short commands she issued like a drill sergeant every once in awhile. The new exercises tested his stamina, but Clay gritted his teeth and kept his mind on the prize. A cool down with his Ice Princess's warm hands attending to his muscles and the rare pleasure of having her touching him willingly was heaven.

Almost willingly anyway.

It wasn't much, but he'd settle for all he could have right now. Clay Mammoth settling? What would the boys think of that? He could barely comprehend it himself.

A half an hour later he was rewarded with a cool down that began, and ended, much too quickly. Her fingers were attentive to his worn out muscles, making him relax as well as stimulating him beyond what he once thought he was capable of handling. At one point, her hand moved up massaging his upper thigh. Having not an ounce of control for that heated excitement that lay between his legs, Clay felt himself move toward her. He went from dying for a simple massage to hoping she didn't notice his reaction at all. Maybe she was able to ignore his hardness. He certainly couldn't.

"Done. See you Monday," she said much too soon. Her bag was on her shoulder; and her feet were taking her down the stairs by the time he said goodbye, leaving him experiencing something much more than a lack of sexual satisfaction.

This—whatever it was, was not an easy situation to find himself in, but a bit of frustration in his system was a whole lot easier to cope with than the anger that had once lived inside of him.

The anger had begun to dissolve when he had finally come to the realization that he would return to the game he loved. It would simply take patience. That quality, he was in short supply of. Patience, he realized, he relied on Icie for.

He would also have his Ice Princess once and for all. Something else that would take a bit of simple patience.

"Just who are you kidding, man?" Clay asked himself out loud. There was nothing simple about his recovery, or Icie.

Icie couldn't get out of Clay Mammoth's house fast enough. She was so preoccupied with the relief a few days free of Clay's presence brought that she was halfway down the steps before she realized that she had gone straight past Ray without a word. She turned walking up a few steps.

"Ray."

"Oh, hey there, Icie." He seemed to be preoccupied himself.

"I haven't seen you lately"

"I've been pretty busy."

"I noticed. You've been coming in late every night. You're supposed to be here for me, Ray"

"I know. I know, but I have been here."

"Long after ten o'clock when it doesn't make a difference."

"Sorry, what have you been doing? Locking yourself in your room, I bet?" he smiled, knowing her so well.

"Pretty much."

"Sorry."

"You said that already." Icie took a good, hard look at him. He seemed to be himself but then again…, there was something different. "Are you okay, Ray?" She had to ask.

"Yeah, but I'm in a hurry. Can we talk about this later, Icie girl?"

"Sure, we're still on for Monday, right?"

"As always. I can't wait to see what you've got cooked up for us." He rubbed his hands together in anticipation.

That was a bit strange, but Icie was too relieved to get away from Clay to worry much about it. They would catch up with each other on Monday at dinner.

Less than a half an hour later, Icie entered her quiet home going to the stereo to fill in the silence. Louis Armstrong's voice filled the room. It wasn't Michelle's high pitched nonsense, but it did the trick. Icie needed to revel in Louis's deep, soulful timber. His voice reminded her that no matter how she felt at this moment she truly did live in a wonderful world.

She fixed herself a cup of soup. Not exactly the satisfying meal she had cooked Monday evening, but good enough.

Uh, she didn't mean to think about Monday.

She wanted to erase every minute of that day out of her mind.

How could she have been so stupid?

Friendliness killing sexual tension?

Ha! She had been fooling herself. At least it hadn't taken long for her to realize that fact. Just a few moments alone with Clay outside of their professional relationship was all it took to kill that ridiculous idea. And what exactly had she done? Invited Fifty-one-out-for-fun Clay Mammoth to make a move.

And Lord, did he make a move!

A warm shiver went through her as she remembered it all. A body she had wanted to reach inside, and a kiss that had answered all her wonderings. Answers she really didn't need to know.

Not feeling up to hanging around her empty apartment and dwelling on Clay, Icie changed into her one piece swimsuit, grabbed her gym bag and was out the door. She arrived at the YMCA and even found a parking space without any trouble, but she had to dig inside her purse to find the membership card she hadn't used in over two months.

"Well if isn't Miss Freeze herself."

Icie forgot about her purse, letting it slide down her shoulder as she grinned up at the tall thin man standing before her. "Hi Tim." Icie was always happy to see her old classmate.

"Finally showed up for a workout, huh?" He gave her a hug.

She hugged him right back, even threw in a squeeze. No tension, no problem. Why couldn't it be that way with Clay? "You know how that goes. Time to do everything but—"

"Exercise," he finished for her.

"I haven't talked to you in ages. How have you been?" It would be wonderful, she realized, if she could transfer her feelings for Clay to this tall pleasant man before her. She liked Tim. He was a nice guy. Single. Talented. Successful. And handsome in his own way.

He nodded. "I've been okay but you, I see, have been very lazy."

"Partly, I've got a new patient." Icie slipped her bag back onto her shoulder trying to stop herself from comparing Tim to Clay. Tim was nothing like Clay who had that in-your-face handsomeness women died for. Tim was handsome but had a more laid back take-a-step-away-to-see-for-yourself kind of attractiveness.

"That's nothing new," he told her then added as an afterthought, "I've got a new client."

"Nothing new for you either." Icie went back to digging in her purse.

"You've got loads of clients."

"True. Too many if you ask me."

"Found it!" Icie flashed her membership card. "Where are you working out today? With the weights or on the track?"

"Neither one, I just came from the treadmill. I was on my way out, but I'll walk with you. We've got some catching up to do. To the pool right?"

"Yeah, I thought I'd do a few laps." To wash Clay Mammoth out of my head, she thought, determined to have a normal conversation with an old friend without that football player breaking interference and pounding into her brain.

"It's hot enough for it."

"Who are you telling? I soaked in a bit too many rays getting out of my car and into wherever I was going"

"I hear ya, but it's almost August, the worst is yet to come."

"Summertime in N'awlins, don't you just love it." They laughed.

"So tell me about this new patient of yours," he asked.

Icie normally gave Tim a little summary of her patients giving a few details, adding a bit here and there about their personalities. It was all part of the process Tim had told her. The process that would guide him to accurately depict each of her patients on a wall in her office. A few years ago, before Tim had been in such high demand, she had hired him to paint a mural. It was a simple design; fluffy white clouds, a wide open field, bright sunshine. A picture that inspired hope, a bright, new beginning. That was what she wanted to represent for her patients. In the time it took for him to paint the mural, he had watched from the sidelines the progress of one of her patients and without realizing what he was doing had added the little boy to the scene.

Icie had loved the idea. From then on, Tim asked about every one of her patients, stopped by to meet them at least once so that he could do a sketch without any of them suspecting a thing. And then he would show up to add one more person to the mural. The big, grassy field was getting crowded, but there still was room for more.

"Icie, your patient. Tell me about your new kid."

"My kid? Why do you always call them my kids?"

"Because you take them under your wing, guide them and allow them to go on to live their lives to the fullest. Exactly like any good parent would do."

He had it right. "How do you know me so well?"

"No biggie, I just do. The patient?"

They had just reached the doors to the locker rooms. "Meet me by the pool."

Icie would love to tell Tim about her patient, her new kid as he called him. Could she? She put her things inside a locker and went to the pool. Tim was pacing up and down.

"Something wrong?" he asked her.

"No, I just don't think I can tell you about this kid."

"Why?" He looked insulted. "How am I supposed to paint the kid if you don't tell me about—" he paused.

"Him," Icie supplied.

"That's a start. At least I know its a him."

Icie laughed at that. "It's complicated," she sobered.

"Alright." And that was the end of it.

Tim was such an easy person. Why? Oh why? Stop it Icie, she told herself.

"Are we still on for next week?"

"Mmmm?"

"The painting, in the evenings. You're almost through with rehabilitation for Antonia, Neisha, Corey and Roy right?"

"Yeah, just about. How do you remember all their names?"

"It's easy, these kids are special. They go through great pain, endure and succeed. That's why I paint them. That mural is a memorial."

"That's sweet."

"That's because I'm a sweet kind of guy"

That was true, but then again not so true. An image of Steve and Clay talking and admiring the Crescent Symbol reminded her of something. "Not to everyone."

"But to you. Friends are important."

"How about potential clients?" she asked. "Anybody in particular."

"What does the name Clay Mammoth mean to you?"

"Him."

Icie almost laughed out loud. She knew all the adjectives that him implied.

"You know him?" Tim asked.

"You could say that."

"He called my studio and expected me to drop whatever I was doing to paint for the Mighty Mammoth."

This time Icie did laugh. "You didn't like him too much, did you?"

"On the field he's one tough brother. On the phone—lets just say he hasn't heard from me yet."

"So you've gotten so famous you can pick and choose."

"Famous or not, that's what I've always done. It's why I paint for you, Icie. Why I still work for you."

"But I haven't paid you since the first time you painted."

"That doesn't matter. Six-o'clock every day next week to paint?"

"Every day except Monday"

"Okay, see you then." He gave her a peck on the cheek and was on his way. That peck should have felt like something. But it didn't. Too bad. Tim was a friend and would only be a friend.

Icie swam, practicing her strokes. The water gliding past her was a cooling comfort. By the time she finished, she was happier that she had come. The exercise both energized and relaxed her; removing the tension of the past week. It was unfortunate that Clay Mammoth, and whatever he'd done to make her want him physically, seemed to be a stubborn stain that was not easy to remove.

Monday.

Icie hated for this day to come around again, yet she looked forward to it. She needed to talk to Ray. All her Clay problems were a minor annoyance compared to her concern about her friend. She had tried to call him a few times this past weekend but he was never home. Whether the home was Clay's or his, Ray was nowhere to be found.

As soon as she entered Clay's house, Icie ran up the stairs and into her room throwing her things onto her bed. She headed down the hall straight to Ray's room. She still had time before her first session with Clay began. She knocked, but got a response from the wrong door. Clay poked his head out of the room a few doors down.

"You're early."

"I know." Icie tried to suppress the thrill she felt at just hearing his voice. "Have you seen Ray?" Clay closed the door behind him with a slow confident stride, and started moving toward her. Any other person looking at the sure way he moved would never have suspected that he was still in the rehabilitation stage of his injury. He had only been relieved of his crutches a few days ago but there he stood the epitome of a supreme athletic body. Icie would have preferred that he answer her question from where he had stood a few moments before. But what could she do? Run away?

No, she'd practice.

Practice suppressing all the silly tingles and throbs that flicked on like a light switch whenever he was near. And standing near was exactly what he was doing. That and smiling. Maybe he didn't hear the question. "Have you seen Ray?" Icie asked again.

"No, not once today." He leaned against the wall a sure sign that his leg was probably bothering him a little.

"Have you been using your leg too much?"

He shook his head no in a slow masculine way that sent a rush of tingles down her spine.

Practice, girl, hold it together Icie reminded herself.

"Is something wrong?" he asked her.

"No, I just wanted to find Ray"

"You're not going to find him here."

"That's obvious."

"I heard him leave early this morning."

"I thought you said you didn't see him?"

"Hearing is not seeing."

"You could have said what you meant." Icie wasn't up to playing word games with Clay Mammoth. "Look, I'll meet you up in ten minutes," she told him, going back to her room.

That didn't go too well Clay had to admit. He was trying to get her to talk to him, make her linger for a while because once the therapy session started upstairs she was all professional woman, drill sergeant, and coach. That meshed into one tough woman. If he was going to change her opinion of him, Clay had to take advantage of every moment he could catch her outside of a therapy session. He shrugged. There would be other opportunities. After all the woman did live in his house five days a week.

Clay went to the elevator and straight to the mirrored wall. It felt good to see himself without those crutches. He eyed his image from head to toe. Did all those months of forced inactivity take the edge off his athletic skills? Seven months into the year and he hadn't played a bit of football since that fatal Super Bowl game, unless he counted the one that was the cause of him missing training camp right this minute.

Clay took a deep steadying breath, a growl rumbling inside his throat. He was oaky. Healing took time. If he could train himself to slam into a running bulldozer of a player from any opposing team without flinching, then he could train himself to have patience. And his skills? Clay had nothing to worry about. The skills he possessed were ones that he was born with. They were instinctive. That's how his dad had always described them. The man was wise. Clay still missed him sometimes.

The sound of feet pounding on the stairs drew his attention away from himself. As he turned toward the sound, his eyes once again caught the blank wall on the other side of the room. That wall should not be so plain. By now the spot should bear the Crescent symbol. Clay had to contact that Long artist again. He had offered to pay the man double what he normally charged, but all he would say was that he was booked up and would call back when he was available.

"Let's get started," Icie told him without once looking in his direction.

Clay walked over, careful not to put too much pressure on his knee. As he knew it would, the session began and progressed with Icie in command. Clay didn't know why but when she was in professional mode his Ice Princess held a sort of power over him making him want to do whatever she wanted him to do.

At first he had thought it was his determination to get back to the game he loved. Then Steve was here as a sort of distraction. Now there was no Steve, no distraction and no reason why he couldn't start a bit of flirtation during the session.

No reason except that Icie would not stand for it.

Flirting with her might push her to quit. Something she said she'd never done before. Clay admired that. He wasn't a quitter either. Fifty-one might be known for having fun, but he wasn't one to give up easily. Which was exactly why he knew he would once again feel Icie pushing into him with her entire body as if she couldn't get close enough, as if she couldn't feel enough.

Now that was something worth working for. He had never had so much woman in his arms. Not because she wasn't one of those skinny model types he was used to, but because she was so natural. The way her breath caught on a sigh, her softness, her irresistible reaction to a kiss. What would happen when he really demonstrated the skills his hands possessed? Somehow he knew that sleeping with Icie would be as different, and special, as that one little kiss that had left him wanting her constantly.

"Okay we're done."

"What?"

"We're done. The session's over."

Done? Had he missed the cool down? Had he actually daydreamed through his favorite part of the session?

"I'll see you at three."

"Wait. Don't go yet. Come promise me something."

She paused without turning around. "Don't start that stuff again, Fifty-one."

"I'm not starting anything." Clay had forgotten about the come promise mess he started.

"I thought you might be interested in meeting me halfway."

"Halfway to what?"

To heaven he wanted to say but knew that would sound either too cocky or too corny.

"Hallway to having a decent patient/therapist relationship."

"An indecent relationship is actually what you're looking for."

"I'm much deeper than that."

"Prove it," she told him, and without turning around she bounded down the steps and headed to her jeep, leaving him until the evening session.

"Prove it? Oh, I could prove it," Clay whispered to himself, then got busy. He called a sign painter; contacted the Blue and White shop that specialized in Crescent gear; and ordered a few things online not once questioning why he was going to so much trouble to prove himself to a woman that he once suspected of being a gold digger. "I guess," Clay said out loud to the empty room, "because now, I suspect that there has to be so much more to her."

She was much deeper than that.

Clay knew he was right. He believed it, as sure as the fact that he would be a starter, playing defense on Thanksgiving day with his fellow teammates.

CHAPTER 9

Later that same day, Icie was once again waved through the gates of the Eastover subdivision by the security guard who had come to know her face. She wished that the guard didn't know her face so well, and that she didn't have to stick to that ridiculous therapist-in-residence clause in the contract she had signed. Clay hadn't needed her once at night during the last few weeks. And he had survived weekends without her presence, but still she was stuck with spending the week in Clay Mammoth's house. Something she probably could have weaseled out of with a positive report of his progress if Coach Barnes hadn't barged in on her moment of insanity in the kitchen that night.

After witnessing her and Clay in what could only be described as a lovelock, he insisted on every letter of the contract be followed. Icie felt like releasing a Mammoth growl. Instead she blew out a tremendous breath. Though the situation with Clay was frustrating, she had to admit, overall there were some good things happening around her. Three of her patients were officially signed out of her care having fully recovered from their injuries. Neisha, Corey and Roy were all looking forward to starting school in the fall and as Roy told her; "Do regular kid stuff." Icie could feel her eyes fill. They had all said their good byes but promised to come back for a special farewell party after Tim added each of them to the mural of course.

As Icie turned down Crescent Drive, Clay's doing she was sure, she felt less tense. Knowing that she did her best to get her patients where they needed to be gave her a natural high. She was still on guard, still committed to practicing her resistance to Clay. But even thoughts of her trouble with Clay couldn't dampen her mood. Ray, on the other hand, still worried her a little, but tonight she'd have a long talk with him. Icie was going to find out why he was acting so mysteriously.

Icie pulled into her regular spot at the end of the long drive. She immediately noticed the large sign in the exact space she parked everyday. Considering the fact that it hadn't been there in the last few weeks or the last few hours she couldn't miss it.

"Fifty-one," she read. What? Was she in his spot now? If she was, too bad. He couldn't get out to drive anywhere anyway. Icie stopped directly in front of the sign. She read it. And read it again. Icie burst out laughing. How true it was. It had to be from Ray. The sign highlighted exactly why she felt so good about herself right now. That's why she hadn't seen Ray lately and it would explain why he had been acting so strange.

He must have had this surprise planned and wanted to keep it a secret.

Icie carried the makings for tonight's dinner as if the bags were light as a feather. She went straight to the kitchen and decided not to run around hunting for Ray again. Instead she'd get right into making the pot of gumbo, Ray's favorite. She had planned on starting before going up to work with Clay. It was just the matter of making the roux, peeling the shrimp and throwing all the other ingredients together so it could all simmer until dinnertime.

She was humming the wonderful world song as Louis Armstrong's voice played in her head and her fingers worked on peeling the two pounds of shrimp she had bought. Clay popped his head inside the door.

"What's going on?"

"Shrimp's going on," Icie answered, still on guard but too happy to be stiff and cautious.

"Dinner?"

"Gumbo," was all she said to that, neither inviting nor forbidding him to join them tonight.

He looked at his watch. "Are you sure you're going to finish this before our session?"

She had twenty minutes. "Of course, all I need to do is finish peeling the shrimp, make the stock, chop the seasonings—"

"—chop the sausage, and make the roux. I know you're the best damn therapist in the world but how are you going to do all that in twenty minutes?"

"Watch me."

"Step aside," he commanded. "Let me at those shrimp. Gotta keep us on schedule. You go do something else."

Not wanting to be in his company but wanting to serve the gumbo tonight as a thank you to Ray, Icie accepted his offer after a moment's thought. He could peel the shrimp on that end of the island while she threw the seasonings into the food processor on the other side of the kitchen. After all, this was a big kitchen. It was also a big kitchen last Monday a voice inside her head reminded her. And this time it wasn't Louis Armstrong's.

But now they were cooking. They're hands were occupied. What could happen? Clay Mammoth could happen and you know that. Suppressing the thought, she turned her attention to the food processor. As she started the roux, Clay put the shrimp heads in a big pot full of water and set it on the stove to boil. They worked in silence, both of them moving around the kitchen not once touching or saying a word to each other.

I'm here if you want me Clay silently transmitted with his eyes.

I don't want you, even though I want you is the response Icie threw back at him with hers.

All the ingredients were added to the huge pot on the stove, the island was cleaned and clear before they finally spoke.

"Done in under twenty minutes." Clay was looking at his watch. "You know, this really wasn't necessary. We could have started the session a little later."

"And mess with your schedule? No way. My muscles are used to working out at eight and three."

Icie laughed. Clay could be funny when he wanted to. "I understand. See you upstairs." This time Icie looked at her watch, "in three minutes. I forgot the bay leaf."

"Don't be late."

"I promise that I won't. I need your muscles working with me, not against me." And not on me Icie added silently as she continued to smile at him.

"Come promise me something else."

"Fifty-one," she said in warning. Clay had to mess this up. She was feeling good, even looking forward to the session instead of dreading it. Icie thought that they finally understood each other.

"Come promise me that you'll come up wearing the same smile you have on right now."

That wasn't bad. He didn't ruin it after all. "I'll try. But don't expect anything else."

He nodded and left the kitchen. That was…different. Icie didn't know what to think about it.

She found the seasoning and added two leaves to the pot, stirred and lowered the fire.

She grabbed her lab coat, the one she had worn earlier for her young patients. With words of celebration written all over it. It was her traditional final session coat.

Jogging up the stairs, Icie wondered what she'd wear to Clay's last session. While the words spread across the coat were congratulatory she would probably need something more powerful to convey the relief she was bound to feel by late October.

"Thanks," Clay told her as soon as she entered the gym. "For what?"

"Wearing the smile."

"Let's get this session started." Her smile widened. "Anything for the best damn physical therapist in the world." Clay was on the table beginning the sequence of warm-up exercises when she asked, "That's the second time you've said that. You must have seen the sign Ray put outside?"

"Number Fifty-one the best damn therapist in the world?"

"That's the one."

"Who said it was Ray?"

"It has to be Ray. Who else here would do something—"

"To put a smile on your face?" Not smiling now, Icie nodded.

"Try me."

The smile disappeared. "Why did you do that?"

"Just because."

"Why?' she asked again, honestly confused by the gesture.

"Why not? Do I have to have a motive?"

"You're all motive, Fifty-one."

"Sometimes yes and sometimes no, Fifty-one."

"That's your number." Icie did more than lose her smile. Her shoulders stiffened, a tension inside her building up once again.

"Yours too, therapist number fifty-one," he said slowly. We have something in common."

Not knowing what to say to that, Icie spent the rest of the session issuing instructions, giving standard encouragement and the quickest cool down she could get away with.

"I'll see you at dinner;" Clay called as she left the room.

Icie couldn't tell him he wasn't invited. He had helped to make the meal. "Sure," she said before taking the stairs down to her room.

That went a lot better than he thought it would. The same woman who would barely look at him this morning smiled at him, even with him until he made her mad. Then she even invited him to dinner. Well sort of invited him to dinner.

Clay took the elevator down and went to his room to get ready. He showered, shaved and pulled himself into a pair of long pants. Then he went on the internet to kill time, checking out the season's schedule. For the first time, Clay was able to look at it without his stomach twisting in frustration because of the number of games he was going to be forced to miss.

Progress was slow, but there was progress, both in his career and in his personal life with a woman he was finding himself wanting for more than the sexual satisfaction he knew they could share.

Icie was…different.

Tired of waiting, Clay left his room and went to the elevator. In the kitchen he heard her on the phone. He stood out of sight as he listened to her side of the conversation.

"You're where?"

A pause.

"Who's Victoria?"

A longer pause.

"I've already invited him."

A beautiful laugh.

"You're right, he invited himself."

A much longer pause.

"I'm always nice. It's him you ought to be telling that to. I'll take a rain check this time, Ray, but if you stand me up again there will be no more Monday night dinners for you."

When Clay heard her say goodbye, he walked into the kitchen. "That gumbo smells ready."

"It is, grab a bowl and come dish out what you like."

"I like a little of everything." Clay couldn't stop himself from taking in the everything she was blessed with. The everything he wanted to have in his arms again.

"Help yourself."

"We're eating without, Ray?" he slyly asked already knowing the answer. "He's out, again." Icie sat down at the table, having already filled her bowl.

"Same lady friend or new lady friend?"

"The same."

Clay filled his bowl and came to sit across from her. "You don't look too happy about it."

"This is not like Ray"

"It isn't?"

"In the last few years he has not missed one Monday night dinner."

"He hasn't?"

"No, and I think he's been avoiding me."

"Uncle Ray? He's been around, Miss Ice. Not as much now as before. But he's still capable of being preoccupied with his new friend. I kinda like the idea of him having a love interest."

"Hmm," she said as she stared into her gumbo.

"Oh, I understand, now."

She put her spoon down in a slow precise movement. "What is it you think you understand, Fifty-one?"

Not a wise thought to voice Clay realized and immediately attempted to take it back. "I'd better not say, Fifty-one." She gave him a sideways look.

"See what I mean. I don't want to make you mad. Then you'd put that hazel-eyed frozen stare on me. I'd get a chill, catch pneumonia, and have to go to the hospital. I don't want to go there again."

"It's the middle of summer; and my stare doesn't do a thing to you."

"That's what you think." If he were to tell the truth, it did a couple of things to him.

"Out with it!" she persisted. "What is it that you understand so well?"

"You won't get mad?"

"No."

She said she wouldn't get mad but somehow Clay knew that no actually meant yes.

"Well?"

He was thinking, trying to decide whether to lie or tell the truth.

"Out with it!" she repeated.

"You're jealous." There! He said it.

She sat still and calm, showing no signs of being mad. But she was. That frozen stare was directed right at him and it did not waiver. "My gumbo's getting cold," she remarked at last and began to eat.

Clay took her lead helping himself to the hot French bread on the table, emptying his bowl and refilling it again. "That's the best gumbo I ever made," he told her coming back to the table attempting to make some conversation. It had been a mistake to tell her what he thought about how she felt about Uncle Ray dating. "But," he continued trying desperately to drum up some conversation, "it's not the best I ever had. The best I've ever eaten was from my dad. Oh, he could make a pot of gumbo. It's the best I ever tasted in my entire life."

"I know."

Icie was looking at him, a fondness, a remembrance in her eyes that Clay was sure was in his as well. "We have something else in common besides a number don't we?"

"A love of Mr. M.'s gumbo? I loved the man more than his gumbo. He was like a father to me."

Clay dropped his spoon into the bowl, the gumbo forgotten. "What does that mean?"

"Nothing I should have said, obviously."

"He was my father. I loved him."

"I'm sure you did," she answered him. "Look, eat all the gumbo you want. I have some place to go."

"I'm done."

Icie stood and dumped an almost full bowl into the garbage disposal. He watched as she quietly put the huge pot into the fridge. "Don't wait up for me," was all she said before leaving.

Progress before dinner?

He had pushed forward ten yards and gained another first down.

Progress after dinner?

Two penalty flags and now ten yards behind, right back where he started.

In other words, no progress.

Forget this. The woman was too difficult. She really was an ice princess. And who was she to question whether or not he loved his father? Clay banged a fist on the table. He needed to do something.

He went up to the gym and put himself through an hour long workout building his pecs, his biceps, even his abs in an effort to reduce the annoyance he felt at the way the evening ended. After an hour he was tired, but it was the good kind of tired. A satisfied kind of tired. Too bad that this was the only kind of satisfaction he could get.

He went back to his room, showered again then sat out on the balcony risking the wrath of the mosquitoes. The air was humid but once in a while a warm breeze hit him.

Mind empty, Clay was content to sit, his legs propped up on another chair; swatting at mosquitoes, and breathing in the warm night air. A sense of peace fell over him until his mind began to fill. It was a slow filtering of images that sank into his brain before he realized that his thoughts were focused on one thing, one person.

Like a slow rewind he saw Icie walking away after telling him not to wait up for her; her deep concentration on the shrimp she deftly peeled, her smiling face when she gave Ray credit for the sign he'd had made for her; the cold look of anger when she let him know what a mistake it was for him to kiss her; and the breathless I-want-you-more expression she wore just after he had kissed her.

The pictures continued to move backwards until a crystal clear image of Icie, lying close to his father in a hospital bed flashed and held. That was the day his dad had died. The same day he had met Icie for the first time. Clay remembered it all; the loss, the hurt, the pain, the anger. He let all the emotions wash over him then purposely fast forwarded to his favorite image. Icie's eyes staring at him with wanting. They certainly didn't resemble icicles then. Clay stood, almost too fast, putting too much weight on his knee. Suddenly he wanted to see her again. Where the hell was she? She was supposed to be here in this house in case he needed her. It didn't matter that he hadn't needed her once during the night, that the clause in the contract was an unnecessary precaution. She was suppose to be here. That was all that mattered.

He left his room going up to the gym and on to the other side of the house where another balcony gave him a view of the driveway. He sat in the darkness watching the spot where he'd put the sign himself, watching the empty space before it. Clay didn't have to keep his vigil for long. Icie's jeep pulled into the driveway. The bumper tapped the sign making it wobble. Clay wondered if she'd done it on purpose.

Probably.

Feeling foolish for watching and waiting for a woman he had already decided was too difficult to deal with, Clay moved to the elevator. One last scrimmage, one last encounter to show that she didn't bother him at all was what kept him lingering in the hall.

"The Ice Princess returns," he announced rather dramatically

"Good night, Mr. Mammoth," was all she said as she walked away. The lab coat was gone. A pair of tight blue jeans hugged her hips and shaped her bottom. Clay watched as the satisfying image moved away from him.

"I hope it was a good one for you."

She paused a second, twisted her head in his direction and said, "Oh yes, yes it was."

Clay squelched the urge to go after her to find out exactly what she had meant by that. Instead, he found himself in the gym where once again he spent another hour working out his frustrations.

Every night, every day was the same. She didn't talk to him unless she had to. She didn't smile at him at all. And of course that was fine because she was much too difficult a woman to have anything to do with. That's exactly what he kept telling himself.

And what made her so difficult?

The fact the she didn't want him. Unfortunately Clay still wanted her. Which was why he couldn't stop himself from asking about her new evening adventures. Work was where she claimed to be going every night. Clay wasn't sure he believed her.

Which is why he sat on the balcony night after night this past week waiting to see her headlights. Waiting to see her bump the sign that still stood in the driveway. She was doing it on purpose. The thought amused him. And if he was honest with himself, the woman amused him too.

She also made him crazy with a wanting he had never experienced before. Then there was more. Clay wanted to know what was going on behind those hazel eyes. And he definitely wanted to know what was going on with her right now. Period.

Which is why, after fours days of watching her walk away from her post, Clay decided to follow her. It wasn't going to be easy. He hadn't driven a car in over seven months and hadn't been officially released to drive yet. But hey, what could a little movement hurt? The sessions Icie had been putting him through lately were more demanding than driving a car.

He wouldn't take his Porsche; Clay knew using the stick shift and handling the powerful engine would be too much of a bother. He compromised for the Lexus.

As soon as Friday evening's session was over; Icie went to her room as usual. Then, donning a pair of dark shades and a football cap, Clay went straight to the garage and as quietly as he could, slipped inside the car.

The car was warm, but not as hot as it would be if it had been parked out in the sun in the middle of a New Orleans summer. It was so good to be behind the wheel again. He wanted to savor the simple feel of the steering wheel beneath his hands but instead backed out clicking the garage door closed behind him.

Clay drove past the security guard at the gate, parked and waited near the entrance of the subdivision. A few minutes later Icie's jeep appeared and Clay followed.

Icie took the interstate. Clay was right behind her. He tailed her trying to pretend that he wasn't tailing her. He could be any driver moving along behind her. She took the Claiborne exit heading uptown and soon parked in front of a building across from a hospital.

So maybe she had been going to work.

Clay passed the building and made a U-turn coming around in time to see her enter the building. She wasn't wearing the lab coat and had changed into a t-shirt. The way she was dressed, Icie couldn't have been going there to actually work.

He found a spot in the patient parking lot and got out. It felt good to be somewhere other his house.

Clay casually entered the building and scanned the lobby. No sign of Icie. The directory caught his eye. Clay traced a finger down the list, stopping as he quietly read out loud, "I. C. Ellis Physical Therapist."

Clay laughed. That had to be a mistake. Her initials couldn't spell ice. The name Icie was strange enough. Shoulders shaking he walked down the hall finding her room as soon as he turned the corner. The door was cracked open. Icie was talking. She was talking in full animated sentences. Clay didn't think he'd heard so much from her at any one time before.

He opened the door just wide enough for him to enter. Icie was straddling a desk chair; her elbows resting on the head rest as she talked to a tall skinny looking somebody doing something to the wall.

Was she getting her office redecorated? Was that why she deserted him every day? The skinny somebody looked at him and said to Icie in a deadpan voice that carried across the room, "You've got company."

She turned toward him. She wasn't looking at him with frozen nothingness now. There was surprise and if he wasn't mistaken, concern in her face. "Fifty-one? What are you doing here?"

"The Mammoth. I thought that was him," was all the man said before going back to doing whatever he was doing before he had spotted Clay at the door.

Icie was across the room and standing in front of him before he could move two steps.

"What are you doing here?"

"How did you get here?"

"Did Ray bring you?"

"Where is he?" She was stretching her neck to look behind him. Clay ignored all her questions taking a slow walk around the room. "So this is where you work?" He walked between a set of parallel bars, bounced a hand on a huge rubber ball, avoided stepping on the mats laid in one corner of the room, and picked up some interesting looking blocks and toys on a shelf. He turned around to find Icie right behind him.

"Well?"

"I was curious to see where you work."

"That answers one question."

"You've got a nice cheerful place here," he told her; stalling. Not because he was afraid of her wrath but then again because he was afraid of her wrath. Not so much afraid, uncomfortable was the word. Clay didn't care for her hazel-eyed stare landing on him.

"Now you can answer the others."

"Who you got working back there?"

Icie turned her head in the direction of the skinny guy and almost immediately back at him. "A friend."

"You put your friends to work?" Clay moved closer to the guy on the other side of the room as he talked. He was enjoying this little game of stalling. She wasn't angry or cold and was actually talking to him. And yes, she was concerned.

"Only the good ones. Now tell me—"

"I just realized something."

"What?" she asked, obviously thrown by his quick change in subject.

"Every friend of yours I've met so far has been a man."

"So."

"So, do you have any girlfriends?"

"N—yes, I mean, of course."

"Of course," Clay agreed wondering if she had some weird fixation with men. She had been friends with his dad, now Uncle Ray, Steve and this guy whoever he was. Why couldn't she be friends with him? Although friendship could only be the ice breaker for the two of them.

We're not talking about me," she quipped. But Clay wasn't paying much attention. His focus was on the guy and the wall. That skinny guy wasn't just painting the wall. He was painting on the wall.

"Fifty-one."

"Yeah what?" He gave her half his attention while the other half moved with him to the wall as he studied the bright vibrant colors and the realistic quality of the field and foliage.

"Is Ray with you?"

"Uh- no." He was now right at the wall, nose to nose with a little boy's face that had been painted on the wall.

"How did you get here then?"

"I drove." Clay was making his way across the mural. A suspicion turned into certainty as he moved toward the man painting at the other end of the wall.

"You what?"

Icie was standing in front of him. The hazel-eyed stare that usually made him uncomfortable was directed at him now. Funny he wasn't at all uncomfortable with it this time. Placing a hand on each of her arms and holding them in his grasp, taking in the heat of her skin, Clay leaned forward to whisper in her ear. "I drove."

"But you're not supposed to," she told him after catching her breath and blinking her eyes once.

Then twice.

Forgetting the mural, forgetting the man standing a few feet away Clay told her; "I know. Are you going to punish me?"

They looked at each other for a long moment. Clay could feel the same vibrating tension in the air as that night in the kitchen. She broke eye contact staring down at his nose before stepping back.

"You need something more than punishment. I should quit," was her quiet reply.

"You can't."

"I know I can't."

"Not because of that contract, but because you always finish what you start."

Icie had something to say to that just like he knew she would but before she could get it out the skinny guy was saying, "So, this is your new kid, huh, Icie?" He was rubbing his chin with his forefinger and thumb holding the paintbrush as if it were an extension of his hand.

Clay's head shot up. "Kid?' Clay looked from Icie to the man he now knew to be Tim Long. "Have you two been talking about me behind my back?' Here stood before him the man he had been dying to meet, dying to get to agree to paint for him, and what did Clay do? Demand to know if they were talking about him.

"No, Icie wouldn't tell me who you were. A few clues, a little common sense, and I figured it out." He turned back to the mural. "You two can continue your conversation. I wasn't listening."

"We can tell how much you weren't listening." Icie was smiling at the guy who gave her a salute with his paintbrush before going back to work.

Clay didn't care for this little exchange. It was too full of familiarity. Exactly how familiar was she with this guy? Jealousy gripped him hard as he walked back to the door.

Icie stopped him, a hand on his arm, her head pressed close to his. Clay inhaled. Her hair smelled like coconuts. She had it in that ponytail of hers that she liked so much.

"Fifty-one." She was talking to him.

"Tim's way on the other side of the room. He can't hear us so explain your business here."

"So you call him Tim." Remember; no unnecessary tackles he told himself. "You don't call me by my name."

"Mr. Mammoth, why are you here?"

He was getting the hazel-eyed stare and the frosty tone. "Fifty-one's better than Mr. Mammoth." She just looked at him. "Have you two been friends long?"

"We went to school together."

"Dated?"

Her eyes blinked before she answered. "— Elementary school together."

"You see him often?"

"What can I do for you? Why are you here?"

"I was bored, and curious so I—"

"You followed me. You followed me here?" Her voice actually raised a notch. "No wonder I didn't see a sign of you anywhere before I left."

"You were looking for me? It's nice to know you care."

"I was not," she declared. "I'll call you a cab so you can get home."

"That won't be necessary." He grinned inside when he saw her blink before he walked back to where the artist was carefully painting. "Hey Tim!" Clay was across the room before Icie realized that he had moved. "Things slow down for you yet? I still want you to paint that mural of the Crescents Emblem."

"The one with you on the sidelines."

"That's the one."

"Tim's got clients coming out of his ears," Icie said standing next to him.

"You could put in a kind word for me," Clay responded.

Tim chuckled, "I think I can squeeze you in."

Clay was surprised at his compliance; Icie seemed shocked. "Can you start this weekend?" Clay jumped at the opportunity.

"No," was all he said, offering nothing else.

"Monday morning?" Clay asked.

Tim looked from him to Icie, a slow smile spread across his face before he answered. "Fine." Then he went back to work.

Strange. What could Icie possibly see in this guy? Clay had no clue. If there was anything between them, he would find out for sure. Starting Monday, he would be a careful, silent observer. Clay turned to Icie practicing his careful silent observer look. She was not pleased.

"Are you happy now that you've gotten your way?"

"Yeah, pretty much."

"Good. Now that your curiosity's satisfied, and you have what you want, and you refuse to take your therapist's advice to take a cab home, please leave my office."

"Just as you wish, my Ice Princess. This has been a productive Friday evening. I can't wait to see both of you first thing Monday morning." Clay's eyes moved from Icie to Tim Long only to return to Icie again. "I can't wait until Monday morning," he whispered; a finger grazed her cheek before he walked away leaving the door open.

"Why did you do that?" Icie turned on Tim. "You told me you had tons of clients. Why did you accept his offer?"

"For the entertainment value." Tim kept right on painting as he answered.

"Entertainment?"

"You two are fun to watch."

"Tim, that's not funny."

"Maybe not to you." He turned to her twirling the paintbrush between his fingers. "For me it's entertaining." Tim twirled the brush once more, dipped it in a bit of paint and went back to the mural before adding. "I figure, if I could never get you to look at me twice, I might as well enjoy watching Mammoth try."

"That's not true."

He turned her way again, his face blank but serious.

"Okay it's true. My life would be a whole lot easier if I had feelings for you instead of someone like Clay Mammoth."

"You do have feelings for me. It's called friendship. I realized a long time ago that friends was all we'd ever be."

"Some friend you turned out to be today."

"I'm one of the good ones, remember?"

And he was. She and Tim stayed in the office until he put the finishing touches on Corey. He had one more of her patients to add and the mural would be finished for the party she would have for the kids next Friday. Icie wished she were celebrating the end of her work experience with Clay Mammoth instead. She told herself she would trade one Clay Mammoth for one hundred kids any day.

CHAPTER 10

That's what she told herself. But with time to think over the weekend, Icie finally admitted to herself that there was more than simple sexual tension between them. There was something about Clay that called out to her. And to make matters worse, he was her patient. She could not get involved with a patient. She had never had to deal with this situation before.

Icie parked in her usual spot in Clay's driveway, putting on her brakes just before hitting the sign. Bumping it every time she parked was a childish way of getting back at him.

But then again the sign was merely a reflection of the truth. She was his fifty-first therapist and she was damn good at her job. So what if they had a few things in common. Nothing would happen between them. Nothing could because she wouldn't allow it.

Icie jogged up the steps, stopping at her room to leave her bag. This situation would be a whole lot easier if she wasn't in-residence, but butting heads with that stubborn loud mouth coach was not something Icie cared to do.

She was heading up to the gym when Clay called out, "Good morning, Miss Ice."

She spun around. "Good morning, Mr. Mammoth."

"It is a good morning, don't you think? It can be better; but only if you come promise me a few things."

"Please, I should be extracting promises from you." *A promise that you won't kiss me again, visit my place of work or hound me with your presence any longer than necessary.* These promises came pouring into her mind, though she would not say them aloud.

"That sounds painful. Would this extraction be any worse than the exercises you've been putting me through?"

"You might think so."

"I tell you what. I'll make those promises to you without even hearing what they are if you make one for me."

Icie thought about that for a second. She wouldn't tell him the promises she had in mind but she could come up with a few others. She'd made compromises with her patients before. This shouldn't be a big deal, but every encounter with Clay was always filled with a million other thoughts and emotions. She was always uncertain about where to go with him. "I'd have to know what you're asking first."

"One promise, that's all."

"Let's hear it."

"I'm missing training camp right now."

"I know." This was the first time he'd made any mention of football and what he was missing by being injured. Icie found herself listening harder. She could feel herself moving toward him, giving into him, wanting to help in what ever way she could.

Her eyes became keen as they honed in on his face, his body language. She could see how just mentioning training camp had turned his face into a hard plane of painful acceptance. He was tense and completely immobile as he stood before her. Icie would only agree to a reasonable request of course, but she could almost hear herself saying yes already

"I haven't told anyone else this, but it feels weird not being there. I feel empty. I'm supposed to have a team. I'm supposed to be part of a team. I am a defender with nothing to defend."

Clay turned his face away from her a second. Icie had never seen him like this before. She hadn't thought about the loss he might be feeling.

"Look, I have to do something, anything to get the feel of the game even though—especially since—I'm not there. I need to be surrounded by the sounds of football, and I don't want to have to fight for that."

"I understand what you're saying," she told him, her soft heart already pouring out to him despite not knowing exactly where he was going with this.

"During our sessions I want to watch some tapes. Get the sounds of football around me."

"Okay." She nodded again seeing nothing strange in his request.

"And I want—"

"You asked for one promise," Icie reminded him, afraid her soft heart would agree to something she'd be sorry for later.

"This is all part of it." Clay took the few steps separating them, his brown eyes looking into hers until she was forced to focus on his nose. "To get into the feel of the game I ordered a few football jerseys. I want you to wear one during our sessions. Like a sort of uniform."

"I don't know," she answered slowly taking a step back.

"You wear one every day already don't you?" That pained look of longing was replaced by a coaxing grin that probably coaxed a few too many things his way. "It'll make me feel like we're on the same team."

"We are."

"No, we're not," he stated in complete seriousness, a bit of longing showing on his face once again but only for an instant.

"Close enough," was all she could say to that because he was right. They weren't exactly on the same team. He was working hard to get back to his game.

She was working hard to get away. "How do these jerseys look?"

"You've seen them on TV right?"

"So the one you want me to wear is exactly like the ones on TV? No holes, no special cuts in certain places."

"No just a regular ol' jersey with the number fifty-one on it of course."

"Of course." Icie stared at his nose a minute longer. He had a really nice nose. She was starting to get attached to it.

"Well?" he asked.

"Okay" she agreed seeing no harm in wearing a jersey even though they would end up looking alike. Here she was agreeing to having something else in common with Clay. What was happening to Princess Ice? Steve would say she was just being herself. Hard as ice on the outside, sweet as a princess within. Icie wished she could actually be the Ice Princess Clay claimed her to be. Hard and cold with her nose in the air.

"Good. They should be here by this afternoon. Now tell me what you want me to promise."

"No more driving until you're released by the doctor," she told him, needing no time to think about that one.

"Fine."

"You were mighty quick to agree."

"Once I make a bargain I'm committed."

"That's good to know. You also have to agree to follow all my orders."

"Orders?"

"Instructions. Is that better?"

"Much better."

"Have you seen Ray?" Icie asked having been guaranteed her promises, she realized that she had spent enough time talking to Clay outside of their regular session.

"No, but your friend Tim Long's upstairs. He's been here since Six this morn—"

She was gone, running up the stairs as if she'd find life's biggest secret up there. Maybe she would. Tim Long might be it for her. Her man, her life, her secret.

Clay caught the growl that rumbled in his throat with that idea. He took a few steps toward the stairs to go after her before he realized that he wasn't supposed to take the stairs.

Instructions. He had to follow them. A commitment was a commitment. Clay forced himself to walk to the elevator cursing the slowness, the inactivity it forced him into. More than anything he wanted to get into some kind of physical release. Which meant, he was ready for today's session.

She walked past him going straight to the bench slapping it with the palm of her hand.

"Follow instructions, we've got a warm up to do."

"If you say so." Clay looked from one to the other. There was something there. He still wasn't sure what.

"Fifty-one. We've got a schedule, remember? The one your muscles like."

"I need to put this tape on first." Clay slipped the tape into the VCR. The National anthem played as a well known singer belted out the words with passion and reverence. The Crescents burst out onto the field. Clay saw himself whole and full of athletic power. He shook his head in pity for the image of himself on the screen. A young man who had no idea that his life would change before this game ended. Here was the Super Bowl game that was the beginning of a huge change in his life as he once knew it.

"Are you sure you want to watch this particular game?" Icie was behind him.

"Yeah."

He had to.

Clay needed to be reminded of who he once was, what he was still capable of and that even though life sometimes threw wild passes at you when you aren't ready there was still a chance of you stretching your fingers to catch it. He was going to catch it. His career; his life and maybe a bit of Icie's, "Let's give these muscles what they're waiting for;" Clay announced going back to the bench beginning the sequence of warm-up exercises before she could make it back over.

Clay had looked forward to seeing Icie today. He wanted to talk to her; had tons of questions to ask her now, but they were all forgotten. Seeing himself on the screen and opening his feelings to her had thrown him into a contemplative silence. He hadn't meant to get so serious; he just wanted her to wear the damn jersey. It was all part of his plan to prove that he was more of a man than she thought he was.

Funny how easily the words had slipped out. They had come so easy that at first, he was embarrassed by them. It had taken him a minute to get a grip on himself.

Was he embarrassed now?

Not at all. Somehow sharing his feelings with Icie was as natural as breathing. As natural as the exercises she was guiding him through. Yes, he was getting better. His knee moved more naturally. The pain had lessened. He was not sweating through a few baby exercises, he was moving forward. Moving on! He was going to make it to the field.

A growl rumbled in his throat.

"Fifty-one! That's it! No more! Stop!"

He heard her; but he couldn't stop. It felt so good to move, to exercise the knee that had put him through so much.

"Stop!" he heard her say again. Clay felt a staying hand on his upper thigh. He immediately froze. "What happened to following instructions?"

"I got carried away," was all he could say.

"I was thinking about having you carried away."

Was that a smile that crept onto her face? Clay wasn't sure. She was looking him straight in the eye a second ago, but then her eyes had moved down.

"What was that noise coming from your throat?"

"My power growl?"

"It was a growl alright." As Icie talked, she eased right into the cool down continuing the conversation as if that were what she'd always done. "You do that growl thing often?"

"When I feel the need." Her warm fingers moved across his skin relaxing his muscles, caressing his soul.

"And the power; I suppose, is simply a part of you."

"Right."

"Mmmm. Well, that's it; we're done for this morning. I was trying not to work you too hard there, Fifty-one."

"Don't hold anything back on me."

"I don't need to when you got that power growl going for you."

"No, I guess not."

"Ready, Tim?" Icie called over her shoulder.

"Been ready for the last ten minutes," Tim answered.

"And what were you doing with that time?" she asked, turning away from Clay to talk to the artist.

"I think you already know."

Clay felt as if he had been pushed aside; she was done with him and was now ignoring him.

"I hope you're enjoying yourself," she was saying.

Clay wasn't enjoying any of this.

"I'd hoped for more entertainment, but there's still time."

Listening to the two of them, Clay wasn't sure what they were talking about. What he did know was that he had been left out of the conversation for far too long. "You can take all the time you want. Stay," he told Tim. "You don't have to leave yet."

"Yes, I do," was all he said to Clay before asking Icie, "Are you shopping for the kids today?"

"No, tomorrow; wanna come?"

"Yeah."

"Fifty-one, I'll see you this evening," Icie said to him before jogging down the stairs.

"Tomorrow," Tim Long told him before disappearing behind her.

Clay felt left out, deserted. The sounds of a cheering crowd drew him to the television. On the screen, Clay saw himself sprawled on the ground. He remembered that moment like it was yesterday. He had just tackled a running back after he'd caught a forty yard pass.

To be able to do that again.

To hear the fans praising him with their cheers.

He loved that sound. Clay stopped the video and turned the set off. In the quiet of the room there was something else he found that he longed for; something else he hoped to hear again. The sound of Icie talking to him in a relaxed, natural way. Her hands touching him, healing him inside with her gentle touch.

He must be going soft. At least that's what his head told him. His heart told him something else, something much more commanding.

Clay took the elevator down to the kitchen. He fixed himself a sandwich, then did something he'd never done before. He walked out his front door and took what couldn't be called anything but a slow stroll. For the first time, he traveled on foot through the subdivision he'd lived in for the last two years.

He took notice of the homes in his neighborhood seeing the various similarities and differences. Some of the houses were smaller than his, others twice as big. One quality they all had in common was the understated wealth on the outside. The houses resembled the wholesomeness of the All-American home, but with perfectly manicured lawns and an overall display of wealth that came through loud and clear. Some, if he remembered correctly from when he first looked into buying a home here, were extravagant showcase homes inside, a contrast to the houses outward appearance. Those were more for displaying what you owned instead of living with what you have. His house, he supposed, was somewhere in between.

After walking a few more blocks, Clay decided to head back home. The fresh air was nice but the humidity was starting to get to him. He should have started doing this a long time ago. He needed to build up his stamina, deal with the heat and over time make longer trips around the subdivision. Clay was liking this idea. He needed to strengthen his knee. Besides, this little enclosed community was his home, why not get to know it a little better? After having had a taste of being out last weekend, Clay knew he couldn't spend much more time cooped up inside.

He came home in time to find a FedEx delivery guy at the door. The jerseys. This was going to be fun. It was all part of his plan to get Icie to look at him in a new light. He signed for the package but not before the young man, sudden recognition on his face, asked for an autograph. Clay was happy to oblige. He was feeling pretty good right now. Amazing, he thought to himself, what fresh air and sunshine could do for you. Not even the cloud of uncertainty of whatever was between Icie and that Tim Long guy bothered him too much.

"Clay, my boy where ya' been?" Ray called out as soon as he walked through the door.

"Me? I should be asking you that question, old man."

A grin spread across Ray's face, bigger than any Clay had seen in all the years he'd known him. "You young people ask too many questions."

"Is that supposed to mean one question is too many?"

"That's about right."

"Then you better stay out of Icie's sight until you're about ready to confess every detail of your love life."

A thoughtful look crossed his face. "I know exactly what you mean."

"She's worried about you."

Ray's head lifted in surprise. "You've actually noticed that?"

"I'm aware of the people around me."

"Mmm." Ray gave him the wise old man study "Especially a beautiful physical therapist, I suppose?"

"Especially a beautiful therapist who lives in my house but still has a tendency to shut me out cold."

"So, it's been cold between you?"

"As ice."

Ray laughed.

"What's so funny, old man?"

"A picture of you, Fifty-one-out-for-fun Mammoth, getting shut out cold in anything."

"I've been shut out of my game, and been dealing with that alright lately."

"It seems as if you have." Ray's grin twisted into a serious frown. "I haven't been around much to see for myself, so tell me, truthfully, how well have things been going?"

Thankful that Ray didn't refresh his memory by reminding Clay exactly how long it had taken for him to come to grips with his injury and his anger he asked, "Why don't you discuss it with my therapist? You are eating dinner with her tonight, right? You're not going to let her down again, are you?"

"And if it happens that way?"

"I might have to overlook the fact that you're an old man who helped raise me and be forced to set you straight."

"Mmm." His serious expression turned even more serious, worldly even. "Uncle Ray, you can stop throwing that wise old man look my way."

"I don't know what you're talking about. I look like this all the time."

"Old and wise? Not all the time. Only when you think you've got something figured out inside that gray head of yours."

"And I do."

"Me and Icie?"

"You and Icie. I love you both."

"And you're worried that Fifty-one-out-for-fun Mammoth is going to hurt one of the people you love."

"Will you?"

"I don't intend to."

"But you might."

"I don't know what's happening, Uncle Ray. I can't get the woman to look at me. So I can't answer that. One thing I'm sure of is that there's something there." His mind shifting to Tim Long and his need to know if there was something there had Clay adding, "What do you know about Tim Long?"

"Icie's friend? The one who paints?"

"Yeah."

"The one you can't get to do that mural you want so bad?"

"That's the one. I've got him doing the mural now."

"Did Icie put a good word in for you?"

"Just the opposite. While I was trying to let the man know that he could still paint for me, Icie was reminding him about all the clients he had."

"I could see her doing that."

"She did it, alright. Why didn't you tell me you knew him?"

"Icie does. I don't. I mean, not good enough to ask for favors. Otherwise I would have put a word in for you myself."

Clay nodded not doubting him a second. "What do you know about him?"

"He's a decent guy. Always wondered why—" Ray stopped.

"You always wondered, what?"

"Not a thing," Ray told him, realizing that letting Clay think whatever he thought about Tim Long and Icie would be good for him. Clay always got what he wanted too easily. If he wanted Icie, and Ray could see that he did, then he needed to work hard to get her. Icie was the kind of woman he should settle down with, make a family. Clay's dad had wanted it that way.

"You're not gonna finish saying what was on your mind?"

"Nothing's on my mind."

"Alright, I get it, Uncle Ray. I'll let it go for now, but something's still on mine. Are you eating dinner with Icie tonight or what?"

"Don't worry, I'm going to be there."

"Good, me too. Maybe I'll make that peach cobbler for her."

"For her? I don't get any?"

"You can have some; Tim Long can't have a thing."

Uncle Ray laughed. Clay shifted the box in his hands and moved toward the elevators.

"I got something on my mind too," his uncle told him walking a few steps with him.

"What's that?"

"Tell me. How are you really doing?"

Clay stared into a face full of love and concern knowing that Uncle Ray was asking the same question his father would have if he were here. "As good as you can expect from a man who's unable to do the thing he loves the most. You know, I just hope I can still get in there to play the game the way I used to."

"You will," was all his uncle said.

"I have to believe that."

"In the meantime, to take your mind off of it all, get a hobby."

"A hobby? Something like your Victoria,"

"Yeah," Uncle Ray grinned.

"I've got Icie."

"Not yet you don't." An arm rested across Clay's shoulder. "Get a hobby," Uncle Ray advised.

Clay laughed hearing the protective warning in Uncle Ray's voice, then headed to the second floor and opened the package. He took out five of the jerseys, all identical except that in white letters, slashed onto the back of each jersey was the day of the week directly above his new slogan. He read it to himself. The statement was sad but true. But then again, not so sad if he could have Icie. Clay left the package at her door knowing she would stop by her room before the next session.

He went into his own room, wrote a note and taped it to the box. He might get a smile out of this one. Maybe even a whole laugh. Remembering the cobbler, Clay went back downstairs to find Uncle Ray. His uncle was going to take the trip with him to the grocery so that he could buy what he needed to make his famous dessert. Riding down in the elevator, Clay wondered if it were possible to win a woman's heart through her stomach?

Naw, it couldn't be that easy. Besides he still wasn't so sure about wanting her heart.

He wanted her.

Definitely.

Her heart?

A steady beat seemed to pound inside his brain. Her heart and his, together?

"Forget the heart, peach cobbler's all I'm looking forward to right now," Clay told himself as he headed toward the kitchen to find Uncle Ray.

Icie had a very successful session with Antonia and a relaxing lunch with Tim before going to the grocery and then back to Clay's. She threw all the makings for dinner tonight into the fridge. It was going to be simple. Shepherd's pie. If Ray wanted something special then he should show up when he was supposed to.

She ran up the steps moving quickly to her room stopping short when she saw the package at her door. Something was taped to the box. A note.

Our compromise
Come wearing the jersey.
You promised me.
Clay.

Icie felt the grin as it spread across her face.

This was how he was getting to her.

This is why the attraction was more than a sex-starved need to have his body all over her.

Icie dumped the contents of the box onto the bed, then held up a shirt inspecting it for unusual additions despite Clay's assurance that there wouldn't be any. Of course, the number fifty-one in large print dominated the front of the navy blue shirt. She turned it around noticing the day of the week printed on the back and having picked up a Monday shirt, she looked through the others, finding the rest of the week. It wasn't until she held the Monday shirt before her once again that she read Clay's slogan.

She laughed. The man was impossible.

She read the slogan again.

It was his.

It was true, but it was different.

The difference perfectly attesting to his present situation. Icie was more than pleased to wear the jersey.

She hung the others in the empty closet and went upstairs for a second session with Clay.

A tickle of laughter bouncing from her with every few steps, she almost bumped into Ray.

"Hey there, Icie my girl."

"Hey, yourself." Icie was trying to be stiff and angry but Ray usually saw right through her and she was in too good a mood for that anyway.

"I see you're wearing your new jersey."

"You've seen them."

"Clay's wearing his, I especially like the slogan on the back. The boy's been having too much fun in his life. You can help him get over himself."

A sudden thought hit Icie. "Is that why you wanted me to help Clay?"

"Now, Icie girl, don't even think that. I'll see you at dinner tonight."

"You better be there."

"I will."

Icie let him go, already knowing the answer to the question she had just thrown at Ray. He had some hidden agenda. Hidden agendas didn't bother her too much because Icie did what she felt she should do, not what someone told her she should. Although, she had to admit, Ray had used a bit of coercion last month when all this started.

"You're wearing the jersey." Clay said as she came into the gym.

"I promised to, didn't I?' A grin, a remnant of her earlier laugh explosion, was stuck to her face.

"I've been keeping my promises here too."

"Good. Let's get this session started."

Clay sat on the bench. "You're taking that slogan to heart, aren't you, Ice Princess?"

"You bet. Fifty-one-ain't having no fun." Icie sang the slogan with feeling.

"I'm not thrilled with how happy that slogan's made you."

"You can't do much of anything about that. Come on, first set."

Clay began the warm-up exercises but continued to talk, his deep voice becoming rough and intimate. "True, I can't do a thing about how happy you are about the lack of fun in my life, but you've got to realize that this new slogan is only a temporary thing."

"Really?" Icie's grin dropped a notch.

"For both of us, Fifty-one." Clay looked directly into her eyes. He held them even as she fought to redirect her gaze to his nose. She won the fight but not easily, and got through the session by avoiding as much actual direct contact as possible and by studying his nose each time she had to talk to him. Under the jersey her skin was hot and sensitive to the soft material. She knew that touching him would be much too much for her to deal with right now. Nearing the end of the session , closing in on the cool-down, Icie made a professional decision.

"Cool-down," she told him.

"Good, warm fingers to the rescue."

"Not today." Icie told him with a straight face.

"What was that?"

"You've progressed to a point where you don't need a massage cool down anymore. I'm ready to take you to the next level."

"What? You didn't say anything about that this morning."

"Sorry."

"I would have savored my last official cool-down."

"As I said, sorry. Let me tell you about this stretching exercise. It's perfect for strengthening your leg muscles."

"I understand. You're making sure Fifty-one really ain't having no fun."

"Of course not. I'm doing my job. I'm making sure my patient progresses and reaches full recovery."

"Without having any fun?"

"Sometimes life takes you in that direction. Fun isn't everything."

"Whatever you say Ice Princess."

Icie heard the dig but ignored it.

She directed him to sit on the floor as she joined him, beginning her first count as he held the stretches she demonstrated. During the first two counts, Icie could feel his eyes examining her; eating at her already shaky control. He broke her rhythmic count with a question.

"Since I'm being deprived of so much today, how about some conversation?"

"Somebody's got to count."

We'll work around it."

Icie nodded before waving a hand for him to continue and began to count again.

"So, tell me about these kids you and Tim were talking about this morning."

Her kids? Icie had no idea why he would want to talk about her other patients but decided to oblige since they were a much safer topic. "What do you want to know?"

"How many do you have?"

"Four."

"Four!"

"Yes, four," Icie added between counts. Four was way below her normal patient count. What did he expect when she spent so much time with him, when he wanted her as his exclusive therapist?

"They've got names?"

"Antonia, Neisha, Corey and Roy" Icie rattled off the names of the kids she had been working with, some for a matter of months, some over a year. Each of their situations came to mind, each of their happy faces now that they had completed therapy with success. All except for Antonia who still had a way to go.

"Two and two."

"What was that?"

"Two boys and two girls."

"Yes." Icie stood satisfied with Clay's first hands-free cool down. "Session's over," she was relieved to be able to say, having had enough of trying to control the feeling he aroused in her.

"That was quick. We haven't finished our conversation. Come downstairs with me and I'll get you a bottle of fresh spring water. It's free."

That didn't sound too bad but all Icie would want to do with the water is throw it all over her, or him, maybe both of them. "No thanks."

"I'll see you at dinner; then. Uncle Ray promised no disappearing acts today."

"Okay," Icie told him, trying to remember exactly what happened to make Clay a part of her Monday night dinner plans on a regular basis.

"I'm making a peach cobbler."

"Oh."

"We'll be sharing the kitchen."

Oh no, she thought to herself.

"Now that might be some fun."

'Oh, no, no, no, no, no!' she screamed inside her head. This fifty-one was not having any fun, or luck, not even a decent break. Icie gave him a slight wave, not letting on a bit of what she was feeling. She left, dying for some space, some air that wasn't filled with Clay Mammoth.

CHAPTER 11

The kitchen was too small.

Icie never thought she'd say that about a kitchen that was the size of her living room, bedroom and her own kitchen combined. But it was, because Clay Mammoth was inside it filling it with his irresistible attractiveness and promises of fun that would be so satisfying to give in to but...

Remind yourself, Icie demanded,...but damaging to the heart. If she caved in now, brushing aside her obligation as his therapist and pushing aside her better judgment, she would be giving in to more than sexual urges. Her heart was involved now. Too involved.

Icie put the entire package of ground beef into the frying pan. She glanced at him over her shoulder. He was cracking eggs with one hand tossing the shells in the garbage can behind him. Watching the whole process, the cracking, the fingers separating to open the shell, the tossing—Icie was disgusted with the sudden increase of her breathing.

The meat sizzled in the pan calling her attention back to where it should be. She stirred, determined to cook this meal without allowing Clay Mammoth to distract her. Why hadn't he just stayed in his room a little longer? She would have been done in fifteen, twenty minutes tops. She browned her ground meat, made the potatoes, put it all together, added cheese and left it to bake.

Quick and simple.

She'd come down a whole two hours after she had taken a shower and lounged around in her luxurious room hoping to be in the kitchen after he was done. He must have been listening for her because he had joined her in less than two minutes. She stirred the meat again chopping now and then.

Icie couldn't stop herself from peeking at him again. He was making loud grunting noises that would have made anybody curious. Her eyes took a quick but thorough sweep of him. He was still wearing the "Fifty-one-ain't-having-no-fun" jersey, the sleeves rolled up, exposing the bulging biceps as he was actively beating every lump that might dare to exist inside the bowl before him. Why did he have to mix the batter by hand? There was a mixer in the well-equipped kitchen, Icie was sure.

She stirred the ground beef in the pan again. She needed some air. She went to the fridge and stood before it hoping a bit of the coolness inside would do something for her.

"What are you trying to do," Clay called from across the room, "refrigerate the whole kitchen?"

"Of course not," she told him without turning around.

"Well, as long as you're in there grab some butter for me."

Icie found the butter and walked across the room to hand him a stick. They cooked together last Monday with no problem. It could happen again.

But it didn't.

Instead of browning the ground meat, she almost blackened it. She added too much milk to the potatoes and had to cook more because they were loose and runny. She scraped her finger on the grater almost adding a piece of her flesh to the cheese. She was thankful that she didn't bleed, but only scraped the top layer of skin a little. All these little disasters were happening because Clay was in the kitchen with her. It was a sign. Just think of the huge disaster it would be if he was an intimate part of her life. Icie didn't need that kind of fun.

All the ingredients finally together, Icie was ready to put the Shepherd's pie into the oven to bake.

"What temperature do you need the oven on?" he asked.

"Three-fifty."

"Same here. We can put them in together and save using the other oven."

"Do you have a problem with that?"

"With what?"

"Sharing the oven with me?"

"Not at all. Go right ahead."

The muscles in his arms contracted as he lifted the pan of gooey looking batter into the oven. "See, there's still room for the Shepherd's pie. I'll put it in for you."

"Thanks," Icie said to his nose.

"Thirty minutes?"

"Fine."

He clicked the oven light on. "Side by side, dinner and dessert. Both will be delicious, I'm sure."

"I'm sure," Icie repeated.

He stood staring into the oven a moment more before adding, "One pan holds a necessary meal to keep you going, the other a little something extra that makes it complete. They look good in there together, don't you think."

"The food, yes."

"What else would I be talking about?" Clay made a tsking sound before turning off the oven light and walking toward the doorway that was actually a wide area leading to the foyer. He paused. "I'm going upstairs to take a shower before dinner. Need any help in here?"

"Not at all."

"I'll get to my mess after dinner. Leave it alone."

"No problem."

As soon as he was gone Icie went to the sink and turned on the faucet to splash water on her face. Once, twice, three times before Ray said behind her, "Can't drown your sorrows that way, Icie girl."

"Who said I was drowning sorrows?"

"Clay just left didn't he?"

Icie nodded. "My patient, slash house mate, slash cooking assistant just left my side."

"So you two are getting to know each other better."

"That's not funny, Ray"

"I guess not. How are things going between you two?"

"Not the way I'd like it."

"He's giving you a hard time?"

Was he? "No, not any more."

"Then he's cooperating, doing what you tell him he needs to do."

"For the most part." But then again he was doing other things he had no business doing. Making her feel things she had no business feeling.

"I knew you were the one for him. I told him fifty-one was his lucky number."

"Lucky for him, not for me."

"It's not that bad, Icie. Unless there's something you're not telling me. Has Clay done something he shouldn't have? Are you hiding something from me?"

She was hiding a lot from him. How do you tell someone you look at as an uncle that you were having sexual fantasies about his nephew? "Nothing for you to worry about. I'm a big girl and can handle Clay Mammoth any day"

She hoped.

"If you want to know more, then stick around more often."

"Still mad at me about that, huh?"

"Yes."

"You'll forgive me when you meet Victoria."

"I will?"

"Let me tell you about her."

Ray went on to list Victoria's endless qualities while she made homemade gravy to go with the Shepherd's pie.

Dinner that evening went smoothly with Ray continuing to sing the praises of Victoria. She and Clay even shared a quick secret smile at how happy and animated he had become since meeting his new love. They skipped coffee after the meal, Ray had a church function to attend.

Icie had no intention of sharing coffee or anything else with Clay tonight. The peach cobbler did compliment the meal, so Icie complimented the baker.

"The peach cobbler was delicious."

"Not as good as that Shepherd's pie."

"They were both delicious, perfect together," Ray chuckled. "See you two later," he said in a rush, leaving before the last word was out of his mouth.

Ray's parting remark drew their eyes together. They laughed.

"The man sounds like he knows what he's talking about." Clay was the first to speak.

"Ray knows his food."

"There was more than food behind his words of wisdom."

"You want there to be something more than food?"

"I won't deny it. So where does that leave us?"

"Exactly where we started, patient and therapist. Nothing more."

"Guess I'll have to take that for now."

"Forever."

"For the next four months."

Having nothing to add to that, Icie turned to the dirty bowl and utensils he told her not to touch. "The clean up's all yours."

"The cleaning lady will get it tomorrow. Why don't we sit and talk for awhile? I know this nice place with a beautiful view from the balcony."

"Yours, I bet. Good 'night, Fifty-one."

"Until tomorrow, Fifty-one." Icie heard him whisper as she left.

How many tomorrows? At least thirty times four.

One hundred twenty!

One hundred twenty days to resist the heaven Clay's arms promised that could only turn into a living hell in the end.

Clay woke up the next morning feeling good. Icie was loosening up to him. Clay could tell. She enjoyed his little joke with the jerseys; she smiled at him; she cooked with him; she stared at him as if she wanted to do more.

Clay saw it all.

He knew when a woman was interested and Icie Ellis was not only thawing toward him, she would be melting in his arms before long.

The only concern he had were the kids she'd mentioned. Four. That was a lot. And where did she keep them? Did they stay with Tim? Clay slipped on his Tuesday jersey and went up to the gym.

Tim was already there. The giant sketch of a football field almost complete. "Morning."

"Yeah," Tim waved a brush at him.

"How's it going?"

"It's going."

Clay stood next to the guy for a few minutes more before realizing that he might be disturbing him then stepped away. Icie came breezing into the room. Her eyes skimmed over him searching the corner of the room where she knew Tim would be, and dashed over full of noise. The excitement in her voice sounded exactly like that—noise.

She rattled on with him a good fifteen minutes as Clay watched. The speck of jealousy Clay already felt for the man doubled in size.

"Morning, Fifty-one." She finally decided to speak to him.

"Morning," he told her, and then could think of nothing else to say. The session progressed, warm-up, exercise, cool-down All done smoothly, quietly, but with a strain that hadn't existed before. Clay knew it was his fault. He was jealous. He was angry. And the best thing he could do was keep his mouth shut because if he opened it now he would be sorry for what would come out later. But it was hard to do. Clay wasn't used to holding much in.

"You've been mighty quiet today," Icie said to him after making a few marks on her chart.

"So you noticed," he told her.

She nodded once but didn't say another word to him. "Time to shop," she called over to Tim. They left together and this time came back together for the evening session.

"I thought you were done for the day?" Clay asked Tim, disgusted to see the man's face again so soon.

"I wasn't."

Clay was getting tired of these short answers, and was now sorry that he had begged this man to come into his house. He didn't like him spending so much time with Icie. What had they been doing together all day long?

The evening session went much like the morning, then every day after the same. In the morning Tim would be there, Icie would rush over to talk to him, work with Clay in silence and dash out again only to return, again with the interfering man in tow.

It was the most frustrating situation he had ever been involved in. His daily walks around the neighborhood and the few minutes he spent talking to an elderly woman walking her dog were the only distractions he had.

By Friday Clay began to feel that he had only imagined a thaw on Icie's part. She had effectively frozen him out using Tim as interference, just like she had tried to do with Steve.

Clay wasn't having it.

After the Friday evening's session he told her, "You're mighty quiet today"

"This has been a pretty quiet week, don't you think?"

"Not when you're talking to him." Clay's head jerked in Tim's direction.

"We're friends, we talk."

"What are we?"

Icie let out a long sigh before answering. "Patient and therapist, remember?"

"Pardon me, I must have forgotten. Can you, my therapist, stay a few minutes to talk to me?"

"I'm sort of in a hurry. About what?"

"Concerns."

"Fine. Let me tell Tim."

Tell Tim, tell Tim, a tiny voice mocked inside his head. Clay's eye stayed on them. He watched her talk with him a good five minutes. Watched her smile at him during the entire five minutes when she had given him, Clay Mammoth, not one lift of her lips nearly the entire week.

Then she kissed him. It started on the cheek but eased into a lip lock. Icie swatted at Tim glancing at Clay with a bit of embarrassment.

From where he stood the kiss had been much too heartfelt, much too intimate. The swat nothing more than a play at chastisement.

No way! Clay was not going to tolerate this. She was not going to kiss that man in front of him again. "Icie, I'm waiting," he growled.

She patted Tim on the back, a soft little caress freely given that Clay would have died for. Tim left, a smirk plastered on his face. Clay wanted to plaster something else on his face.

"What are your concerns?" She stood before him asking the question as if she hadn't just flirted with Mr. Skinny right in front of his eyes.

"How can you kiss every man you know, but me!" The last thing he expected to say was now being said. Fine. It was something he needed to know.

"What are you talking about?"

"Kissing!" Clay couldn't believe she had to ask.

"What about it?"

They were both shouting now and Clay didn't care. Icie was his, she just didn't know it yet. "I want to know why it is so easy for you to kiss every man you know except me!"

"I don't kiss every man I know."

"I've seen you kiss Steve, Uncle Ray and just now, that artist guy you know so well."

"Tim?"

"You know exactly who I'm talking about." Clay forced himself to speak slowly attempting to control the jealousy inside of him that was pulling his insides until they were as taunt as the lace in a newly sewn football.

"Yes, Tim, and…" she paused.

She was calm once more exhibiting a control he envied. "I've even seen you kiss my father!" Clay heard himself say barely believing that he had stooped even lower by becoming a whiny child.

"He was on his deathbed. I was saying goodbye."

"That's what you say now!" Didn't he know when to stop? "It's the truth."

"What about the others?" Obviously he did not know. "That's none of your business."

"But it is." He was making it his. He was already acting like a whiny child why not add demanding to the list? Not a demanding child, but a man demanding that she open her eyes and see what they could have.

"How?"

"Because you kissed me, and that one kiss I shared with you took me so deep inside of you that I have to have—" his voice lowered to a half whisper; "more." Icie said nothing for a long time. Finally, Clay insisted. "You have to give me more," and more softly, "Why won't you give me more?"

"Because—" she was staring at the middle of his face.

"Don't stop at because." Clay reached a hand out to her. It softly landed on her shoulder. She shrugged it off taking a step back.

"Because kissing you again is going to put me exactly where you want me."

"That's right. In my arms and in my life."

"For how long?"

"For—"

She looked him up and down as if she already knew his answer. But there was no way she knew his answer because he didn't know it himself. Well, don't stop at for;" she goaded.

"For as long as we want."

"Then that means for never."

She looked into his eyes for a moment then glanced lower. She was always doing that lately. It was another thing that he didn't like, Clay realized.

"Do you have any concerns that would apply to your injury?" Her voice was cool and professional.

Clay stood, silently yearning for his brain to work, to think, to put together some words that made sense, that would keep her away from Tim Long a little longer. Nothing came to mind. "No," was all he could say.

"Good bye then," Icie told him before pounding down the steps, leaving him full of regret. He had opened his mouth and he was sorry for every word that had crashed out it.

Almost.

Clay went to the other side of the room planning to release his frustrations with exercise. He found himself a few feet from the unfinished mural. An image of Icie and the artist having an intimate conversation, a replay of the kiss flashed through him. He needed to get out of this room. Forgetting about caution, safety and what was best for his knee Clay pounded down the stairs just as Icie had done, but louder. The sound drummed in his ears. It was a satisfying noise that matched the growing growl in his throat.

He was outside. Clay scanned the driveway, knowing that he wouldn't see her car, but cursed at its absence anyway The sign he had made for her stood lonely as he, but at least it stood. It was going to be there as long as he wanted it to stay, and Icie was going to be here for as long as he needed her. He had not given up yet.

He took his usual route through the neighborhood, walking faster, farther and much longer than usual.

He had to.

If he stopped moving, Clay knew he would do something really stupid like hunt Icie down, only to find her, Tim and their four kids having a cozy little dinner or something close to such a familial scene.

If she had a family, then it would make sense for her to want nothing to do with him. Too bad Clay didn't want any of it to make sense.

He soon found himself right back in front of his own door. He also found Ray walking out of it. "Where are you off to?"

"To a little party Icie's having at her office."

"A party?"

"For her kids."

"Her kids." Why hadn't he thought to ask Uncle Ray before? "Does she really have four?"

"For now."

"She wants more?"

"Always did, always will. Look, Clay, I'm already late and I still have a cake to pick up. Save the questions for later."

"One more. Who else is going to be at this party?"

"The kids, family Tim…a few other people I guess."

"And you."

"Me, too. Do you want to come? I'm sure Icie won't mind."

"I'm sure she would. I don't want to intrude."

"If you change your mind give me a call. I can swing by to pick you up."

"Sure. Have a good time, Uncle Ray."

Clay went straight up to the gym ignoring the half finished mural and went to sit on the bench where he and Icie began many a session. If he didn't know himself better he could have sworn he was feeling a little bit depressed.

Clay Mammoth didn't get depressed.

He got angry.

He got even.

Or he'd play it easy by taking himself away from a bad situation.

Icie wasn't a bad situation. She was good. And Clay wasn't talking about her curvy figure or beautiful face. She was a strong woman. A caring woman. A secretive one.

Secrets. She had a lot of those. That would mean she was also intriguing. That's why he had to know her.

Clay was so lost in thought that he hadn't realized that he had gone through the entire warm up until he had completed the final set leading into his regular exercises. He didn't stop but continued the routine exercises. What could it hurt to go through them one more time? He stopped short of doing the knee lifts that usually left his muscles quivering.

Then he went to his room to shower. The steam from the hot spray having no positive effect on him, Clay decided to do the only thing he could think of that would possibly make him feel a little bit better.

He had to see them.

He had to see Icie, her kids and this closed-mouth Tim together. If he saw a nice happy family he would leave well enough alone.

Remembering his promise to Icie about following rules, Clay called a cab, absently wondering if the extra exercise and use of the stairs meant that he had broken the rules? Not that he hadn't broken rules before, but breaking Icie's bothered him a little.

Simple solution.

He wouldn't tell her. She wouldn't know, which meant nothing was broken.

The mural was beautiful but hidden so that she and Tim could make a grand presentation. Everyone was eating. The face painter was there, the clown was making balloon animals, and Ray had come with the cake long before the kids and their families had arrived.

"Princess Ice, this is sooo much fun." Neisha the most cooperative, quietest child she knew ran up to her. Icie was not at all surprised by the declaration, but when the soft little voice demanded, "Tell me what the surprise is," she was impressed with exactly how far her patient had come with learning to walk again as well as how much she had come out of her shell.

"I can't do that, but I can tell you where." Icie pointed to the white sheet covering the wall on the other side of the room.

"Are our pictures really on the wall like the other kids?"

"They're done."

"I want to see first." Corey came over; the most demanding of the three.

"That won't be fair;" Roy injected.

"We'll all see the mural at the same time," Icie promised. "Won't we, Mr. Tim?"

"Sure," Tim answered. "All of us." He jerked a finger in the direction of the door.

"No, it can't be," Corey whispered in awe.

"Impossible!" Roy yelled.

"It's that football Mammoth guy!" Neisha said running across the room before any one of the boys moved into action. Seeing her run with such spirit when a little over a year ago she could barely walk, spread a ray of pride through her heart. It even softened the instant jolt of excitement that flashed through her at the sight of Clay unexpectedly standing inside her office door.

"Looks like more entertainment to me," Tim whispered into her ear.

"What's he doing here?"

"Providing me with my other half of entertainment. You're kinda boring by yourself, Icie."

"Cut that out, Tim, I've heard enough of that from you a!! week long." And she had. Every day as they walked out of the gym together he'd hum the 'Let Me Entertain You' song and always had a thing or two to say about what was happening between her and Clay.

Icie wished she knew. The nothing she wanted to happen was trying to turn into a something. Icie stood on her toes trying to see above the small crowd of parents and kids surrounding Clay.

"What have you got going on over there, Icie girl?" Ray asked.

"I've got nothing going on."

"Then you?" he asked Tim.

Tim was leaning against the wall humming.

One of the parents turned away from the crowd, made eye contact with Icie and came rushing over. "How did you do it, Miss Ellis? Clay Mammoth! This has made Corey's day!"

"His day? More like his year." Corey's dad came behind his wife to say. "Clay's here? He came?" Ray asked standing on his toes trying to see through the crowd himself.

"I'm happy to hear that," Icie told the parents. "Who invited him?' she whispered to Ray

"I did. He looked so sad and lonely going into that big house all by himself."

"Going into the house, from where?"

"Walking I guess."

"Walking from where to do what?"

"I don't know, Icie girl, ask him."

Icie spun around to do just that, but stopped cold at the sound of a great disappointing "Awww" and the back of Clay's head as he went out the door. "Where did he go?"

Ray shrugged.

Tim grinned continuing to hum even louder.

Roy came over giving all the explanation she needed. "We asked for autographs and he said he'd be right back."

Sure he'd be back. Icie believed that as much as she believed that he was capable of following the simple rules that she asked him to follow. Icie saw red. She didn't invite him here, but he came. What for? To disappoint her kids. He was not going to get away with treating her kids like this. Her feet took her out the door and outside the building in no time. But he was gone. Probably driving in that Porsche of his now. Breaking another rule. The man was impossible.

"Icie? Why'd you run out of there like a bat out of hell?" Ray caught up with her in the middle of the sidewalk.

"I was trying to catch Clay!"

"He'll be back."

"No, I don't think so. The only reason he came was because he was curious. He wanted to see what I was doing. He saw a little kids' party, got bored and left. You gotta remember he's the hot shot jock player who's always out for some fun."

"It may seem that way" Ray quietly said, "but there is more to him."

"What more, Ray?" Icie swatted at a mosquito that had landed on her arm. "With Clay it's what you see is what you get."

"No, there's more there that you can't see. You just don't want to admit that. That's why you're so mixed up about him."

"Mixed up? What do you know about it Ray, you've been playing a disappearing act on me lately."

"With good reason." Ray waved a hand across his face swatting at few of the pesky blood sucking bugs.

"Victoria, I know. I'm happy for you, but this change in your love life must be tampering with your perceptions."

"Not at all. I know you, Icie, and I can tell when something's bothering you."

"These mosquitoes are what's bothering me right now."

"Clay's bothering you."

"Because he's the worst patient I ever had."

Ray gave her an exasperated look that turned into an uncomfortable gaze.

"I'm gonna just say it."

"Go on."

"True, he's probably bothering you because he's the worst patient you ever had, but he's also the strongest attraction you probably ever had too."

"Ha!"

Ray folded his arms as he threw the look of wisdom down on her.

"Ha!" she said again with more heat, forgetting to play it calm and cool.

"The kids are shouting cake," Tim called out standing just inside the building.

"Let's give them what they want. Clay's already disappointed them once tonight."

"If he said he'll be back, he'll be back," Ray insisted.

"I have to see it to believe it." Icie walked back into the building.

"This is getting better and better," Tim said behind her. Icie gave him a cold stare which he laughed at. Now she remembered why she and Tim could never get together. His dry sense of humor about everything drove her crazy sometimes.

As they cut the cake and unveiled the mural, an abundance of ooooh's and aaaaaah's filled the room. The parents took pictures of the kids standing next to their likeness, took pictures of the kids standing next to her and Tim and, just when Icie thought Clay and his promise to return was forgotten, she heard Corey say, "Mom, save a picture so I can take one of you with Clay Mammoth." But of course Clay Mammoth did not show up again.

Her kids were merely disappointed, but Icie felt a deep anger and hurt that she had never experienced before. Outwardly she said her goodbyes, gave her kids farewell hugs, and received promises of letters and pictures; inwardly she was boiling.

Tim saw the danger inside and did not hum another note to the song she was tired of hearing. He hugged Icie before leaving. "Call if you need me. If you want, I can always paint an extra finger, toe, or leg on Clay's mural."

Icie did smile at that thought but it faded quickly. "I'll let you know about that," she told him.

"I'm sorry, Icie," was all Ray could say. "I'll wait while you lock up."

She nodded. Icie had already cleaned most of the mess, leaving the trash and a spill or two for the cleaning crew.

"Wait till I get my hands on that, boy" Ray said as they walked to their cars.

"Don't. I'll handle it."

"I believe you will. I wouldn't want to be Clay right now."

Icie got into her car giving Ray a final wave. She was angry, more angry than she had been in her entire life, but she was also disappointed. Before tonight she had begun to believe that Ray had been right, that there was more to Clay. She had sensed it just as she'd seen the potential and capabilities inside all of her patients.

But she hadn't wanted to see a deeper side of Clay. She hadn't wanted to believe it existed, because then she would have to make a decision about what would happen between them.

Everything was working out for the better. Her perception of Clay had been off. There actually was no deeper side, he was shallow and selfish, and now she was going to be able to tell him off in good conscience cutting him and his determination to make something happen between them into shreds.

CHAPTER 12

Tired after leaving the party, Icie didn't go storming to Clay's house. She wanted nothing more than to relax in a hot tub and have a quick meal, because she hadn't eaten a thing during the party. She needed an early night.

She was fulfilling her wish in exactly that order. The bath had relaxed her. Her meal had taken only ten minutes to prepare. She sat at the table to enjoy her salad and grilled cheese sandwich, already daydreaming about her soft, welcoming bed.

Icie lifted the first forkful of salad to her mouth only to drop it with disgust. It landed on her plate with a clang synchronized with the ringing of the telephone. Before she was halfway to the phone she paused.

She knew; somehow Icie knew who was on the other end of the line. Icie quietly stood next to the ringing phone.

It was insistent, exactly like the man. It was annoying, definitely like Clay. But this sound, this insistent, annoying sound that rattled her was something she could control, something she could stop. With a satisfied grin Icie picked up the receiver.

"Hello," she grated into the phone.

"Don't hang up—I know you don't want to talk to me, Icie, but—just don't hang up."

He sounded strange, as if talking was a strain. Something was wrong. "Ray!" she shouted into the phone. He had left the party at the same time she had. Did he get in an accident on the way home? "What's wrong with him?" Icie tried not to panic but long fingers of dread ran up her spine.

"Nothing's wrong with Ray."

"Nothing?"

"He's fine as far as I know, Icie. It's…"

Intense relief landed her into a nearby chair.

"It's what?" Icie asked, fear and worry easing from her now that she knew nothing was wrong with Ray. Anything else Clay had to say she didn't particularly want to hear.

"It's me."

Icie should have known. It was always about him. No matter how charming or hot he was, Clay was still a selfish brat. "What about you?"

"I'm in pain."

"Is that it? Is that all? You should expect to be a bit sore. We've started some new exercises. You've been using some new muscles."

"It's more than that—"

"You're right, it probably is; you were doing a bit more than you should have today weren't you? You had no business following me, showing up at the party, disappointing my patients."

"Yeah, I should have known they were your patients." He dragged out the last word as if it were killing him to talk.

"Of course they were my patients. You are not my only patient. I told you that when this whole thing started. But of course such information didn't concern you, so you ignored it. Just like you ignored your promise to come back to give my kids those autographs you promised them. Why did you show up in the first place? I didn't invite you."

"I know." His voice was deeper than usual and held that growling sound he made when he exercised.

"So what could you possibly have to say to me? How can you have the nerve to call me tonight?"

"I'm sorry. I tried." The sounds of a deep breath pushing past clenched teeth came through the line.

That sound was an indication that something was seriously wrong. At the back of her mind the thought began to filter through, but still all she could say was, "Sure you did."

"Will you close your mouth and listen to me, Miss Physical Therapist?"

The mention of her profession reminded her of her responsibility to him.

Icie normally listened to her patients. Why was she dismissing his problem without hearing him out?

Because he had disappointed and hurt her.

Because he wasn't a young child with a young child's needs and wants. He was a man with a whole other set of needs and wants. He was also her patient and she had to listen to what he was saying. "Okay, tell me about what's wrong."

"It's not just soreness. I've been getting these spasms."

"A tinge here and there is normal."

"It's more than a tinge, Icie—" he suddenly sucked in a huge breath. "Clay? Are you okay?" She could hear him breathing, not exactly breathing. He sounded like he was pulling in huge gulps of air.

"I'm hanging in there, but, Icie, I need you here."

The plea in his voice went straight to her soft heart. He was hurting. "What you need is a soak in that hot tub you've got hidden away in that huge house of yours." She said calmly thinking to suggest a simple cure that he could use until she got there herself.

"That sounds good, but I don't think I can make it there."

That was not a good sign. When a mighty two-hundred twenty-five pound athlete confessed to not being able to walk he was in more pain than he was letting on. "Where's Ray?"

"Uncle Ray never came back. I guess he's staying home for the weekend."

He was probably right.

"After this evening—. After not being able to make it back—"

"What do you mean not being able to make it back?"

"I went to buy some footballs to sign for the kids, but then these spasms hit me and I told the cab driver to bring me home instead."

"Home? You should have come back to the clinic." A cab. He had taken a cab. That meant he had not ignored her rules.

"And let those kids see me barely able to walk? No way."

So he had an explanation, and a good one at that.

"Icie, I didn't want to call. I wouldn't have called, but this is—" he stopped. The same harsh breathing sounds filled the line.

"I'll be over." Icie hung up the phone and raced to the door, her uneaten dinner forgotten. Clay must be in extreme pain. She'd seen the man bounce back from a head-on hit that would have knocked out an elephant. Had she pushed him too far? Had she mixed her personal anger with her professional ethics? Did she subconsciously seek revenge by pushing him too far too fast?

No. She did not. That was not her way of handling a situation. Icie prided herself on her professionalism. Her career, her reputation, was her life. These spasms were most likely a result of his inactive muscles resisting new activities. That didn't stop her from caring about her patient and doing something to relieve the intense amount of pain he seemed to be in.

Icie was at Clay's door in less than fifteen minutes. She unlocked the door using the key she had been given a few weeks ago. "Clay!" she called hoping the spasms weren't so severe that he had ended up hurting himself. He could have fallen and banged his head, burst it wide open or maybe he had gone into a coma because he had knocked it so hard. "Clay!"

"I'm in here. The kitchen," his voice called out to her, heavy with pain.

Icie jumped over three huge bags of footballs sitting in the foyer and was there beside him in an instant. He must have fallen because he was on the floor, hands fisted at his sides, sweat pouring down his face, his leg visibly shaking. Icie sat beside him with no thought of anything but relieving the pain he was suffering. She laid him flat by gently pushing at his chest and began to work on his knotted muscles with sure firm fingers.

"It all started so quick. I was sitting in the cab on the way back…" Clay attempted to sit up.

"No, not a word" she told him, having no problem looking him in the eye to issue the command. She gently pushed at his hard chest once again with one hand as the other continued to work on his muscles. When he complied without a sound, worry ran through her at an even faster pace. He shouldn't be having this reaction, not from the exercises they'd been doing, not even from driving last weekend.

"Deal with why later," she whispered to herself, "concentrate on the patient."

"What did you say?" Clay's voice, raspy and rough came at her.

"Nothing, I was just talking to myself."

"How about talking to me—" the sound of air rushing past his teeth came to her ears before he added, "—instead."

Of course. How could she be so dense? Icie told her patients stories all the time, even sang to them, anything to keep their mind off the pain. And Clay's muscles were so knotted there was no doubt that he was in intense pain.

What to talk about? What was comforting? The mural? No, he didn't like Tim.

Football? No.

Mr. M.? A big no.

Michelle. Yeah, her crazy little African Grey parrot. "Icie. Talk." Clay grunted at her.

"I'm talking, I was just trying to decide what Michelle story to tell you."

"Michelle?"

"My pet, an African Grey parrot. She was given to me by—a very special friend. Now let me tell you, this was no ordinary bird. Michelle could not only talk. She did some really interesting tricks. A lot of them got her into serious trouble, too." Icie went on talking even when she started to perspire. She was dripping with sweat and her hands were sore. Still she continued to massage his leg long after the muscles loosened, relaxing as they should beneath the smooth brown skin.

She should stop, but Icie didn't. She didn't know what kept her going.

Guilt?

Maybe. She shouldn't have judged him without hearing his side of why he hadn't showed up tonight. "Then one day—"

He was sitting up, both of his hands gently gripping her wrists. "Thanks, you can stop now."

It was so good to hear his voice free from pain. Tired, but free from pain. She sighed, and sat on her bottom, relieving her knees of the pressure she'd put on them. His hands moved down to her own, holding them in a light grasp. "Take a look at your hands, Icie."

She did. They were curled and stiff. She slowly opened and closed them feeling her fingers resist, pain shooting through them as she forced them to move. "I'm okay, no permanent damage."

"I hope not. Those hands are special."

Now why did he have to say that? Icie didn't have time to think about it because he was talking again.

"After all this, am I able to say, 'I'm okay, no permanent damage,' when talking about my leg?"

"Definitely. You're still standing tall on that road to recovery."

"I don't feel like it."

"Of course you don't. Your muscles just finished screaming at you. They were only trying to get your attention."

"A less painful way would have been appreciated. Look at me. I feel like a weak little nothing. Look at you, you're a mess from taking care of me."

Icie ran her finger over her hair that had been pulled back into a ponytail. It was still intact. "I know I don't look like a beauty queen, but hey, I was working here."

"No, you sure don't."

"Thanks."

"What I mean is, you look tired. I'm tired. What do you say we both go into that hot tub?" He pointed his head beyond the kitchen.

That didn't sound like a bad idea. Her arms were aching, her fingers as stiff as ever.

Warm soothing bubbles surrounding her, loosening her muscles and Clay sitting across from her. Then again that didn't sound like a good idea either. "You've got a hot tub back there?' she stalled.

"Yeah, besides the one upstairs, I've got one in my room, too. How about it? You did suggest it earlier. It will be good for both of us."

It would be good therapy for her patient, not to mention her. He looked so worn out. What could he possibly do in his condition? Not make a pass she was sure.

Icie stood, her knees cracking in the process. She helped him to stand. All two-hundred twenty-five pounds of him. They got as far as the nearest chair which Clay fell into with none of the athletic grace she knew he possessed. Icie was a strong woman but Clay was too much man for her to carry.

"So, how do we get to this hot tub?" she asked.

"I can walk but I'll need a little help."

"As you just saw, I'm not much of that."

"I never thought I'd say this again, but I need those damn crutches again." Icie didn't want to laugh. She tried to hold the smile back but it popped out anyway letting loose a roaring sound that must have been contagious because Clay was laughing too.

"This is a sad, sad day," he finally got out. "I fell on my butt and couldn't get up, I wore my therapist's fingers to the bone, and I can't even walk a few feet."

"Not so sad. You've got some good points there still."

"I've got good points. If I remember correctly, at one time you couldn't think of any"

"I didn't have enough time then."

"Alright then, tell me anything. Go on make me feel good."

"You're as heavy as an ox and you've got a chest that's solid as a rock." She shouldn't have said that, but too late, she had. Icie was almost too tired to care but decided to end with, "and tomorrow's another day."

"Yeah, but will you be there to save me again?"

"What?"

"Tomorrow and the rest of the day. It's the weekend."

"Yes it is."

"You'll stay, right? Just in case it happens again."

"I can only promise you a few hours," Icie replied not sure what motivated her compliance. Devotion to her patient or that guilt she was feeling earlier. She left to find the crutches.

With a crutch on one side and Icie on the other they managed to reach the hot tub built inside a sort of sunroom. She helped him sit on the edge of a wooden deck and watched as he slid himself inside.

"Aww, this is wonderful," he moaned as Icie set the timer.

"Twenty minutes, that's all." she informed him.

"Thirty."

"Twenty-five and don't push it."

"No pushing the woman with the miracle fingers."

"That's right."

"And I thought I had magic hands…" he trailed off.

Hearing that reminder of the night he had kissed her, Icie almost left the room. But duty to her patient and her own aching muscles convinced her to take off her sandals and slide into a spot across from Clay. She began to relax allowing the bubbles to do their work. Her mouth broke out into a grin as she realized that they were both wearing shorts and a t-shirt. Not hot tub attire but neither one of them cared.

The silence grew long and comfortable. Icie felt herself drifting somewhere between sleep and wakefulness.

"Thank you," Clay told her.

Icie opened her eyes to see the bubbles swirling all around, dancing on Clay's bare chest. When had he taken his shirt off? "You said that already"

"That was for the massage, for getting rid of the pain. I want to thank you for, what did you call them? The Michelle stories. She sounds like a character."

"Oh yes," her response was an agreement and a tribute to the display of bare-chested excellence before her.

"I'd like to meet her one day."

She pulled her eyes from his chest to focus on his nose. "That's impossible."

"Because you won't let me into your house? You already kicked me out of your office once."

"No."

"Then I can come to your house?"

"No, yes. I didn't say that."

"What did you say?"

"That you couldn't meet Michelle."

"Scared I might teach her some new bad habits?"

"No," Icie paused, this would only be the second time she'd said this out loud. "Because she's dead." Telling Ray hadn't been easy because losing Michelle had been so fresh, the loss so new. It had been like losing the last part of Mr. M. that she could see and touch daily. But just now, telling Clay hadn't been so bad. Watching someone writhe in pain as you massaged their knotted muscles tended to alter a relationship. Then again it was something more. The tilt of his head, the way he held her gaze had reminded her of Mr. M. Had made her want to talk to him. Beyond that, he was all Clay.

"Recently?"

"Yes."

"Then Michelle must have been the loss Uncle Ray talked about that first day."

Icie was surprised with how quickly he made the connection. She was surprised that he would remember something that didn't directly involve him.

His eyes caught hers transmitting a mutual understanding of how she had felt, how she still felt. They shared a moment of closeness, one that held them even closer than the one time she was in his arms, even though there was a few feet of water between them now.

"Clay! Where are you?"

"Well, speak of the devil," he whispered, "back here Uncle Ray," Clay called turning toward the open door.

"Isn't that Icie's car out there? Did she chew you up and spit you out yet for that little disappearing act you played today? I would have never suggested you come if I had known you would be such a disappointment." Ray walked into the sunroom as he talked. "Icie," he stopped in his tracks.

"What are you doing here?"

"Clay had some trouble. He called. I came."

"And he's still in one piece." Ray's eyes darted from one to the other almost dancing. Was that a pleased look of satisfaction she saw on his face? "Doesn't look like he's having much trouble now."

"The trouble's over. This is what we call the relaxing aftermath," Clay answered for the both of them.

"Then you're okay now," he asked Clay immediately turning to Icie to ask, "right Icie?"

"He'll live," Icie said.

"I'm kind of worn out. I'm spending the weekend at my place. Call if you need me." Icie could have sworn she saw a grin covering his face before he walked out the door. "I'll see you two later." He gave a backhand wave but turned back to ask, "What's with all the footballs at the door?"

"They were for the autographs."

"I get it," Ray waved once more and was gone.

Clay and Icie called out their own goodbyes as he walked out the room.

A long contented silence fell between them. Icie had never felt as comfortable in Clay's presence as she did now. Eyes closed, body relaxed to the point of feeling boneless, Icie went to the effort of raising an eyelid to check on her patient. Opening one eye and squinting to keep the other one closed, she found Clay looking at her in exactly the same way. They laughed. The room turned silent once again, the churning of the bubbles the only sound until they too stopped, leaving the warm water still and quiet.

"So tell me." Clay's deep voice filled the room, his movement disturbing the water sending a little wave her way, "How did you meet my father? How did you come to love him?"

The question surprised her; not just because Mr. M. was a touchy subject between them, but because of the way he asked. He did not demand. There wasn't one ounce of accusation in his tone. Clay was sincerely asking about her relationship with his father. The block that she held against him began to sway, prompting her to tell him.

"Actually, I met Ray first."

"I didn't know that."

"Your dad was around, I just didn't know it then. Mr. M. was in the back seat of the car."

"What did Uncle Ray do, hit your car or something like that?"

"No, I was a toll collector working my way through school. Every night at exactly three a. m, Ray would drive through, pay the toll and leave a tip."

"That must have been nice."

"It was. Nice and strange. It started out with Ray giving me a five dollar bill, making a comment about whatever book I had in front of me. I was studying of course, always studying. Then he'd drive away without getting his change. I held it for him that first night."

"Why didn't you just keep it?"

"It wasn't mine to keep. The next day when I tried to give it back to him he wouldn't take it. Ray told me to use it to buy textbooks."

"Did you?"

"Yes, indeed. I had a student loan but it didn't cover everything."

"Parents?"

"I never knew my dad. My mom, she died not long after I finished high school."

"That must have been tough."

"I was fine." Icie waved a hand toward him trying to brush off Clay's sympathy for her. She had been better off without her mother who drank away every bit of money they ever had.

"Tell me some more about these early morning visits."

"I was slowly getting to know Ray. He was friendly and his visit broke the monotony of the night. Have you ever tried to stay awake in a toll booth at three o'clock in the morning, your only company the books you had to memorize for a test you felt you were doomed to fail?"

"Can't say I have. Have you ever tackled a running back ten yards to the end zone rolling into the side-lines, a bench your only brakes?"

"Can't say that I have."

Their laughter filled the room sending vibrations across the water and a sweet new feeling of enjoyment between them.

"I need to get you out of this hot tub," Icie told him.

"We both need to get out of this hot tub, but I would rather go against the entire Rams offensive all by myself than leave this warm heaven."

"Do you mean you want to sit in this water long enough to turn into a wrinkled prune?"

"What I mean is, I don't want to break whatever magic is happening right now."

Icie didn't expect him to say that. She was having similar thoughts, not sure that Clay was feeling the same magic. They had somehow moved to another level. The sexual tension, as usual, was a steady throb between them but not the most dominant feeling at this moment.

Clay got out of the hot tub on his own without her help or the aid of the crutches. He leaned against it for support. They both stood in the sunless sunroom dripping wet but unfazed by that little inconvenience. Icie was looking up at the sky having a clear view from the skylight.

"Aren't the stars amazing," she said to him. Then, "Clay?" When he didn't answer.

"Yes, they are," he finally said, but he wasn't looking at the sky. His eyes were plastered on the vivid outline of her breast. The white t-shirt and light-weight bra had turned transparent. The cooler air had hardened her nipples. Clay's direct heated gaze made them stand out even more, if that were possible. She couldn't move, her nipples tingled, ached even. The gentle throb of tension that had been held in check was building into a powerful rumble of want.

Want?

Icie didn't want this.

Not now. Not when they had finally found some steady ground to stand on. Releasing this sexual tension would be wrong. Clay's gaze lifted. His eyes held hers a second. Asking.

Icie forced herself to turn away. "We should have asked Ray to bring us a couple of towels."

"Are you sure you want a towel?"

Was she sure? She was positive. "Yes," she said out loud acknowledging Clay's subtle way of asking if she really wanted to turn away from him. Suddenly cold, Icie wrapped her arms around herself covering her aching breast.

"If you look in that closet behind you, you'll find some towels." He sounded so disappointed Icie could have sworn she had snatched from him something near and dear to his heart.

She grabbed a few towels and handed one to him. She wrapped one around her waist and another over her breast before turning to face him again. "I should have a change of clothes upstairs."

"I'm pretty sure I do, too," he told her obviously trying to make a joke. "That means we're headed in the same direction."

Clay followed her out of the sunroom. Icie studied him a moment over her shoulder just to make sure he was steady on his feet, she told herself. They went through the kitchen and stopped at the elevator.

"No stairs?"

"No," Icie shook her head pressing the button to call the elevator. The doors opened. They both stepped inside. Clay's shoulder brushed against hers. That accidental touch was all it took for the tension they both felt to reach its breaking point.

The break pushed hard muscles and soft flesh against each other. Clay's back was to the rear wall of the elevator. He had pulled her against him, but he didn't need to hold her there. She pressed into his hard body her lips placing sweet marks of passion on the chest she had admired earlier.

His hands found her breast. Her breath caught, the tingling sensation surrounding her nipples intensified as his hand grazed her there, his palms pressed into her soft skin and Icie felt as if she was melting. She didn't know if she could stand much more, if she could stand at all. All this and she still had her clothes on.

Clothes.

She should be putting clothes on, not thinking of taking them off. What was she doing? They could not have a sexual relationship. It wasn't just a matter of whether or not she wanted to. It had never been that simple.

Clay was her patient.

Without a second's more thought Icie did what she knew was best. She slowly backed away. Her fingers lingering on smooth brown skin as she moved away from him.

"Icie, where are you going? Where do you want to go? Your room? Mine?"

"Neither one, Clay. You know we can't do this."

He shook his head but stayed where he was, his back against the wall almost as if it were holding him up. "Why not? I want this. You want this. What's stopping us?"

"You're my patient. This isn't right. And things were going so well between us tonight. Something like this could ruin everything." The elevator doors opened. Icie stood against the doors keeping them open.

"The, this you don't want to have anything to do with wouldn't happen to be the amazing sex we could be having right now?"

"Exactly."

Clay muttered a few words under his breath that Icie was glad she couldn't hear.

"Are you done with the muttering?" she asked.

"No. I've got a question for you. Since we won't be indulging in any amazing sex, what are we going to do with this intense chemistry between us?" Clay slowly moved away from the wall. "Tell me, what exactly," he came a few steps closer, "are we supposed to do with it?"

"Ignore it," she answered blinking and swallowing a startled breath. He was a big man. Icie knew that, but now he was a big man who was intentionally releasing all of the magnetic sensual power that attracted her to him to begin with. It was all out in the open. Could she ignore it or him?

"That's impossible," he stated simply.

"You wouldn't be the first person to attempt the impossible." Recognizing the sharp degree of determination to change her mind in his eyes, Icie knew she wouldn't be able to ignore him. She stepped away from the door and walked down the hall to her room.

Clay didn't follow her. She quickly changed, hung her wet clothes in the bathroom and was out again in time to see Clay slap his wet towel at the wall. He looked as sexy and as irresistible as he had when she walked away from him a few minutes ago. "What are you doing?"

"Waiting for you."

"And passing the time swatting at the wall with a wet towel?" Humor was an excellent way to ease unwanted, out of control emotions. It worked on her patients. Humor could also ease anger or fear in an instant. Maybe it would help her ignore the fact that she would love to be back in the elevator pressing hot kisses on the very bare, very much exposed chest of steel before her.

"No, one of those roaches was flying around in the hall again."

Roaches, a safe subject. "You'd think a man who owned such a beautiful house could keep the roaches out of it."

"These aren't regular roaches. It was one of those New Orleans summertime cockroaches. Ray must have left his window open again. I can't stop the things from coming in if they see an open window. Impossible, don't you think."

"True, that's the way some things are."

"Us?"

"I thought we had this conversation already."

"We weren't finished."

"What about us?"

"Are we an impossibility forever?"

Shouldn't it be that way? Icie wasn't sure she'd meant forever. Not when he made her feel as if she needed to be inside of him. She wanted to know him more. There were small evidences of another side to his nature that weren't so completely self-absorbed. It came leaking out once in awhile.

His concern for Ray. That sign he'd put out for her last week that she had finally stopped taking pleasure in hitting whenever she parked, his help in the kitchen, the footballs for her kids.

"Buzzz, time's up. You are taking much too long to answer. That tells me that we are possible."

"For as long as I'm your physical therapist that can't be."

"Fine, I don't want to fire you because then I won't be able to see you every day. I will just have to suffer and wait for us to be together."

"That's still a maybe. I don't really know you, Clay."

"We can fix that. We can devote the rest of our time together as patient and physical therapist getting to know each other, becoming friends."

Icie found that she wanted to do that. Besides his athletic ability, just what was it that made Clay so special, to Mr. M, to Ray, Crescents fans? Why was she so attracted to him? Move away from the attraction she reminded herself. "And working on getting you back on the field," she said out loud for both their benefits.

"Of course. Why don't we start by going downstairs to share a cup of coffee together."

"Coffee?"

They were both remembering the last time they had coffee together.

"Just coffee," he assured her.

"Are you going to change out of those wet clothes first?"

"That might be a good idea."

It was an excellent idea. Icie was not sitting down to a have a cup of coffee with a man who was half naked. Especially when she knew exactly how warm and hard those muscles on his chest felt. "Can you handle getting changed by yourself? What I mean is, are you sure you're okay now?"

"What if I said I wasn't?"

"Then I'd help you like I would any of my other patients."

"I'll manage on my own," he told her. "I don't want you to think of me the way you think of any of your other patients."

"Believe me, that's something that is impossible. I'll see you downstairs."

His legs still wobbly, Clay walked down the hall as fast as he could. He hated this lingering weakness. After having Icie witness the humiliating situation he found himself in today, Clay did not want to show her any other sign of fragility.

It was all his fault anyway. Clay pulled at the shorts that were plastered to him, got them past his hips and landed on the bed shifting sideways to finish the job.

He made the decision to take that extra walk, the extra long walk when he knew he wasn't supposed to. He was the one who came home so angry and jealous that he went through every exercise in their normal routine, twice. He wouldn't tell Icie that though. Maybe he'd tell her about the walk. She could assume that was the cause of the spasms.

Dressed in a dry t-shirt and shorts, he took the elevator down. The scent of fresh brewed coffee was a relief. Clay had feared she would change her mind and leave before he could make it to the kitchen. Without a word he took a seat and watched as she carried two mugs of hot coffee to the table, wisps of steam rose from the cups.

First the hot tub, now coffee, Clay could honestly say that the melting had begun again. But it was a completely different kind than he had planned. Instead of a quick reaction like butter on a hot skillet, Clay was looking forward to a slow double boiler kind of melting used to turn chocolate into a smooth creamy treat that was worth the wait.

She sat across from him and smiled. Icie was smiling at him, not Ray, or Steve, or Tim Long. Yeah, Icie Ellis was worth the wait. Clay suddenly remembered something that brought a grin just as big to his face.

"Does pain do that to you?"

"What?"

"Put such a happy look on your face. I've seen that same kind of look on your face once before. During a game your helmet flew off after you hit the ground and the cameras did a close-up on you."

"I took someone down with me I hope."

"Of course. Would Fifty-one do anything less? It's too bad that this time you slammed into pain and had no one to take with you."

"Yes I did," Clay reached for her hand having to almost pry it from her coffee cup. "She was there with me, and even helped to ease the pain with her presence, stop it with her touch." Where these words were coming from Clay did not know, but they flowed out of his mouth so naturally. He liked the sound of them, so kept going. "Her name is I. C. Ellis."

"I was only doing my job."

"And then some. Tell me, what does the C in Icie Ellis stand for?"

"It doesn't stand for anything. C is the second letter in my name."

"The initial."

"You saw that at the office, I suppose."

Clay nodded enjoying the rare look of surprise on her face. "Exactly."

"Let's talk about something else."

"Not interested in sharing an embarrassing middle name?"

"Isn't the first one strange enough?"

"I've gotten used to it. It fits you."

"Oh yeah, the Ice Princess bit."

"You've got to admit, you're cold and hard when you're running me through those exercises."

"I have to be."

Clay moved in closer, his arms leaning across the table as he looked into her beautiful face. "But there have been a few times when the Ice in Ice Princess has melted away." He caught her eyes for a second but they shifted down almost as quickly as they had connected.

"What were we talking about?" She lifted the coffee mug to her lips. "Names, that's right. There's a story behind how I got my name, you know."

"I never doubted it."

"Do you want to hear the story?"

Clay nodded loving the easy manner she had with him now. She wasn't stiff or cold, just relaxed. "I'm listening." Clay leaned back, content to let her get away with changing the subject.

"I was born on one of those rare days during winter when New Orleans got cold enough to see a bit of ice."

"I'm getting the idea."

"My mother was a little bit—different from most people. When the nurse brought me into the hospital room for first time, my mother claimed that she handed me to her and said, "Here's a warm bundle of joy on an icy cold day."

"Okay, that makes sense."

"It would have been more sensible to latch onto the word joy as a name, not icy, but as I said before, my mother was unusual."

"That explains the name. What about the initials."

"The name wasn't enough. My mother made sure my initials spelled I. C. E."

"Ellis was convenient."

"Too good to pass up."

"She thought so," Icie agreed. "The C?"

"You can see your way to not finding that out."

"What if I tell you what my middle name is?"

"It can't be worse than mine."

"Believe me, it is."

"Okay, shoot."

"Ulysses"

"That doesn't sound too bad. Clay Ulysses Mammoth. It's got a kind of style. It's classy. Your dad had a hand in that I bet. Mr. M. was very classy."

"Up to a point. What do my initials spell?"

"C. U. M. Oh no!" Icie burst out with a loud laugh that filled the room. "Do you put your initials on anything?"

"Nothing."

"Oh, Clay, I'm so sorry. Mr. M. couldn't have known."

"He had always claimed he didn't realize it at the time."

"You didn't believe him."

"I don't know. My dad always had a crazy sense of humor."

"He did."

They shared a quiet moment. Clay was lost in thoughts of his dad, regrets that he hadn't made the most of the last few years he had with him. He wondered what Icie was thinking. What memories she had. He wanted to keep her talking, to keep her with him in the kitchen where he felt warm and cozy and at home with her there.

"Earlier, in the hot tub, you were telling me about how you met Uncle Ray and my dad. Why don't we have a second cup of coffee while you finish the story?"

She agreed, seeming to like the idea and Clay certainly did. He could do this all night long. Even knowing that the conversation wouldn't turn into a sex charged night between the sheets.

He refilled the mugs, returned the pot to keep it warm and asked, "And those toll-booth tips? Did they get any bigger?"

"Bigger? Ray started handing me tens and twenties. I tried to give him his change, but when that didn't work, I tried to force him to come through without giving me any money at all. I had saved the tips and decided to use them to pay for any future tolls they would have to pay. That's when they started going through the toll tag booth."

"That sounds like something they would do. But why didn't you just keep the money?"

"It didn't feel right, especially when Ray handed me the hundred."

"Why were they giving you all this money?"

"That's what I asked. Ray told me it was because he thought I was a hardworking girl."

"You were working in a toll booth."

"And studying in a toll booth."

"I understand. My dad took pride in education."

Icie went on to explain how she had never met his father yet. Uncle Ray told her she had a secret benefactor who wanted to supplement her education. Clay could see it happening. Uncle Ray and his dad discussing ways to help a hard-working stranger just because she looked like she needed help.

"I started to get worried. I didn't want to tell my supervisor; but I wanted them to take the money back. Ray told me the benefactor—"

"My dad."

Icie nodded, "—would only take it back if I met with him in person."

"And you did."

"I was scared to death. I was all alone in the world. My mom was gone. I lived to work and study. I had no life."

"But you went to meet them anyway."

"In a very public place."

"Where?"

"At the House of Blues."

"My dad loved jazz and that club."

"I know."

"He must have really been impressed by you. After knowing you, I can see why." The words that were coming out of his mouth. Clay kept surprising himself.

"Thank you," she told him holding his eyes for only a second. "That's exactly what he told me after I made my own assumption."

"Which was?"

"Well, my first impression was that they were dirty old men looking for something from me I had no intention of giving."

"Did you tell them that?"

"No, I laid the money on the table that they had given me as tips, and told them I wouldn't join them unless they took it all back."

"They took it back, right?" Clay asked.

"Yes."

"That explains a lot. Do you know that my dad has a trust fund set aside for you? It was in his will."

"Ray told me."

"And I tried to keep it from you by contesting the will. I wasn't successful, you know."

"Something else Ray told me. I haven't touched it."

"I'm sorry I misjudged you. I didn't know."

"You also didn't take the time to know."

"No, I didn't. The fault's all mine. Forgive me." She wasn't looking at him. She was, but not so that he could see her hazel eyes. He wanted to see her eyes when he asked for her forgiveness. He had never asked anyone besides his father for this, so he needed to see her eyes when he did. Clay had been horrible to her. He had been childish and had called her horrible names labeling her before he knew anything about her.

He'd called her fat, when he was too blind to see the beautiful sturdy curves of her figure.

A gold-digger, when he didn't even try to see her giving nature.

A tramp, when the only love she gave his father was the kind he should have given to him himself.

Reaching across the table Clay took her face in his hands and said once again, "Forgive me."

She said nothing at first, but after a few intense moments spoke words that sent his heart beating faster than he thought possible. "I never thought I could. I've actually hated you sometimes, but yes, Clay Mammoth, I can forgive you."

She could. She really could. Her eyes were filled with forgiveness. "Thank you." He leaned over and kissed her. His lips brushed against hers moving slightly as they connected. This kiss was different. Not like before. Not full of passion and heat. It was a tender kiss of appreciation.

Icie sighed making that breathy little noise he was coming to enjoy hearing whenever he kissed her. "This has become some night. Where do we go from here?"

"On."

"We go on," Clay repeated when she gave him a questioning look. "Or we could go on up to my room and finish—, not a good idea," he finished when she threw a whole different kind of look his way. "Well then, go on with the story."

Icie did go on, "I stayed."

"At the House of Blues."

Icie nodded, "We talked, enjoyed the music and ate dinner together. By the end of the night I realized that they weren't dirty old men. I also found out your dad was dying of cancer."

Clay's heart skipped a beat. "He told you."

"Yes."

"He told you he was dying!" Clay's voice rose.

She slowly nodded her head, her expression full of worry. But now, despite his new found feelings for Icie, despite tonight's revelations, this bit of news was throwing him back. Back to the hurt and pain of that day when he himself found out that his father was dying. He stood, the chair flying back behind him. His legs still weak Clay leaned forward using his arms for support. "My own father told a perfect stranger that he was dying when he didn't tell his own son until it was almost too late for me to say goodbye!"

"You didn't know?"

"No, but you did."

"I thought you knew."

"If I had known I would have been there for him every step of the way."

"Clay," she brushed her fingers, her magic fingers against his forearms. They were soothing, soft, comforting, but he didn't want that right now, "don't take it so hard. He had Ray and me."

Clay jumped back from her touch forcing himself to stand tall and straight before her. He was angry.

At her.

At Uncle Ray.

At his father most of all.

"He was supposed to have me, too!" A jealousy Clay just now realized that he had always had of Icie was pounding through him.

The jealousy that made him hate the sound of her name whenever his father mentioned her.

The jealousy that hit him when she was at his dad's side the day he died. The jealousy that drove him to say the awful degrading things he had said to her at the hospital and the graveyard.

The jealousy that was about to make him say something stupid right now. After all these years it was still there. "Icie, I think you had better leave right now."

"We can't end this night like this."

"We have to or I'm going to regret the next thing that comes out of my mouth."

"I'll go, but," she took his face in her hands and asked, "forgive me for knowing something you of all people should have been told."

Clay wanted to put his arms around this wonderful woman that had come into his life, but he didn't. He needed to be alone. He needed to work through his anger. This time he wasn't going to take his anger out on his damaged knee or the beginnings of what could be the most important relationship in his life.

CHAPTER 13

Icie was home. She threw away the dinner that still sat on the kitchen table. She slunk around the house feeling as if all the happenings of this one day had taken weeks instead of hours. She went to her room and flopped face down on the bed.

Clay didn't know.

Everything made sense now.

Clay hadn't ignored his father when he was dying. He was merely living as any twenty-something-year-old football star would. Enjoying life, dropping in to see his father once in a while, thinking he had all the time in the world to spend with him later.

Icie understood his anger. Right now she was feeling a little bit of it herself.

"Mr. M. Why did you do this to your son?" she moaned into her pillow. Icie turned onto her back staring at the white ceiling. Her body was exhausted, her brain was tired and her heart hurt because she wanted to help Clay, to comfort him. He wouldn't let her. Not yet anyway.

She closed her eyes trying to allow the exhaustion to take over, but flashes of the day appeared behind her eyelids.

Clay yelling at her for kissing Tim.

Clay on the floor in pain.

Clay's bare chest with bubbles clinging to him and she herself clinging to that very same chest inside the elevator.

Clay swatting at a cockroach. Icie laughing.

Clay kissing her. Icie moaning.

And finally, Clay, the man she was coming to love like no other man, hurting and angry.

Icie turned onto her stomach once more, bunching the pillow under her chin. Mr. M. must have had his reasons for keeping the fact that he was dying of cancer from his son, but Ray had to have known. He should have told Clay. Ray should have at least told her that Clay hadn't known. That would have been enough to keep her from judging him so unfairly.

Icie rolled off the bed and headed to the front door. She had a thing or two to say to Ray. But by the time she got to the door, she realized that it was not her place to confront Ray. Oh, she was going to have her say, but it was Clay's right to have his say first.

She went back to her bed, forced herself to calm down and after long moments of quiet wakefulness drifted off to sleep. Icie awoke feeling almost as tired as she had been last night. She would see Ray today but wouldn't say a word unless she knew Clay had already talked to him. Then she would see Clay. As much as she wanted to stay away from him last weekend, she wanted to be with him twice as much today

Morning came as gloomy and depressing as last night's discoveries. Gray clouds layered the sky but spots of blue here and there cheered her, even encouraged her to go on even though she had no idea exactly what is was she was going to do.

Icie drove to Ray's house. He lived in a fairly new constructed subdivision in Eastern New Orleans, or 'in the east' as it was called, not far from Clay. She knocked. The door opened almost immediately.

"Were you expecting someone?" she asked getting a good look at Ray. His face was worn, his eyes red and strained.

"I thought you might be Clay."

"Have you seen him? Have you talked to him? Was he okay? Are you okay?"

"I'm fine, Icie. Come on in. This is the day for early morning visitors."

"So Clay was here."

"Yeah, he came about an hour ago. That boy wasn't too happy with me."

"He's not a boy. He's a man, Ray"

"I know that, Icie girl, I guess I'll always think of him as a boy." Ray shrugged his shoulders with a weary half smile, moving his hands as he spoke. "Manuel's boy. My good friend's boy. That boy over there, he's my nephew."

"Ray I can have some understanding of why it might be difficult to see it, but you can't be blind to the fact that he's a twenty-nine year old man."

"Almost thirty, his birthday's in October, right before Halloween."

"I didn't know that." Icie did not have the heart to lay into Ray like she had planned to. He seemed so sad, so regretful.

"Manuel was worse with it than me, you know. Especially after his wife Louise died when Clay was barely two years old. He looked after that boy. Clay was his life. That was probably part of the problem."

Icie sat or the sofa grasping Ray's hand, gently tugging so that he sat down next to her. "Tell me about the problem, Ray"

"Manuel didn't want Clay to know he was dying. He wanted Clay to live his life as free as a young man should. He was proud of that boy.

"That was very unselfish, but unfair."

"I thought so too, but Manuel was slick. When he found out he was going to die he told me the news and asked for one last favor from me. I promised right away, no questions asked."

"You promised not to tell, Clay."

Ray nodded, his hands covered his entire face, his shoulders slumped The burden of that promise still hung on his shoulders. Icie wrapped an arm around him. Ray's hands moved over his face a few times, up and down. The friction of skin rubbing against skin the only sound until he spoke again. "I didn't think he should keep the news from Clay, but it was a death wish, Icie. My hands were tied. I felt bound. And now the b—" Ray paused "—the man hates me."

"Clay doesn't hate you. He's angry and he'll come around."

"Maybe, but for now, he hates me. How about you?"

"I can never hate you, Ray. I'm not happy. I'm disappointed, but at least some things are clear to me now."

"You've got a good heart, Icie."

"A soft one. All this confusion and hurt was not necessary. This promise to Mr. M. had me making a lot of assumptions that were not accurate."

"Who was it that made these assumptions?"

"Me. I alone made them," Icie said, knowing what he was getting at. Never make assumptions he had told her on more than one occasion. "But life would have been easier if you had straightened them out."

"A promise is a promise, Icie girl."

"Okay then, I could partly blame myself, but if you had told me Clay didn't know about Mr. M, things would have been different between us."

"Manuel and I pretty much ruined that, huh? I've been trying to fix things."

"By throwing us together! I knew it!" Icie stood. Ray was going to admit to his matchmaking.

"Don't get all upset, Icie girl, cool it down, think of your name."

Icie almost laughed at that. He hadn't teased her about her name in a long time. But she held strong, showing him her cold face. "And why shouldn't I get upset when someone's trying to run my life?"

"I'm not running anything. I was desperate when I asked you to work with Clay. It just so happens that this was an opportunity to get you two together, to discover, he held a hand up before continuing, "on your own, how good you are for each other."

"Ray."

"You are good for each other. I know it. Manuel thought so, too."

"You two discussed this back then?"

"We talked about a lot of things before he died. Why do you think he was trying to get Clay to come home all the time."

"I thought he was pining away for his son. Instead he was playing matchmaker."

"It was more than that. Icie, he risked having Clay home, coming up on him at his weakest moments. You remember how sick he was after radiation."

"Yes, I do." She answered, remembering well the frail body of Mr. M, sick and weak, after the treatment that he hoped would prolong his life.

"And his hair. He had to explain why he suddenly decided to go bald. Manuel had been so proud of his full head of hair. No receding hairline."

"He had complete hair loss instead."

"He risked a lot just trying to get the two of you together."

"And it never worked out."

"That doesn't mean it can't now."

"It can't now, I'm his therapist. He's my patient. There are professional ethics involved."

"I understand all that." Ray stood pacing the living room. "Just get to know him better."

"I've already decided to do that."

"Good. I'm glad we had this talk. I wish my talk with Clay had gone better."

"I was easy. I'm a softy and you know it. Clay will come around." Icie wrapped her arms around her old friend.

"I know it. I just hope it doesn't take too long."

Icie left, declining Ray's invitation to coffee. A few minutes later, at Clay's door, Icie thought twice about using the key. Last night he had asked to be left alone.

She wasn't here in a professional capacity, so what was appropriate?

The door swung open. This was a day for swinging doors. "Drive me somewhere," Clay told her. He was dressed in a black suit and filled the door completely. When she said nothing he added, "I'd do it myself but I made this promise to someone…"

"No problem. Where do you want to go?"

"The cemetery."

"Good. Okay. Good."

"Yeah, good."

Seeing Clay's face twisted in such a way that nothing in this world—at this moment—was good in any way, Icie wasn't sure what to say next. She turned to go back to the jeep with Clay following behind her.

They rode in silence.

Clay not speaking.

Icie not speaking because he wasn't, and had no idea what to say to him anyway.

The silence took over, filling the inside of the jeep completely as if it was necessary to exist. Glancing over at Clay once or twice, Icie realized that it was. The crunching of the jeep's tires rolling on the graveled path of the cemetery felt like an intrusion to the noiselessness surrounding them.

Icie parked, ironically, in the same place she had four years before as she waited for the crowd to disappear so that she could say one final farewell to Mr. M.

Clay's face turned toward her for the first time since they had gotten into the jeep together. But not for long. His head twisted in the opposite direction, toward his father's grave, then back to her before easing from the jeep without a sound.

Icie stayed put. Smart enough to know when she wasn't needed. This was between father and son. Even knowing this, Icie wanted to roll down the windows of the cool air-conditioned jeep so that she could hear what he was saying. Because he was saying a lot.

Clay was moving up and down in front of his father's grave. His hands were fisted, his arms swinging through the air with the words he threw at the unresponsive gravestone. Icie could hear the rumble of his voice but could not make out the words.

Suddenly another kind of rumble brought her attention away from Clay and up toward the darkening sky. The clouds looked as if they were ready to release a downpour, and Clay was still in the midst of his own. He took no notice of the sudden wind, the second clap of thunder or the flash of lightening that crossed the sky just before the first fat drops of rain came splashing down.

Icie got out of the jeep wanting to help Clay, wanting to warn him, wanting to comfort him in some way. But he looked to be in no way ready for that yet. The weather seemed to be a parallel force in tune with his emotions. Icie could almost feel them vibrating as one with the next clap of thunder.

So she stayed where she was, leaning against the door as the rain fell, soaking her completely. She didn't care about getting wet. Her attention was focused on the pain and hurt of the man she had come to love.

He was suddenly motionless, his hands still fisted at his side. He began slowly pacing in front of the grave site, rain dripping from every part of his body. Icie was getting a little nervous. He was now moving with an awkward gait, his anger had seemed to keep him steady.

What if he slipped on the gravel surrounding the grave and hurt himself even worse? She needed to go out there and stop him before he did make matters worse. She needed to get him out of the storm before lightening decided to strike him for yelling non-stop at a dead man who could not defend himself.

By the time Icie reached his side Clay was standing still once again. His hands were no longer fisted with signs of rage but were held open and waiting. Icie took one of his hands in her own and held it lightly grazing his palm with her thumb.

"What are you doing here?" he asked her distract-edly.

A shiver ran through her at the nearly identical question he had asked her at this same place four years ago, but now, said in a much different tone, having a totally different meaning. "I brought you here."

"Yeah, I remember." He looked straight into her; claiming her eyes, for a searching gaze she could not divert to his nose.

"It might be a good idea for us to leave now," Icie suggested.

He turned from her to the grave and back again. "That would be a good idea. Why don't you come home with me?" he said without taking a breath.

Icie nodded pulling him with her back to the safety of the jeep and into the soft giving folds of her heart. She took a deep breath as the realization that she deeply loved and cared for this man sank inside of her as easily as the rain that had soaked her clothes.

As they drove down the graveled path of the cemetery the rain lessened, turning into tiny dots of moisture that hit the windshield, then into nothing at all. Icie eased into traffic accepting the silence that had once again filled the jeep. Only this time, it was free of the tightly held anger that had dominated the drive not so long ago.

The security guard at the Eastover gate passed them in. Icie parked in her usual spot.

"Thank you," Clay told her, his deep voice raspy, almost raw. "I needed to do that."

"I could tell." Icie wanted so much to say more, to do more for him. He looked so tough, so strong, a man in control, but at the same time somehow vulnerable, needy.

"I could use a woman's touch." He paused, "I said that wrong. What I meant to say was your touch. Only yours."

Icie didn't dare open her mouth to respond to that. Despite the fact that he had first said 'a woman's touch' before becoming more specific she was still close to saying something like, "I want whatever you want." Of course she said nothing.

"I guess you still don't want to sleep with me?"

Icie twisted her head no, even though her heart, her body begged her to shout yes loud enough to bust a hole in his eardrum. She couldn't. Not when all Clay was asking for was casual sex.

"I guess that patient/therapist thing is still in the way huh?"

Icie shook her head yes, still not trusting herself to say much of anything, but eventually with his eyes trained on her holding one of those you-can't-deny-me-I'm-amazing looks he was famous for, Icie slowly forced out a few words. "Among other things."

What Clay was asking for was something she wanted so badly, a pain of want slid straight through her. But she numbed it as she usually did concerning things that were beyond her control. Icie was an expert at freezing out what she wanted most, in order to do what she knew would be best for her because this was not the way she wanted to give herself to a man.

Love…

A commitment…

Marriage with nothing standing in the way of a lasting relationship. That's what she wanted.

Icie deserved nothing less.

Despite the fact that she was in love with this man, she would not give of herself until she could honestly do so. Until he was willing to do the same himself.

"Still willing to spend the day with me?" he asked looking like a little boy asking for a treat he knew he was going to get.

"Yes," Icie answered. How could she refuse something so simple?

They entered the house and went straight to the elevator. Stepping out together, their shoulders brushed bringing to both their minds another moment nearly the same as this.

"I'll meet you downstairs."

He nodded, Icie moving toward her room as he called down the hall adding, "Yell, if you need anything. A towel, clothes, a few warm kisses…"

Clay wasn't sure whether or not she had heard the last few words, his mouth quirked up at the thought anyway. He could use a few warm some-things. This news about his dad knowing that he was dying and hiding it from him had left him feeling cold inside.

Clay knew he had died of cancer but had always thought that it was sudden. He had assumed that his dad had been diagnosed so late with the disease that there was nothing that could be done for him. All along he had been suffering with it for two long years.

He slowly pulled off his wet clothes ignoring the aching twinge in his knee. He toweled off and threw on some shorts and the first shirt he could put his hands on. A out together, of the ones he had had made for him and Icie.

Him and Icie.

Man, he needed her right now. Right this second. If it was nothing more than to see her smile, that would do for now.

Clay threw on the shirt and, barefoot, walked down the hall as quickly as his achy knee would let him, stopping at her door He knocked.

She didn't answer.

Damn, he'd run her off.

He didn't bang on the wall or yell in frustrated anger like he would have done just a few weeks ago. He needed to think.

Clay walked back to his room and sat on the edge of the bed, resting his elbow on his uninjured knee to do some delicate thinking. A tricky task, because he had never done any of this kind of thinking about any woman before. What had there been to think about before?

With Icie, there was too much to think about now.

He didn't know how long he sat there, but some time later there was a sound at the door.

Clay ignored it, his mind swarming with gift ideas that would possibly be good enough to give as an apology for wanting someone too much.

That sounded ridiculous. How could you want somebody too much? "Here's a thick terry cloth robe to cover every inch of your beautiful body and smother all those wants you keep telling me you don't have," said the imaginary card he wrote in his head.

What he'd like to get was this classy piece of black silk that was barely there...

"Clay?"

The door opened a pinch. The only part of his body that moved were his eyes which carefully glanced to the side.

She laughed at him before asking, "Why didn't you answer?"

"I didn't hear you. I thought you left, and what's so funny?"

"That pose."

Clay looked down at himself. He didn't know what she found so funny about it, but if she was enjoying herself he'd keep the pose a while longer. He was just relieved to see that she was still here.

"And why would I leave? I told you I'd stay with you today," she laughed again.

"What exactly is so funny?"

"You looked like a football playing David, the famous Greek sculpture.

"I know what you're talking about. You don't have to spell it out. I did finish college. But you got it wrong."

"I don't think so."

"I know so." Clay pulled off his jersey and threw himself back into the pose. Better?"

"Yes," Icie said out loud but then no to herself. All that golden brown exposure was a bit too much. "A bronze David would make a lot of hearts go wild."

"How about your heart?"

"I can't have that," she said with too much cheer as she sat down next to him. "How about putting that jersey back on?"

His bare chest bothered her. Good, he thought as he slipped it over his head. She was sitting on his bed. Clay wasn't sure what this meant. Was she throwing him mixed signals or was he simply mixed up. He didn't move a muscle. He didn't reach for her hand that was but an inch or two away from his. He didn't take advantage of the perfect view he had of the rise of her breast as they peeked out of the v-neck jersey she herself had changed into.

And a quick peek was all that he indulged in before looking back at her face as he tried to figure out what was going on before he made a move he would be sorry for.

"But I'd like to know how your heart is doing."

"My what?" Clay asked completely confused now.

"Your heart. This news about Mr. M. Your dad. How are you doing with that now?"

"Not bad." Now he was on track. She was worried about him.

"Are you still angry?"

"Some, but I'm better." He was much better. He had been angry at Ray, at his dad, even her. But he had worked most of it out of his system. Time would take care of the rest.

"If you need to talk, I'm here," she said before standing.

"There's nothing to talk about. I'll be okay."

"You talked it all out at the cemetery then."

"That's about right." Clay had no desire to talk about any of it right now. He wanted to talk to Icie, be with her, see exactly what it was that made her a princess. She was definitely one, if not by blood then at heart. Her concern about him was proof enough.

"Okay then." She was walking toward the door. "You didn't answer me before, why did you think I had left?"

"You didn't answer your door."

"I was in the shower; then I went down to make some coffee. When a half hour passed—"

"A half hour?"

"Yep, I was starting to think you didn't need me around."

"No, no, no, never. I was just in here thinking."

"The David thing."

"Yeah." For the first time not sure what to say, Clay suggested, "Want to drink that coffee you made, maybe make a little lunch? I didn't have any breakfast."

"Yeah, all I had was a few drops of rain water myself."

"Ha!" Clay stood. "Was that a joke Princess?"

"As a matter of fact, it was."

"Then I'd better give you a few lessons."

They made lunch together moving around the kitchen as if they had done it a million times.

Lunch was a quick meal of tuna salad sandwiches and chips. Clay was enjoying her company. Having put to the side his all out determination to have Icie sleep with him, Clay found that he was enjoying her company more than he ever had before. He wasn't saying that he preferred this innocent kind of enjoyment over the serious fun they could be having between the sheets, but it was a whole lot better than not having her with him at all.

They lingered at the table and talked, or didn't.

Clay sat in the hot tub while she sat on the deck as they read the newspaper and talked, or didn't.

Clay challenged her to a session of the video game madness. Icie whipped Clay's animated football team so badly that he was embarrassed by his defeat. So embarrassed that he forced her to sit through two hours of real football footage highlighting the many talents of number fifty-one.

And they talked, or didn't.

They took a very slow walk through a small portion of the subdivision, Clay taking her on an abbreviated version of his usual route. They waved to the nice old lady with her dog as they passed by. They talked in whispered tones on the way back to Clay's house.

Something they did a lot of today.

Icie told him about her struggle to stay in school, her career, her patients, even more Michelle stories.

Everything.

Except her childhood. She did not want to depress the man. Her goal today was to keep his spirits up. Keep his eye on recovery. Besides those were sad old memories best forgotten.

"What do ya' say, chauffeur?" Clay had asked.

"Chauffeur you where?"

"I've been talking so much you're not listening any more. The first signs of boredom."

"I'm far from bored." Which was true. Icie was enjoying his company getting to know the real Clay as Ray put it. "And I'm listening now."

"Mmm, that's good to hear."

They stopped at his front door having finished their walk. "Okay, okay. You've been talking about your little patients with so much heart, I know my disappearance the other night must have disappointed them."

"It did. Me too until I found out that you were writhing in pain on the kitchen floor."

"There was no writhing," he said in complete seriousness.

Icie reversed the wide grin that was dying to pop out on her face into a frown that she hoped was as severe as his. "I agree," she nodded, "there was no writhing." Icie swallowed before asking. "What were you saying about my patients?"

He stared at her a minute more before accepting her concession. "I'm glad we got that straight. Now these patients of yours, do you think they'd mind if we paid a visit to each of their houses to deliver some autographed footballs?"

"Clay!" Her arms were wrapped around his neck.

Clay was so surprised, that he didn't know what to do with his own hands. They stretched out on either side of him almost afraid to touch her.

Should he touch her?

Hey, she was touching him. His hands easily slid around her waist. He sighed in contentment.

"That's a wonderful idea!" she said into his shoulder before backing away. She slipped out of his arms and was inside the house before Clay realized he was holding onto nothing more than air.

"I'll call to make sure they're all home. You get a black marker and start signing."

She was now gone completely from sight.

Clay stood where he was, still stunned by her reaction and his reaction to hers. He loved the way she had spontaneously hugged him.

Icie had touched him because she wanted to.

She felt comfortable enough with him to freely touch him. That was no professional-I'm-you're-therapist touch there.

Clay loved every minute of it. If he was lucky he could probably get a few more like that before the day was over.

Not long after, they set off in Icie's jeep, both wearing their football jerseys. The first house they stopped at was of the little girl who was the first person to greet him the night he crashed the party. She smiled up at him shyly before whispering, "Defending the Crescents!"

"And fighting the foe," Clay answered, offering to the little girl, who went by the name of Neisha, the football Icie had been holding for her.

He talked to Neisha a bit, finding he enjoyed the short conversation, took a couple of pictures, and shook the little girl's parents' hands before leaving the happy family to go to their next stop.

It was pretty much the same at each house. Icie introduced him to a happy child; he spent a few minutes talking, took a couple of pictures, and said goodbye to the excited families. Clay watched as Icie's face got brighter with each visit.

He was doing it.

Clay was showing her what a nice guy he was and without having any ulterior motives. For the moment anyway.

"Clay, you have to know what you did has been so special to these kids."

"It wasn't much." And it actually wasn't, a few footballs, a few moments of his time. Hey, he even found that he enjoyed it himself.

"It was more than you think. Thanks."

"You're welcome."

They drove back to his house as the sun set, ending one of the most enjoyable days he had spent in a long time. The natural high gotten from truly making someone feel wonderful filled him up inside with such an immense feeling of satisfaction that Clay almost forgot the hurt and anger he felt toward his dad and Uncle Ray.

Icie pulled into the driveway but made no move to get out.

Clay didn't either.

He didn't want the day to end. "You know, I had a slight misunderstanding about your patients," he said ready to confess his reason for crashing her little party last night, if only to keep her with him awhile longer.

"You did?" She turned the engine off and twisted her body around to face him. "What was that?"

"I thought they were your kids."

"Oh!" A weird sort of choking laugh flew out of her mouth. "You did?"

"Your real actual kids, yep."

"Uh-uh." She let out an all out laugh before asking, "What gave YOU that idea?"

"You and Tim Skinny kept saying, 'the kids this,' 'the kids that'. I thought they were yours."

"Tim Skinny?" She laughed again. "That's what you call him now?" Icie didn't wait for an answer. A sudden look of understanding crossed her face, then a whole football stadium full of amusement.

"Mine?"

Clay raised an eyebrow as a sign of admission.

"Ours?"

He gave a slight nod attempting to appear as cool and laid back with his admission as possible.

"Mine and Tim's?"

"Pretty much," he heard himself say in a low mumble.

"There is no way, we're just friends. Tim has never made me feel the way…

She stopped freezing her mouth shut.

"The way, what?" Clay asked already knowing she meant him. Glowing inside because he'd made at least a ten yard dash toward getting pertinent information out of her

"What nothing," she told him. "I can't believe you thought I had kids. Wait till I tell Tim, talk about entertainment."

"Don't even think about saying a word of this to Mr. Skinny."

"How are you going to stop me?" She looked at him with a playful dare in her eye.

"You think I can't?" Clay asked.

"I know you can't. I'm not one of those he-men you face across he field—"

"You got that right."

Icie obviously made her own interpretation because she was saying, "I think it's time for me to go now."

"Don't."

"I should go."

"You should stay. It's almost Monday."

"That's one whole day away. One whole day to myself," was what she said to him, but her eyes, her body language told him she wanted to stay.

"You can't tell me you didn't have a good time today."

"You're right; I can't tell you that, and I won't tell you much of anything. Besides I've got church tomorrow."

"Take me with you."

"You're kidding?"

Did he look like the devil himself, Clay wondered. "You'll stay, in your own room of course, and tomorrow I'll join you in worship."

Icie seemed to be considering his suggestion. "A little praying might do you some good."

Icie couldn't believe it, but she decided to stay.

Clay had somehow lulled her into feeling as comfortable with him as a sentimental Jazz tune softly vibrating in a still quiet room. About an hour later, she found herself sharing a feast of Chinese food Clay had ordered for dinner.

They sat in front of the big screen TV in the den and watched hour after hour of movies together; sharing the sofa but not touching. Close enough so that Icie could hear each breath that Clay took, but having no need to get closer.

There was a closeness between them that was stronger than the sexual tension that had always existed between them.

Sexual tension that was still there, still an intense part of this new relationship that was developing but was now banked, held back to make room for simply being together.

Neither one of them moved an inch to clear away the dishes or reach for the remote to turn off the set. They were both too tired to move so they spent the night sleeping on the incredibly soft recliners built into the leather sofa.

CHAPTER 14

Icie woke up to the insistent sound of Ray's voice and a not so gentle poking on her shoulder.

"Icie girl, get up."

She opened both eyes a crack, unable to get either one of them fully functioning. "What?"

"What?" Ray repeated. "What is right. Take a look at the morning paper. What do you have to say about this?" Sunday's paper, with the added contents of comics, coupons and store advertisements landed on her lap with a soft thud. The unexpected weight and presence of the offending object forced her eyes open.

Icie looked down and stared at the front cover until it came into focus. There on the left hand side of the paper was what looked like one of the poses Clay had taken with Roy, their second little visitor. Icie read the caption in a low whisper; "Clay Mammoth, no longer in hiding, is he now out for a little fun? See Sports."

Icie didn't have much time to digest the info. or turn to the sports section to see what other tidbits they had on Clay before he called out to her; his voice heavy with sleep, "Talking in your sleep, Princess? I know one of your secrets now."

Icie and Ray both turned to him. Clay's eyes were still closed but he had shifted on the recliner and his entire relaxed body was turned in their direction. Ray seemed somewhat worried, but Icie didn't think this kind of coverage was what Clay or his coach should be concerned about. If anything this was positive publicity.

Firing fifty therapists, that was bad publicity.

Signing autographs and giving out a few footballs to kids completing rehabilitation, good publicity.

"Well, you got nothing to say to that, Princess?" Clay's sleepy gaze was directed at her.

Without turning her head, Icie glanced at Ray who had moved to the other side of the room. He was motioning her to be quiet about him being there, which was ridiculous. Before Ray could make it to the doorway leading to the hall Icie told Clay, "There is nothing to say to that because I don't talk in my sleep. I was talking to Ray."

"Uncle Ray!" Clay sat up. "What's he doing here?"

"Leaving," Ray said and was gone.

Clay hopped up and followed behind his uncle stopping at the doorway. When he saw there was no need to go any further, Ray was gone. He turned to her, a mixture of anger, frustration, and something else spread across his face.

Icie went up to him and put a hand on his shoulder, "Maybe you shouldn't have done that."

"Maybe he shouldn't have kept that fact that my father was dying a secret."

"Maybe he had a reason. Did you give him a chance to explain?"

"Maybe I didn't want to listen to any reasons. Maybe there aren't any reasons good enough to justify keeping that kind of secret from me."

This was a good time to back down. She wanted to tell him about the promise Ray had made to Mr. M, but it wasn't her place to tell. Clay needed to hear this from Ray, not her. "Maybe you do need some prayers," she told him. "We'd better get ready for church."

"Maybe you need some common sense," Coach Barnes' loud timber rolled down the hall.

"Why do you keep invading my house?" Clay asked the man now standing directly in front of them.

"This is no invasion. I was invited inside by that uncle of yours." Gray hair flying, the coach moved past them, spun around the room once and asked, "A romantic dinner in front of the TV?"

"That's none of your business. Why are you here?"

"Because some things are my business." Coach Barnes held up a copy of the Sunday paper a finger pointing at the picture Ray had shown her earlier.

Clay walked over and read the caption. He even smiled. "Okay I know you're press shy about certain things going on with me, but this is nothing to worry about."

"Nothing?"

"Icie did you see this? That's a nice picture. That lil' boy Roy he was something else."

"Yes, he is. The picture's why Ray came over." Icie looked at it again over Clay's shoulder. "He was showing me the paper." Icie went to get her copy.

"Did you happen to read the Sports section yet, Ice lady?"

"As a matter fact, no." Icie gave Coach her best Ice Lady stare just to make the insult true.

"Why don't you read it to us?" Clay suggested, his teeth clenched. "Clay Mammoth, one of Crescents star players has been nowhere to be found since the draft and still, no appearance during training camp sessions with only brief mention of a slow recovery from coach of the Crescents, Gregory Barnes."

"See, I know how to keep my mouth shut and have a low profile."

"Let me see that," Clay took the paper from the older man.

"But recently he has been seen about town, attending a celebration for the personal success of a few young children needing rehabilitation. Even going so far as to deliver autographed footballs to the same youngsters at their homes. Could Clay Mammoth's own mysterious injuries and slow recovery have caused him to open his heart out to others in similar circumstances?"

Clay stopped reading. Icie looked from one man to the other. "I don't get it. What's wrong with the article? This is all good publicity, right?"

"Right up until the last few lines," Clay told her.

"It can't be that bad. Read it."

"Or is his interest another one of his numerous exploits centering on Fifty-one- having- some-fun, for these children all have one thing in common. They are all patients of a beautiful, talented physical therapist that Clay Mammoth now has his eye on."

Both men looked positively explosive. "I don't take offense," Icie told them.

"But I do!" Clay said a deep growl rising in his throat. "Who did this? Who even knew we were visiting your kids?"

Icie had a suspicion, but she wasn't going to say a word to Clay just yet. Roy's dad, if she remembered correctly, worked with the paper.

"And why do you care about this?" Clay was shouting at his coach. "My love interest never bothered you before."

Love interest? Icie thought to herself. He was considering her his love interest.

She sat as the two men argued negative publicity for the team. Reaching for the copy of the paper Ray had brought in, she read the small column for herself. It wasn't all that bad. She read it again. The words somehow calmed her; bringing to mind Clay's good side.

"Well, tell me this Mr. Hothead," Coach demanded.

"Speak up, Coach, your little football star is listening."

Icie laughed out loud at that.

Coach Barnes was not amused.

"What are you going to do about the law suit The Walton Football Company is going to throw at you. How do you think that kind of bad publicity will affect the team?"

"What are you talking about?"

Icie was wondering the same thing.

"Since you are "in hiding" as they say in the paper, The Walton Company couldn't get in touch with you so they called me early this morning demanding to know if you autographed only Walton footballs."

"Did I?" Clay turned to her.

"I don't remember." Icie put the paper aside.

"I can't believe I forgot about that." Clay left the den and headed to the garage where they had stored the bag of footballs.

"What's the problem?" Icie asked.

"Endorsement," was all he said and all he had to say.

If Clay had an endorsement with Walton, then he most likely could not sign footballs made by any other company.

When Icie walked into the garage Clay was digging through the huge white bag. Coach was quiet for a change.

"I've got Wilson, even Nerf, and one Walton."

"I hope that means you signed all Waltons. I'll call the kids and ask."

"While you're at it, ask who tipped off the media."

Icie left the men in the garage, the coach's loud voice following her as he said to Clay, "You know you're going to have to make some kind of statement. Show your face and tell your fans when you're coming back."

"Yeah," Icie heard Clay answer. He would be going back before she knew it. Her time with Clay would be short. His progress was good except for that one episode with the spasms. He'd soon make it back on the field. That thought depressed her.

Icie called all her patients breathing a sigh of relief when she hung up with the last confirming that all the footballs signed were Waltons. She also discovered the culprit responsible for the story in the paper. Not Roy's dad, but a friend who also worked at the paper, and had happened to be visiting the day they came over. Roy's father apologized for mentioning anything to him at all.

Icie went back to the garage to tell Clay the good news about the footballs and what she had discovered about the source of the article. He was standing at the front door. "I'm just making sure the man leaves my house. I understand his worry about keeping up a positive image for the team, but he's making me crazy with these little unexpected visits," Clay told her without turning around.

"I can tell."

He closed the door behind him. She made him crazy too, but he wasn't going to say that out loud. "Did you find out anything?"

Icie told him. He nodded his head. "I do need some prayers, some in thanksgiving and some for patience."

"Don't forget about forgiveness."

"I'm just starting out, don't push me on this one, Princess."

Icie liked the way he now called her Princess, leaving off the ice. "I had to get that one in. Ray's—"

"Understood," Clay cut her off. "It's time for church right? I don't want to be late when it's my first time back in years."

"Then you might have to go to confession."

"No, doubt."

They got into the elevator together and parted in the hallway on the second floor. Clay walked in his room thinking about the many things he had done in his life that he would need to confess.

He felt a need to change all that. His relationships with women could not be called relationships. They were more like 'hello, goodbyes' He didn't want that with Icie. He didn't know exactly what he wanted with Icie. More than a 'hello, goodbye,' but then again he definitely wasn't looking for a forever. He wasn't ready for a forever in anything.

Icie drove them into the city to the same church Clay remembered going to as a boy. The same place his dad had his final funeral mass.

The over-crowded parking lot and flow of people entering the church was exactly the same. People in the community loved this church. Clay remembered the soulful music and the homily preached with such feeling that it kept people going, giving a spiritual uplift to last the week.

Clay and Icie parked a few blocks away and made it into the church just before mass began. A few people recognized him and waved but were more interested in getting inside the church to find a place to sit.

Icie lead him to a small spot where they were able to squeeze into one of the back pews. Mass started. The music and the energy of the people around him began to stir something inside of him. But it wasn't until the homily that he was able to identify just what that something was. It was more than memories; it was closer to a revelation.

Selfishness.

That's what the homily was about. The priest said the word once and it rang inside his ears.

Selfish.

That one word pretty much said it all about him. He had been selfish with his time which was why he hadn't noticed that his father was dying. He did what made him feel good no matter what it was or whom he disappointed or hurt.

Until recently.

Clay looked over at Icie. Until a Princess looked down on him and made him think twice about himself. He couldn't hurt her because of what he wanted from her.

Unselfish. That was his new word. He had already decided not to push Icie into doing anything she didn't want to, but he now made a promise to himself to think about what she wanted. He had to try to be less concerned about what he wanted from her and more accepting of what she wanted. Icie's needs and wants, not his.

That might be hard, but Clay cared about her more than he had any other woman. At the end of mass they left church, Clay shaking a few hands before making it out the door.

"Where to now?" Icie asked.

"It's a hot day. I feel like a swim. How about you?" he asked.

"That sounds like a good idea. I was going to add swimming to your exercise program. It's good for your knee. The exercise will strengthen it and increase your range of motion without danger of impact and—"

"—and it might be fun."

"That too."

"Do you have a swimsuit?"

"'Fraid not."

Clay thought about offering her one of the many he had hanging in the cabana near the pool but didn't feel right about that. Icie wasn't a 'hello, goodbye' girl. She deserved better As a matter of fact when he got home he'd get rid of them all, give them to good will or something like that.

"Besides," she was saying, "I don't need to get into the pool."

"Of course you do. It's a relaxing pastime and you can't expect me to get into the pool by myself when it comes time for my sessions."

"You've got a point there. I guess I'll have to buy myself a new suit."

"I'll come with you to help you pick one out."

"No, you're not. I do this alone."

"Whatever you say, Princess."

Icie looked at him strangely but pulled into traffic without comment. She dropped him off at the house. Clay dashed, if he could call the slow lumber his knee allowed him to take a dash, inside and went straight to the cabana. He grabbed the dozen or so swimsuits and threw them into one of the recycling bins he kept near the kitchen.

He pulled a package of frozen chicken breasts and burgers out of the freezer and went to fire up the grill. Loading the charcoal and pouring on the fluid brought Uncle Ray to mind. They'd spent many an evening here after Clay had injured his knee the first time. Maybe he should call him and invite him over. But the idea of actually following through on that thought brought back the twist of anger that had overtaken Clay earlier this morning when he found Uncle Ray talking to Icie. He simply couldn't.

He was still too angry. There was within him a great respect for the man that helped raise him, and Clay was not sure he would be able to keep that same measure of respect in tact when talking to him.

He wasn't ready. Not yet.

By the time Clay heard Icie in the driveway, he had some decent pieces of meat cooked and a few buns toasting on the grill. He called to her, waving a spatula in the air.. "Hey, Fifty-one, back here!" She tossed him the same irresistible smile she'd given Steve, Uncle Ray and even Tim Skinny. The same smile he had always wanted exclusively for him.

As she came closer Clay noticed that her lips were wider, her hazel eyes brighter than they had ever been when she wore that look of joy and excitement, and they were directed at him. He was the focus of it all. The energy from it knocked the air out his lungs and pushed Clay against the wall behind him.

He leaned against it trying to appear as cool and unaffected as he could. This was what he had always wanted from her, had been so jealous of, but now he wasn't sure he could handle it when she smiled at him that same way.

"Wait till you see the suit I picked out," she was saying as she passed him to go into the house.

"Umm," was the only sound he could get out of his mouth. It seemed to be enough of a response because she waved a hand at him before going inside, that blinding smile that sent his heart racing with fear still dominating her face.

By the time Icie came out wearing the modest navy blue suit, Clay had pulled himself back together.

It was only a smile.

No big deal.

It really didn't look as if her heart was all in it. As if she was waiting for his heart to do something about it.

"Well, what do you think?" she asked, when he said nothing.

Smooth and perfect.

Those were the words that slid through his brain as the spatula he held went sliding straight through his fingers and clanged on the patio brick.

How had he ever thought she was fat?

"You shouldn't have butter fingers near a grill, Fifty-one," she said as she bent to reach for the fallen spatula.

Here, standing before him, practically leaning against him, was a woman whom he wanted like no other woman in his life, but he couldn't have her.

…was afraid of what having her would mean.

….was afraid of what she wanted.

She stood taking away the luscious view that had been driving him crazy for the whole twenty seconds it was before him. "Something wrong?" she asked. "I guess you don't like the way I copied you. I know about these swollen heads you athletes have."

What was she talking about? She had turned to the outdoor sink not far from the grill to clean the spatula so all he had was a backside view. It was a good one. So good, Clay decided he needed to stay in this chair a while longer.

She handed him the cleaned spatula. "Alright Fifty-one, the least you could do is acknowledge my effort here."

Her hand brushed the top of her breast. Clay's eyes locked on a curve that her hand had barely touched. Clay thought about his hands barely touching her there—everywhere. Clay wanted that hand of hers to be his.

"Fifty-one," she said again.

Finally his eyes moved a few inches higher as they attempted to look up at her face. Before he got there Clay discovered what she was talking about. The number Fifty-one was etched onto her suit. Now he understood. "Nice."

"You got one too. Get yourself dressed for the pool. I left your trunks hanging on the door to your room. I'll finish out here."

"Sure," he readily agreed not sure of much anymore. Why was she buying him stuff? That didn't seem right. But not wanting to hurt her feelings, Clay went to put on the suit he found right where she said it would be.

Icie put together a few burgers and chicken sandwiches adding a few knick-knacks from the pantry and the fridge and set the meal up on one of the tables near the indoor pool. At times she wondered if she was doing too much for him.

…with him?

Should she have agreed to swim with him?

"Shut up. You're not working now. Enjoy the day" Icie finally said to herself.

Which is what she did. She and Clay ate lunch, lounged in the pool on a soft floating raft, and even swam a few leisurely laps together. Neither one of them had much to say to each other. They both seemed to be in some sort of mutually accepted reflective mood, holding their thoughts within while still enjoying each other's presence. The only distraction being the attraction, vibrantly alive, each felt for the other.

Throughout the afternoon Icie found Clay staring at her, constantly. Once or twice he looked as if he'd reach over, swim over, once maybe even dive over just to kiss her. She wanted to melt into him without a thought of anything else but thought is what always prevailed.

"You think too much!" her mother used to tell her. "Let yourself feel once in a while Ice Girl," she would taunt. Of course that was during one of her mother's numerous drunken sprees so Icie made sure to take the opposite of that advice.

Which is why she thought before she acted.

Which is why she didn't give into everything that simply felt good.

Hours later, Clay offered her dinner, but Icie declined. She had an early night showering, washing and setting her hair before literally crawling onto the bed where she froze at the sight of Clay bare-chested wearing only the navy blue trunks with the number fifty-one sewn on the bottom of the left leg. He burst through the door, a rolled up newspaper in her hand.

"Don't move, I saw it crawl under the door."

"What?" Icie frozen in the middle of the bed.

"A cockroach. The flying kind."

"Well then kill it!"

"That's why I'm here. There he goes." Clay stomped at the floor with his good leg.

"I got it. You're safe." He began to unroll the newspaper he was carrying. "I guess I really need to keep my balcony doors and windows closed."

"What you need to do is hire an exterminator."

"For one little roach?" He was using the piece of newspaper like a dustpan kicking the dead bug onto the now flat paper Clay went into her bathroom.

"I saw it. There was nothing little about that roach," Icie told him still on her hands and knees, crawling to the edge of the bed. "I can't stand them. Have you ever had one of those things crawl all over you?" Icie heard the toilet flush, but not another sound. She guessed the bug had been flushed away to a watery grave. Still on her hands and knees she turned to the bathroom door. Clay and that bigger than life body of his filled the doorway. He was staring at her, exactly as he had so many times at the pool.

He wanted to kiss her, she could tell.

Icie was going to let him, something else she could tell.

He was no longer at the door but standing beside the bed. Waiting. "I'd love to crawl all over you."

"I know."

"You want me to."

"I know."

"There's nothing I would rather do at this moment."

"I know that too."

"Invite me, then."

"To crawl all over me?"

Clay nodded.

Thoughts began to fly into her head before her mouth could open. The same cautious no-nonsense warnings. Her head was full of them, diminishing though not demolishing the feelings, the cravings she was having inside.

"Invite me," he whispered once again leaning closer toward her; not touching, not making contact with her; using nothing but his voice and his warm breath as it breezed past her ear.

"Okay" she released a deep frustrating sigh. She did want to feel, if not everything then some thing, a little something that Clay was more than ready to give. "Please come and kiss me."

Clay inched in as he stared at her mouth, then stopped. "No crawling?" he asked.

"No, I don't want you to."

"Don't want me to what?"

"To crawl all over me."

"Then you'll have to crawl all over me," he said before easing under her and onto the bed. She was on her hands and knees one minute but somehow he had managed to clasp her hands and pull them over her head as he stretched her body to fit over his. At the same time Clay's lips took her own in a probing heart-searching kiss that threw her into a restless frenzy. Her arms now free of his grasp moved up, down, and all over his body. Her legs pressed against him as she tried to get closer. A growl, coming from Clay forced her to pull back, to pull her lips away from his.

Surprised, and with a tiny pinch of dismay, Icie sat on her heels. She had been crawling all over him. Her entire nearly naked body had been all over him and she couldn't deny the pleased satisfaction she had felt. But Icie didn't let it show on her face. She couldn't get carried away with the moment. She was breathing fast and hard. Her eyes couldn't meet his yet.

"Princess."

They turned to him now. His deep voice a call she couldn't ignore.

"How about inviting yourself over."

Icie knew she couldn't. She was afraid to give into what Clay had to offer. One night? Maybe more? She could not allow herself to give into a bit of fun. "You know I can't," she told him.

Icie watched as a mixture of emotions crossed his face in a matter of seconds, disappointment, relief, and finally resignation. "Then I'll invite myself out." He stood in all his bare-chested glory and left without another word.

Icie didn't understand the look of relief she saw flash across his face. Maybe she was mistaken. Or maybe Clay was as relieved as she was that they hadn't taken this attraction between them any farther.

CHAPTER 15

Determined not to let any of the weekend's revelations, or the special time they had together ruin their professional relationship, Icie spent a few minutes staring at her reflection in the mirror reminding herself who she was and what her job description included.

She visualized past productive sessions with Clay and went into the gym focused on being her best professional self. She gave a distracted wave to Tim, who was once again working on the mural he had begun, and approached Clay with a quick hello and a push to warm up. She did not once make direct eye contact, going back to looking at his nose when she spoke to him, giving him no time to say a word between the instructions she issued for the new exercises and equipment they were working with.

Icie had moved him onto the second stage of improving his knee function. The elliptical trainer, treadmill, incline leg press, and hamstring curls were added to his list of exercises.

An hour later she marked his chart as he went through some cool down stretches and was out the door again and halfway down the first flight of stairs seconds after he was done.

"Icie!" both men called out to her.

She reluctantly trudged back up the steps. She went to Tim first, the easier man to face.

He met her at the top of the steps. "Today wasn't very entertaining." Icie shook her head.

"You okay?" he asked.

"Icie," Clay called again saving her from any lengthy explanation. "I'm fine. Let me see about my patient."

Icie's feet took her across the room to where Clay sat on the mat waiting. She stood before him. "What can I do for you?"

"Don't do this Icie."

"Do what?"

"Turn this gym into the battlefield of the Ice Princess versus the jock again."

"I haven't."

"It feels like it."

Icie didn't know what to say to that. She didn't want to go back to being cold and distant, but after the experiences they'd shared, after being together all weekend long, Icie was unsure of where that put her and Clay now.

"Look." He stood using the bench to pull himself up. "I'm sorry about invading your room last night."

Icie was sorry about that too.

He took a careful step closer. "I'm sorry about kissing again."

She couldn't be too sorry about that. Icie knew it was that kiss that was the main reason she felt so imbalanced right now. "I kissed you back. I even crawled all over you."

"I remember. I was there. We both enjoyed it."

"We did." Icie couldn't deny the truth staring her right in the face.

"But that's where the problem starts, right?"

She nodded.

"I wanted us to go on enjoying each other because it felt so right. You won't, because for you it wasn't right, am I right?"

"Exactly." Surprised that he was speaking so straight forwardly without making her feel as if there was something wrong with the way she felt, Icie's gaze locked with his. She was staring at the face of a man who put worry and fear into the hearts of his opponents, but all she felt was understanding and passion. His eyes held passion for her, but he was holding it back, for her.

"Since we understand each other there should be no reason for a repeat of the kind of session I suffered through this morning."

"Were the exercises too rough?" Icie felt relaxed enough to ask.

"No, the tension was too thick. Even Tim Skinny over there had more to say to me this morning."

"I heard that, Mammoth!" Tim shouted from across the room. "And he's probably heard every other word," Icie told Clay. "I don't care about that. What I care about and want is to be able to talk to you, be with you like we were last weekend."

"Minus the kissing and crawling."

"If you insist. It should be possible for us to be friendly with each other."

Icie had never had trouble with expressing a degree of friendliness with any of her patients before. It was that Clay was so much more to her. That was the problem. But that was also why she couldn't deny him friendship. "Friends," she agreed.

That decision made Icie find the evening session much easier to deal with. They began in the gym but moved on to the pool, not for relaxation but therapy.

They were even able to share the elevator without falling all over each other. Icie changed and went back to the kitchen. She started a simple meal of meatballs and spaghetti for herself, Ray, and she hoped, Clay. The two men had to get into the same house, the same room together to talk.

Sauce bubbling and meatballs rolled and popped into the oven to brown, Icie went to the fridge to get the ingredients to make garlic butter.

"What's going on in here?" Clay asked as she stood in front the fridge.

"It's Monday. I'm cooking dinner."

"For who?"

"For anyone who wants to enjoy a good meal."

"I hope that doesn't include Tim Skinny."

"No, the usual people." Icie closed the silver door placing the butter and garlic on the island counter.

"You've invited Uncle Ray here?" Clay crossed the room standing on the other side of the counter.

"Of course."

"After what he did to me. I thought we were friends, Icie."

"We are, and as your friend I suggest you sit down and talk to him about what he did. About what happened three years ago."

"I can't and I don't want him in my house." He looked like an angry little boy. "You have to un-invite him," Clay demanded.

"Can't do," she calmly answered, "Monday dinners are a tradition I refuse to change. Ray is my friend and since this is where I live during the week this is where he will come today and every Monday whether you like it or not, and I'm thinking you won't like it until you forgive him"

"I can't do that."

"Don't you mean you won't do that?"

"I don't like this." A growl grew inside his throat. "We're finally getting along and this thing with Uncle Ray is going to ruin it."

"Not necessarily. We can agree to disagree."

"Fine. Just keep Uncle Ray away from me," he said as he walked out of the kitchen.

Keeping Ray away from Clay was easy. He was nowhere around during the entire dinner. There was a cloud of sadness surrounding Ray, but not as heavy and dark as the one that had hung over him this past Saturday when Clay first confronted him. Their dinner was more quiet than usual, each relaxed enough with the other to allow silences to fall between them. Ray took one last bite cleaning his plate.

"Mmmm, good as usual, Icie girl."

"Thanks."

"Clay don't know what he's missing. Avoiding me like this has deprived his stomach of some good eatin'."

"It's his tough luck."

"He's still mad. I understand. I would be too. I've got to look at the good side of this."

"There's a good side?"

Slowly the silver lining hidden within that gray cloud surrounding Ray shone bright and clear. "That horrible secret is out. I never felt good about keeping the fact that Manuel was dying from Clay."

"He needs to know that."

"He will, when he's ready. Gotta go, Icie girl."

"Victoria?"

"Of course."

As Ray left, Icie decided to do what she could to get the men together. If Clay would put aside his anger, he could come to understand that Ray did what he did out of love, leaving open a chance for forgiveness.

Weeks passed and Icie wasn't having much luck getting the two men together. Every Monday she cooked something special hoping the smell would draw Clay out, force him to at least come face to face with Ray. But it wasn't working.

Their friendship however, was blooming. Clay surprised her by purchasing another set of exercise equipment he was required to work on. "If I'm gonna work out, you will too," he told her.

So Icie joined him during the sessions making the mornings fly by so much faster. Slowly, the time they spent together went beyond workout sessions. Icie would linger after the morning session and they would talk, completely forgetting their audience of one until Tim would remind her about the time and she would have to leave for her session with Antonia.

In the afternoons, excluding Mondays of course, they would linger by the pool side, sometimes doing nothing more than lounging or perhaps playing a game of cards. They'd even watch a movie if the mood hit them. Clay was becoming such a good friend, such an easy person to know and be around that Icie could almost forget their past relationship.

Their past problems.

Their present frustrations?

Impossible.

She was still suffering with constant urges to not only crawl all over him but to let him have a turn. Especially when she would find Clay staring at her with the look of a man desperate to have what he wanted, both confused and sure of himself at the same time.

Despite the frustrations, Icie wouldn't change the relationship they had been building together for anything in the world.

Icie woke up one morning with the realization that time was getting short. The months were flying by and as autumn fell upon them, it brought milder weather and the final stages of his rehabilitation. Clay's knee was becoming stronger and stronger. He wouldn't need her soon. He actually didn't need her now.

The thought made her heart hurt and her eyes burn. "This is one of the many reasons why you couldn't let things go anywhere with Clay. Pull it together, Icie girl."

Icie's use of Ray's nickname for her pushed that particular problem to the forefront. Two and a half months later and still she hadn't gotten Clay to listen, or to talk about Ray. She had to do something and do it fast.

When she got to the gym, Clay and Tim were in deep conversation. "I thought you finished the mural two weeks ago," she told Tim surprised to see him.

"Skin's here because I asked him to come. I've got this idea for a another mural."

"Another one?" Icie grinned to herself. Skin was Clay's shortened name for Tim who liked it a whole lot better than Tim Skinny.

"Yeah, another one. Why don't you get started without me. I'll be over in two."

"Minutes or hours, Fifty-one? Let's get started on this workout."

"My therapist bellows so I gotta go. Just do what we talked about." Watching the ease that Clay moved and his increased stamina as he worked out on the equipment reinforced her belief that she was not needed. Clay was ready to go back on the field. He was ready to defend the Crescents once again.

Side by side they exercised on the stair climber with Icie wondering why Clay wasn't making a push to get back to practice so that he could play the game he loved so much.

"Happy birthday to—guess who?" Clay was saying as he jumped off the machine, the navy jersey drenched in sweat. Hers didn't look much drier than his she noticed.

"Ray?" Icie asked as she stepped off the machine.

"Me," was all he said ignoring her attempt to put Ray into the conversation.

"Oh," Icie said, remembering Ray saying that Clay's birthday was in October; not to mention the times she helped Mr. M. pick out a present for him. "When is your birthday and what do you have planned?"

"My birthday's in two days and I don't have much planned. I usually throw a huge party for myself, invite everyone over and celebrate till I'm sick. Not this year. My birthday will be quiet and peaceful. Do you want to spend a quiet peaceful birthday with me, Princess?"

Whenever he called her Princess in that deep, deep voice of his, using that soft tender tone that trickled hot wantings through her veins, it was hard to deny Clay anything. Icie was so glad he didn't know that. "Sure," she told Clay as she directed him to use the shuttle that had helped to strengthen his knee these past few months.

"Good. Everything's all set. Be here Saturday at five."

"Where else would I be?" Icie had spent the last few weekends at Clay's, not going home at all in almost a month. She told herself that she had to stick around so that she could find a way to get Ray and Clay together. But Icie knew it was because she was having trouble leaving Clay at all. The time was right. She had to leave him while she could, while the patient' therapist barrier still stood, wobbly though it may be.

Icie got busy. By Saturday she had seen Ray and convinced him to do a little more than sit back and wait for Clay to decide to talk to him. She had gone shopping for the perfect gift hoping that he would understand its significance. It was simple but held great meaning.

When she got back to Clay's house his voice came through the intercom before she could close the door behind her. "Meet me on the second floor, Princess." Icie pushed the door behind her.

The wantings ran free and swift through her entire body as she took the stairs instead of the elevator using the activity to try and burn some of them off. It didn't work, just as she knew it wouldn't. There was nothing that could help her ease the yearning she held deep inside for Clay Mammoth.

At the top of the stairs was an arrow with the message 'This Way' pointing her in the opposite direction from his room. That was a bit of relief.

Clay was waiting by the door of a room she had never been in before. "Happy birthday," Icie told him as she walked inside, taking in everything. A table was set and a delicious smelling meal awaited them. There was even a birthday cake in the shape of a football waiting on the sidelines.

A bottle of champagne chilling in an ice bucket and candlelight filling the room were the only accessories missing from what looked like a romantic dinner for two. "No candlelight and champagne?" Icie found herself asking out loud.

"That's for lovers. We're still friends, still patient and therapist, or has something changed?" he asked her hopefully.

"Now that you mention it. Something has."

He was at her side in an instant. "Tell me, Princess." He had not touched her in any way, but his eyes caressed every inch of her body.

"You're ready to be released. You can get back to your game, get back to defending the Crescents."

"That's good." Icie could have sworn there was a tinge of disappointment in his voice.

"Good, how about great! Fantastic! I was saving the news as a birthday surprise. You're not happy about this?"

"Of course I am." He held out a chair for her. "How much longer do you have to work with me. A week? Two?"

Icie swallowed, her eyes blinked before she answered. "Times up," was all she could manage to say.

"A few days is all we have left then."

"No, I consulted with your doctor, all the paper work's been done. You can start practice Monday morning."

"You did all this behind my back?"

"I wanted to surprise you. This is what you wanted. What you've been working so hard for, right?"

"Yes. No. Of course it is," he told her lifting the covers of the plates to reveal hot steaming bowls of shrimp Creole. "Of course this is what I wanted," Clay said to himself. A chance to get back to the game he loved, to prove he hadn't lost it. A chance to be himself again. Trouble was, he wasn't feeling like his old self. Icie had done something to him. Somehow she changed some vital part of him, ruining the excitement he should be feeling about the best news he'd heard all year. He should be happy. He should be jumping up and down happy, but he wasn't.

"Is the food edible or simply decoration," she asked.

Clay looked up from the bowl of shrimp Creole he had been staring a hole into to gaze into her warm hazel eyes. How had he ever thought they were cold as ice? She didn't hold his gaze for long, she never did. "Dig in," he told her grabbing a spoon himself.

They ate in silence, not saying much to each other. Clay didn't have a problem with that. It was something they'd done many times before. But this silence was different. Wistful longing and unspoken feelings bounced around the room.

Feelings.

That's what he was scared of. What he didn't want to think about. What he wouldn't open the door to no matter how much he wanted her. And Clay wanted Icie.

He could have her now, he was sure. All he needed to do was have her in his arms for a few minutes and Icie would melt for him, into him. There was no patient/therapist barrier to stop them now.

But feelings.

That would do it.

"You're not enjoying your birthday dinner?" she asked.

Clay's tongue moved around his mouth tasting the spices and flavor of the last spoonful he had eaten. "Yeah, it's good."

"That's hard to tell. My bowl's empty, yours is half full."

Clay plopped the spoon into the bowl. "I was thinking. What if I need you this coming week? What if I do too much, too fast at practice and I mess something up? Shouldn't you be here just in case I need you?" Clay was making this up as he talked. He knew he was ready to go back, had known for the last week or two. The problem was he didn't want to be ready and the reason he didn't want to be ready was sitting right across from him and it scared the hell out of him.

"You won't need me, Clay."

Yes he did. From the moment she had walked out of the elevator and into his life till now. He needed her, he wanted her. The hard constant reminder between his thighs never let him forget it. "You don't know that."

"You won't need me."

"Okay, so this birthday dinner has turned into a farewell party."

"Pretty much."

"And the birthday boy can't have his cake and eat it too," he whispered to himself.

"What was that? You're ready for cake? I'll get it."

Icie blinked up at him nervously jumping up to get the cake, clearly as frustrated as he was. Maybe he could have his cake and eat it too. Maybe she was too nervous because she didn't want feelings and emotion all mixed up in what they could have together. They were friends now, it should easier for them to become lovers. Even if it was just for tonight. Better yet, only tonight. As Icie brought the cake over, a play that would make the sweetest touchdown began to form inside his brain.

He had Icie where he wanted her. Every curvy inch of her sat across from him in the hot tub begging him to touch. He had asked her to join him there and talk with him in the hot tub as part of his birthday present.

Clay wanted her to relax. What better form of relaxation was there than warm bubbling jets of water flowing all over you. If that were true, then why was he suddenly so nervous. Icie didn't seem to be. She was almost completely immersed. The tips of her navy covered breast inside the bathing suit she'd bought months ago floated above the water the number fifty-one visible every few seconds as puddles of foam floated by. Clay slowly made his way to her side and simply sat watching her close up as she relaxed with the foam swirling around her.

"Clay, why are you on my side of the hot tub?" she asked in that breathy voice he loved and hadn't heard enough.

"Because I can't kiss you from the other side," he said. She opened her hazel eyes wide. They said kiss me. So he did.

Beginning at the corner of her mouth Clay reverently kissed a path across her lips his body following until he lay above her, covering every inch of hers as the warm water moved over them. A sound that started deep in his pores before building inside his throat erupted into a satisfied growl of pleasure. He found her lips again and began kissing another path across them.

"Touchdown!" Clay heard. It wasn't him. He hadn't said a word. Besides touchdown was the last word he was thinking, though touchdown had been in his plan.

Sweet.

Amazing.

A moment to take slow and cherish.

"Touchdown!" he heard again. No! No! This wasn't a touchdown. This was better.

This was heaven Clay thought, as his hands went on a tactical exploration to seek more from his Princess.

"Touchdown!" he heard a third time.

"Clay, get off me." Icie pulled her lips from his, pushing at his chest. There was a strange catch in her voice.

"I don't want—"

"We've got an audience."

Clay twisted his head to see who had ruined this moment, who had Icie so upset she was shaking in his arms. He eased up to peek over the top of the hot tub using his body to keep Icie hidden.

"Not in the game but still scoring, I see," Randy, quarterback for the Crescents, laughed as he stood just a few feet away.

Clay couldn't believe this. Why were they here? How did they get into his house?

"You in the habit of keeping your door unlocked?" Larry asked, leaning a hand on the edge of the hot tub. None of them had any concern for what they had interrupted, for any embarrassment Icie might be feeling. Why should they? None of them had ever been concerned before. But Clay was now. He was a whole lot more than concerned. He was angry.

"Who you got in there with you?" Larry lifted himself over the edge of the tub to see.

"Put your eyes someplace else man. And the rest of you back off." Clay told his friends.

"Got a shy one?" Joe asked nodding his head in understanding as Larry and Randy took a step back. "Since you didn't look like you were throwing one of your famous parties we came to give you one ourselves," Joe explained their presence, lifting a case of beer and box of fried chicken for him to see.

Clay didn't care why they were here or what they brought. He just wanted them to leave. He could feel Icie slipping lower into the tub. Literally slipping away from him. "Good, now go."

"We're going," Larry backed away, "go on with your own private party. Make it to the end zone, my man."

"Yeah, see you Monday!" Randy called, "Coach says your sorry butt's finally gonna show."

"Yeah, Monday!" Clay yelled back not moving away from Icie until he heard the front door close. When it did, he got up, ran to the door and locked it. When he came back into the sunroom Icie was rubbing herself dry with a huge white towel. Her arms and legs moved fast and hard across her body.

The same body that lay under his willingly a few minutes ago.

The same body that now looked like it was on the way out.

Clay didn't want her to leave but he didn't know how to stop her. He said the first thing he could think of.

"You can't go! It's my birthday."

She turned around and marched right up to him, and held his gaze as she told him, "I am no touchdown!"

"I never said you were."

"I don't hold private parties for jocks and you won't make it to the end zone with me."

"This wasn't—. I didn't—! Oh, hell—I"

"It was. You wanted to and I was going to let you, but hell if I'm going to be used by you, Clay Mammoth."

This was all wrong. This was not how this evening was suppose to end. Sure he'd thought touchdown, but he hadn't meant touchdown, not with Icie. She turned to leave again. Clay caught her by the shoulders, held her and slowly turned her to face him again.

"I was not going to use you, Princess. You know me better than that."

"Then tell me. After tonight, what would you have done with me." Clay had no idea what to say because he had no idea what he would have done with her. Make love to her over and over again until they got tired of each other. Maybe. His silence wasn't helping anything, Clay realized when her hazel eyes turned cold and hard.

"I see you've thought this thing through real good, Clay. I'm making it easy for both of us. Go back to your life. I'll go back to mine. This way no one gets hurt."

"Icie!" he called after her, but let her go. Someone was already hurt. The tears streaming down her face attested to that. The pain ripping through his heart assured him of that.

The sounds of voices outside drew Clay to the front door. Icie came charging back inside before he could even step out of the sunroom. She had a present in her hand. Uncle Ray stood not far behind with a wrapped package in his.

What was he doing here? What was Icie up to now?

The white towel was wrapped around her waist and even though he wanted to shake her for walking out on him, he wanted to pull that towel until he had both ends within his grasp and a willing Princess in his arms again. But Uncle Ray was standing there and Icie was unwrapping the present waving a wooden bowl in her hand.

"This is your present. Take this bowl, pour into it all your hurt and anger, and dump it so that you can listen with half a clear mind to what this man," Icie turned to his uncle, "who loves you like a son, has to say."

She slapped the bowl into his hand and left once again.

Clay stood where he was, still dripping wet holding a wooden bowl with the words 'Free yourself, FORGIVE' carved onto its side. He needed to be free of some of the problems that were pestering him. If forgiveness brought freedom, he'd give it a shot.

"Life isn't easy, is it b——, I mean, Clay." Ray said.

"No, sometimes it's not. We might as well have this talk Icie's been pushing for. Anything you have to say can't make me feel any worse right now." Clay grabbed a towel from the cabinet in the corner of the sunroom and led his uncle to the kitchen, taking his bowl along with him.

"You first," Uncle Ray offered after they both had sat at the table where they had eaten so many dinners with Icie. Clay laid the bowl on the table. Uncle Ray moved it so that it sat directly under Clay. "Gotta be able to catch all that hurt and anger."

So Clay talked. It wasn't easy at first, but soon the words poured out of him letting the man across from him know exactly how angry and hurt he was, how justified he was in having those feelings, how cheated he felt, how hopeless. When he was done Uncle Ray picked up the wooden bowl, went to the sink to fill it with water and poured it down the drain.

"I'm glad you got all that off your chest," Uncle Ray said as he sat himself into the chair and the bowl in the middle of the table. "I know that wasn't easy and this won't be for me either, so don't interrupt, just listen."

"Anything you have to say can't make me feel any worse than I do right now."

But Clay was wrong. Holding a grudge when you are unaware of all the facts, labeling someone the bad guy because it's the easier thing to do and then being wrong about it all made Clay feel even worse.

Icie was right. Uncle Ray did have a good reason for keeping his dad's illness from him. How could anyone remain angry and unforgiving of someone keeping a death wish?

He couldn't.

Clay stood and held his hands out to his uncle, his only family. When Uncle Ray stood to accept the gesture of peace, Clay pulled the older man toward him giving him a bear hug that said more than words could. But he did have words to say, "I love you, man, for being there for my dad and my pig-headed self."

"No problem."

Both men slowly eased back into their chairs their eyes landing on the wooden bowl in the middle of the table.

"That thing works."

"The woman behind the thought is what set things in motion."

"Icie got you here?"

"Surprised?" Uncle Ray asked.

"No, she's been pushing you into almost every conversation we've ever had."

"Conversations? Anything else?"

Clay simply shook his head. "Anything else is ruined and gone."

"Don't be so sure about that."

"I'm sure. Did you see and hear the woman? I've never known her to react with so much emotion. I've never seen her cry."

"That means she cares."

Clay shook his head once with intense certainty. "Icie hates me. She's done with me and is probably thanking the heavens above for being able to get away."

"If you say so."

"I say so." He also knew so. Clay knew he couldn't give Icie what she wanted. It was better for both of them this way.

The Sunday before Christmas Icie was watching the game on TV. It was a home game, the New Orleans Crescents verses the Atlanta Falcons. She hated the Falcons and hoped the dirty birds, as they were called, would get a solid blow to their super egos and undefeated status. With Clay on the field helping to defend the Crescents it was sure to happen.

Clay.

Icie could never have imagined how much she would miss him. Two months and two days later and her heart still yearned for him. Despite knowing she did the right thing and her repeated congratulations to herself on self-discipline and professionalism, Icie could not honestly say that she was truly happy. But if she had given in to Clay she would have been much worse off, she reminded herself.

Yet after knowing Clay and coming to love him, she no longer felt happy with her life as it was. She was still pleased with her job, her career, and her patients, but the rest of her life was so empty. She still had Ray, but he had Victoria.

Icie had no one. There was her Tim, still her good friend, and Steve who she talked to on the phone now and then. But still she felt as if she had no one.

Not one to dwell on what she couldn't have, she let that thought slide away as the players ran onto the football field. She caught sight of Clay immediately, as always. Ingrained upon her brain was the image of how he moved, how he kissed, how he sneaked under her as she enjoyed the feel of his body against hers, how she crawled all over him. She'd dreamed about him so many times in the last two months.

"But having what you wanted wasn't always good for you," Icie said to the TV as the words touchdown and end zone replayed in her ears. She would never be anyone's touchdown.

The doorbell rang and Icie went to answer it. It was a FedEx package. She signed for the package and slowly began to unwrap the small box. She was surprised to find her birthday present to Clay inside. The small wooden bowl was still in tact so he must have controlled his temper enough to stop himself from smashing it. Inside the bowl was an envelope Icie held it in her hands and read it out loud.

"To Princess, From Clay. Free yourself and me. Forgive."

Icie dropped the letter back into the bowl. She sat staring at it as the national anthem played in the background. What did this mean? Was Clay throwing her present back at her? Was he playing some kind of joke that he and his buddies made up? Did he bring this bowl in the locker room as a prop to tell everybody about her? Would he?

Not the Clay she had come to know.

"—land of the free and the home of the brave."

Free and brave. To be free one had to show bravery. Icie picked up the brown envelope, turned it around in her hand a few times before placing her finger under the seal. A loud explosion of a crowd in dismay drew Icie's eyes back to the screen. She dropped the envelope back into the bowl as she saw a Crescent player lying on the ground, injured five minutes into the game.

It couldn't be, Icie thought.

But it was.

Clay's name and number flashed across the screen as the announcer's voice bellowed through the TV speakers, "Mammoth, number fifty-one down. He's been having nothing but bad luck, out half the season and injured again…" Icie tuned out the loud obnoxious announcer Then kneeling right in front of the screen to get a closer view of Clay, she stayed there until he was taken away on a stretcher.

Without a second thought Icie went for her purse and keys turning back to get one last important thing. She drove straight to Baptist Hospital knowing that was the most likely place they would take him. She parked and went straight through the emergency room door where Clay's voice hit her.

"Call Icie, Uncle Ray. Get her over here any way you can, okay. I want her here as soon as possible."

"I'll do what I can." Icie heard Ray's answer.

Icie turned the corner to see a stretcher being rolled away with Clay on

"Stop, wait!" Clay yelled as he spotted her. "You're quick, Uncle Ray." Clay smile up at his uncle, then grasping the handrails of the stretcher he lifted himself to watch her jog down the aisle. "You're here," Clay said to her.

"Where else would I be?" she answered.

"I need you."

"I know. Who else would put up with taking care of you, Fifty-one?"

"I wouldn't want anyone but you, Fifty-one, but what I mean is I need you. Did you get the package? Did you read my letter?"

"I didn't have a chance to yet."

"Sir, we really should get you to—"

"In a minute. This is more important," Clay impatiently told the young orderly at the head of the stretcher.

"Clay, you're in pain, you're hurt. That might be a little bit more important."

"Nothing's more important than what's in that letter and your answer to it. It took me two whole months of being miserable to realize that I couldn't live without you."

"Sir, we're blocking traffic." This time the orderly's voice held a bit of impatience, "Maybe you want to do this in private."

"Okay, wheel me on, but my future wife is coming with me. Grab my hand Princess and don't let go."

In a daze Icie took the hand Clay stretched out to her and walked quickly to keep pace with the moving stretcher. Future wife?

Alone in the room together all she could do was stare at the big man covered in sweat, his eyes full of pain and something else.

"Well?" he asked. "Don't leave me waiting. What do you think? Do you want to marry me? A football player with recurring injuries?"

Stalling Icie answered, "At least it's the other knee." He wanted to marry her. Did that mean he loved her? Clay hadn't said a word about love. He was miserable without her. That was a good sign because she had been miserable without him.

"Forget my leg, Princess. Read the letter."

"I have to get it from the jeep."

"Go on, I'm not going anywhere for a while."

Icie went to the jeep and retrieved the medium-sized brown envelope. She sat as she opened it to find between a sheet of paper, a large navy blue handkerchief folded into fourths. Stitched into it were words. The handkerchief was the letter.

It seems that I have loved you forever; It almost took that long for me to realize it.

Forgive me. I love you, Marry me.

Clay

The words she was looking for, the assurance that Clay was serious when he talked about their getting married sat on her lap written in nylon and cotton. The sheet of paper, she noticed, had writing on it too.

Come to today's game.

Wave this handkerchief so I'll know your answer is "yes", and that you love me too.

It was beautiful.

It was romantic.

It wasn't enough.

Icie needed to see him, to hear him say the words.

The navy handkerchief clasped in her hand, Icie ran back to Clay. Waving the cloth above her head she walked to the bed.

She looked into his eyes having no trouble holding his gaze because it was there that she found all the love he had for her. Despite the pain, it was easy to see. How had she missed it before? "First," she said reaching to lay the handkerchief around his neck, "I forgive you."

"Next?" he asked leaning closer.

"I have loved you with all my heart for a long time myself."

"I was hoping you'd say that." His head rested against hers.

Icie's hand touched his cheek, her lips brushed against his.

"And last?" he asked, his lips still pressed against hers.

"And most importantly, I will be honored to marry you."

"I love you," he leaned back to tell her.

"That's what I wanted to hear you say."

"I'll love you forever."

Icie gently pulled the handkerchief until his lips touched her once again giving him a kiss that melted away all uncertainty, all fears leaving them With a solid core, a love frozen in time, lasting forever.

EPILOGUE

"Where do I put the cake, Icie?" Ray asked.

She pointed to a table she had set up in a corner of the room. Today they were celebrating the recovery of five of her patients. This party was extra special because included in the five was not only Antonia, but her husband.

Clay had suffered such a severe blow to his knee in that game against the Falcons that his ACL, or anterior cruciate ligament, was damaged and replaced with a graft from his patellar ligament in another part of his knee. With both knees weakened by injuries, Clay decided on his own to retire as a football player giving up the game he loved.

It wasn't an easy choice but Icie helped him get through this crisis. For the last four months she had been not only wife and therapist but mentor and tutor. Clay had decided to go back to school to become a physical therapist himself, choosing sports medicine as his specialty.

"Princess Ice," Steve called having come into town for the party and a visit, "Antonia was telling me her favorite story."

"Icie can tell a good story," Clay said as he walked into the clinic carrying a bag of footballs he planned to autograph. He wrapped an arm around her waist and laid a kiss on her cheek.

"You should hear this one. Tell it Antonia," Steve encouraged.

"Yep, entertain the adults," Tim added.

"Okay," Antonia said standing firm and proud on two strong legs. "There was this evil dragon named Claymmoth…"

Icie slowly eased away from the small crowd that surrounded Antonia. She even managed to steer clear of her husband for the rest of the party knowing that he'd have a thing or two to say about that story she had created so long ago. A lifetime ago it seemed.

During the party she'd caught his eye which held a promise of retribution. Nothing to worry about. Retribution, she knew, would be most enjoyable.

At the unveiling of the portraits, near the end of the party, Icie found herself wrapped in the arms of her husband who had snuck up behind her. As the curtain came down to reveal Tim's latest work he whispered in her ear; "The dragon has plans for the princess tonight."

The oohhs and ahhhs of everyone present stopped her from responding, but did nothing to curb the thrill of excitement that ran through her body with Clay's words.

"What am I doing up there?" he asked in surprise.

Tim had painted Clay twice. One portrait showed him as the perfect pro-football player; the other was of Clay walking down the road, a load a books in his hand as he passed an archway labeled LSU School of Medicine. A sign at the entrance also said 'Welcome to Sports Medicine.'

"Have I ever thanked you for being there for me? Twice. I guess that's why you've got two of me up there."

"Of course, you have been my patient two times, you know."

"But I'm you're husband only once. Can we get these people out of here and lock up?"

"Ray and Victoria volunteered to handle that end of the party."

"Great. I always knew there was a reason I liked Victoria."

"I hope that's not the only reason. You do know they're getting married?"

"Uncle Ray, that sly old dog." Clay twisted his head looking around the room for his uncle.

Icie laughed, "Let's get out of here."

"You don't have to tell me twice."

Clay and Icie said their good-byes. When they got home he insisted that they take a slow leisurely shower together. There, Clay displayed, as he had done many times before, the many uses of his hands.

He began with the unhurried removal of her clothes. Icie had never realized that removing a light-weight silk shift with one zipper could be so prolonged or so erotic. The combination of silken fabric, warm, wet kisses and hands that moved expertly over every part of her body melted her bones and left her a throbbing, desperate bundle of nerves that she could only feel.

When the soft fabric had been tossed away. Clay's hands came back sending nerve impulses to the tips of her nipples as each thumb circled and pressed the tips with smooth gentle touches; the rest of his hand hovered above her breasts. Every few moments he'd give each aching handful a gentle squeeze before teasing her nipple again.

Icie's breath caught with each caress. "Had enough?" he asked. "No," she answered, with Clay there was never such a thing as enough. He lifted his body away, his still clothed body. That's not the way Icie wanted him. She knelt on the bed and quickly helped him get rid of his shirt, his pants—everything. Then he pulled her into his warm hard body and half-walked half-carried her into the bathroom.

Lingering.

Lingering is exactly what they did as they show-ered.

There were hands and fingers that made lingering traces over knees, elbows, ear lobes and more.

Gentle strokes on strong, muscled thighs and firm bottoms. Wet, soapy massages that teased and titillated. After Clay turned off the water, his hardness pressed against her, reminding her that the wet body she had skimmed and examined could not compare to what was yet to come.

They dried each other with swift careless swipes of a towel and rolled onto the bed, Clay's protective arms around her. Icie held him as close to her as she could, loving the warm feel of his body completely covering her. But their lingering activities in the shower had left her wet and throbbing, Clay hard and wanting leaving them both with a need for an even closer contact.

"Bring me inside of you, Princess," Clay told her in the deep soft voice she loved, and of course she willingly obeyed guiding the hardness she was once leery of wanting, savoring the deep strokes that came with love, until at last they both experienced the ultimate gift they could possibly give to each other.

Hours later Icie awoke to the feel of Clay's fingers skimming across lips. "Wake up, Princess," he whispered. He pressed a soft kiss on her lips. "What for?"

"I've got something to show you."

"Morning will work."

"No, I've got to show you now. I've been waiting a long time to show you this."

"We waited a long time to make love and look how good that turned out," Icie said without opening her eyes.

"True, it's one of my favorite parts of married life."

Icie cracked her eyes open. "You do look like a happily married man."

"I am. Now make me happier, Princess, and come with me." He leaned his face against hers resting his chin on her shoulder the bristly hair on his chin rousing her in more ways than one. Icie opened her eyes a bit more. Clay looked excited and much too wide awake at four o'clock in the morning. "A few more hours—"

"—will kill me because the delay will mean I will have to wait longer to make love to you again. To have another taste of you, Princess."

That last word, the way he called her Princess did it. "Okay, but this better be good," she warned.

They took the elevator to the gym, Icie using Clay's strong body to hold her up. "We're not going to work out, are we?" she asked, still half asleep.

"No," was all Clay would say, amusement in his voice.

He guided her to the far corner of the gym without turning on any lights, stopping in the same little corner or niche, which she had begun to call it, that had been converted into a tiny room these last few months.

"Oh, the secret," she mumbled.

"The secret is finished and shall be revealed."

The secret was a mural Clay and Tim had been whispering about for far too long, Icie thought. Suddenly, she was awake, the excitement of finally finding out what was behind that sheet eased the sleep right out of her body. She had promised not to look before it was done and had kept her word.

Clay pulled the sheet away and flipped a nearby switch which cast a glow of light directly onto the wall that she couldn't keep her eyes off of. Icie took a step closer and reverently touched the beauty before her. A full size likeness of herself and Clay covered the entire length of the wall, a copy of their wedding portrait. Surrounding it were various scenes of their unsteady road to wedded bliss.

"There's a picture of us working out together," Icie pointed out.

"And one of us cooking."

"And the shirts, Clay, Tim even painted the shirts."

"Check out the pool-side picture and the hospital, where you came running to me before I could even call you."

"Where you told me you loved me for the first time."

Clay wrapped his arms around her squeezing her tight.

Icie turned in his arms to give her husband a kiss that could only begin to show him how much this collage of their life meant to her. Together they sat on the floor, Clay with his arms still surrounding her.

"Every year we can have Skin come back to add a scene or two."

"I'd love that, but, Clay, how did you do all of this?"

"Skin was a big help."

"I'm sure, but he couldn't have known about all of this."

"I gave him some information here and there."

"Look," Icie laughed, "there's you with a towel, swatting at on of those cockroaches that kept getting inside the house."

"Oh yeah, the imaginary cockroaches."

"You mean they weren't real, but I saw the one you killed in my room that night."

"Oh, the same night you crawled all over me when all I did was give you a little kiss."

"Little? There's nothing little about you, Clay. Even your roaches were big, and now you're telling me there were none."

"That one I killed was the only real one, and I pretty much chased him in there."

"Clay!"

"I was a desperate man trying to get your attention. You did things to me I had never experienced before and I was having a little trouble handling."

"I remember."

"I'm having no trouble now. This wall is just the beginning of a long life we're going to have together."

"A long exciting life," Icie agreed. "How should we christen it?"

"With a whole lot of excitement," he answered pulling her with him as he lay flat for a moment before rolling across the floor until she was on top of him, face to face, and chest to breast. "You can start by crawling all over me."

"You don't have to tell me twice," Icie said as she leaned down to initiate the excitement her husband was looking for.

2008 Reprint Mass Market Titles
January

Cautious Heart
Cheris F. Hodges
ISBN-13: 978-1-58571-301-1
ISBN-10: 1-58571-301-5
$6.99

Suddenly You
Crystal Hubbard
ISBN-13: 978-1-58571-302-8
ISBN-10: 1-58571-302-3
$6.99

February

Passion
T. T. Henderson
ISBN-13: 978-1-58571-303-5
ISBN-10: 1-58571-303-1
$6.99

Whispers in the Sand
LaFlorya Gauthier
ISBN-13: 978-1-58571-304-2
ISBN-10: 1-58571-304-x
$6.99

March

Life Is Never As It Seems
J. J. Michael
ISBN-13: 978-1-58571-305-9
ISBN-10: 1-58571-305-8
$6.99

Beyond the Rapture
Beverly Clark
ISBN-13: 978-1-58571-306-6
ISBN-10: 1-58571-306-6
$6.99

April

A Heart's Awakening
Veronica Parker
ISBN-13: 978-1-58571-307-3
ISBN-10: 1-58571-307-4
$6.99

Breeze
Robin Lynette Hampton
ISBN-13: 978-1-58571-308-0
ISBN-10: 1-58571-308-2
$6.99

May

I'll Be Your Shelter
Giselle Carmichael
ISBN-13: 978-1-58571-309-7
ISBN-10: 1-58571-309-0
$6.99

Careless Whispers
Rochelle Alers
ISBN-13: 978-1-58571-310-3
ISBN-10: 1-58571-310-4
$6.99

June

Sin
Crystal Rhodes
ISBN-13: 978-1-58571-311-0
ISBN-10: 1-58571-311-2
$6.99

Dark Storm Rising
Chinelu Moore
ISBN-13: 978-1-58571-312-7
ISBN-10: 1-58571-312-0
$6.99

2008 Reprint Mass Market Titles (continued)

July

Object of His Desire
A.C. Arthur
ISBN-13: 978-1-58571-313-4
ISBN-10: 1-58571-313-9
$6.99

Angel's Paradise
Janice Angelique
ISBN-13: 978-1-58571-314-1
ISBN-10: 1-58571-314-7
$6.99

August

Unbreak My Heart
Dar Tomlinson
ISBN-13: 978-1-58571-315-8
ISBN-10: 1-58571-315-5
$6.99

All I Ask
Barbara Keaton
ISBN-13: 978-1-58571-316-5
ISBN-10: 1-58571-316-3
$6.99

September

Icie
Pamela Leigh Starr
ISBN-13: 978-1-58571-275-5
ISBN-10: 1-58571-275-2
$6.99

At Last
Lisa Riley
ISBN-13: 978-1-58571-276-2
ISBN-10: 1-58571-276-0
$6.99

October

Everlastin' Love
Gay G. Gunn
ISBN-13: 978-1-58571-277-9
ISBN-10: 1-58571-277-9
$6.99

Three Wishes
Seressia Glass
ISBN-13: 978-1-58571-278-6
ISBN-10: 1-58571-278-7
$6.99

November

Yesterday Is Gone
Beverly Clark
ISBN-13: 978-1-58571-279-3
ISBN-10: 1-58571-279-5
$6.99

Again My Love
Kayla Perrin
ISBN-13: 978-1-58571-280-9
ISBN-10: 1-58571-280-9
$6.99

December

Office Policy
A.C. Arthur
ISBN-13: 978-1-58571-281-6
ISBN-10: 1-58571-281-7
$6.99

Rendezvous With Fate
Jeanne Sumerix
ISBN-13: 978-1-58571-283-3
ISBN-10: 1-58571-283-3
$6.99

2008 New Mass Market Titles

January

Where I Want To Be
Maryam Diaab
ISBN-13: 978-1-58571-268-7
ISBN-10: 1-58571-268-X
$6.99

Never Say Never
Michele Cameron
ISBN-13: 978-1-58571-269-4
ISBN-10: 1-58571-269-8
$6.99

February

Stolen Memories
Michele Sudler
ISBN-13: 978-1-58571-270-0
ISBN-10: 1-58571-270-1
$6.99

Dawn's Harbor
Kymberly Hunt
ISBN-13: 978-1-58571-271-7
ISBN-10: 1-58571-271-X
$6.99

March

Undying Love
Renee Alexis
ISBN-13: 978-1-58571-272-4
ISBN-10: 1-58571-272-8
$6.99

Blame It On Paradise
Crystal Hubbard
ISBN-13: 978-1-58571-273-1
ISBN-10: 1-58571-273-6
$6.99

April

When A Man Loves A Woman
La Connie Taylor-Jones
ISBN-13: 978-1-58571-274-8
ISBN-10: 1-58571-274-4
$6.99

Choices
Tammy Williams
ISBN-13: 978-1-58571-300-4
ISBN-10: 1-58571-300-7
$6.99

May

Dream Runner
Gail McFarland
ISBN-13: 978-1-58571-317-2
ISBN-10: 1-58571-317-1
$6.99

Southern Fried Standards
S.R. Maddox
ISBN-13: 978-1-58571-318-9
ISBN-10: 1-58571-318-X
$6.99

June

Looking for Lily
Africa Fine
ISBN-13: 978-1-58571-319-6
ISBN-10: 1-58571-319-8
$6.99

Bliss, Inc.
Chamein Canton
ISBN-13: 978-1-58571-325-7
ISBN-10: 1-58571-325-2
$6.99

2008 New Mass Market Titles (continued)

July

Love's Secrets
Yolanda McVey
ISBN-13: 978-1-58571-321-9
ISBN-10: 1-58571-321-X
$6.99

Things Forbidden
Maryam Diaab
ISBN-13: 978-1-58571-327-1
ISBN-10: 1-58571-327-9
$6.99

August

Storm
Pamela Leigh Starr
ISBN-13: 978-1-58571-323-3
ISBN-10: 1-58571-323-6
$6.99

Passion's Furies
AlTonya Washington
ISBN-13: 978-1-58571-324-0
ISBN-10: 1-58571-324-4
$6.99

September

Three Doors Down
Michele Sudler
ISBN-13: 978-1-58571-332-5
ISBN-10: 1-58571-332-5
$6.99

Mr Fix-It
Crystal Hubbard
ISBN-13: 978-1-58571-326-4
ISBN-10: 1-58571-326-0
$6.99

October

Moments of Clarity
Michele Cameron
ISBN-13: 978-1-58571-330-1
ISBN-10: 1-58571-330-9
$6.99

Lady Preacher
K.T. Richey
ISBN-13: 978-1-58571-333-2
ISBN-10: 1-58571-333-3
$6.99

November

This Life Isn't Perfect Holla
Sandra Foy
ISBN: 978-1-58571-331-8
ISBN-10: 1-58571-331-7
$6.99

Promises Made
Bernice Layton
ISBN-13: 978-1-58571-334-9
ISBN-10: 1-58571-334-1
$6.99

December

A Voice Behind Thunder
Carrie Elizabeth Greene
ISBN-13: 978-1-58571-329-5
ISBN-10: 1-58571-329-5
$6.99

The More Things Change
Chamein Canton
ISBN-13: 978-1-58571-328-8
ISBN-10: 1-58571-328-7
$6.99

Other Genesis Press, Inc. Titles

A Dangerous Deception	J.M. Jeffries	$8.95
A Dangerous Love	J.M. Jeffries	$8.95
A Dangerous Obsession	J.M. Jeffries	$8.95
A Drummer's Beat to Mend	Kei Swanson	$9.95
A Happy Life	Charlotte Harris	$9.95
A Heart's Awakening	Veronica Parker	$9.95
A Lark on the Wing	Phyliss Hamilton	$9.95
A Love of Her Own	Cheris F. Hodges	$9.95
A Love to Cherish	Beverly Clark	$8.95
A Risk of Rain	Dar Tomlinson	$8.95
A Taste of Temptation	Reneé Alexis	$9.95
A Twist of Fate	Beverly Clark	$8.95
A Will to Love	Angie Daniels	$9.95
Acquisitions	Kimberley White	$8.95
Across	Carol Payne	$12.95
After the Vows	Leslie Esdaile	$10.95
(Summer Anthology)	T.T. Henderson	
	Jacqueline Thomas	
Again My Love	Kayla Perrin	$10.95
Against the Wind	Gwynne Forster	$8.95
All I Ask	Barbara Keaton	$8.95
Always You	Crystal Hubbard	$6.99
Ambrosia	T.T. Henderson	$8.95
An Unfinished Love Affair	Barbara Keaton	$8.95
And Then Came You	Dorothy Elizabeth Love	$8.95
Angel's Paradise	Janice Angelique	$9.95
At Last	Lisa G. Riley	$8.95
Best of Friends	Natalie Dunbar	$8.95
Beyond the Rapture	Beverly Clark	$9.95
Blaze	Barbara Keaton	$9.95
Blood Lust	J. M. Jeffries	$9.95
Blood Seduction	J.M. Jeffries	$9.95

Other Genesis Press, Inc. Titles (continued)

Bodyguard	Andrea Jackson	$9.95
Boss of Me	Diana Nyad	$8.95
Bound by Love	Beverly Clark	$8.95
Breeze	Robin Hampton Allen	$10.95
Broken	Dar Tomlinson	$24.95
By Design	Barbara Keaton	$8.95
Cajun Heat	Charlene Berry	$8.95
Careless Whispers	Rochelle Alers	$8.95
Cats & Other Tales	Marilyn Wagner	$8.95
Caught in a Trap	Andre Michelle	$8.95
Caught Up In the Rapture	Lisa G. Riley	$9.95
Cautious Heart	Cheris F Hodges	$8.95
Chances	Pamela Leigh Starr	$8.95
Cherish the Flame	Beverly Clark	$8.95
Class Reunion	Irma Jenkins/	
	John Brown	$12.95
Code Name: Diva	J.M. Jeffries	$9.95
Conquering Dr. Wexler's Heart	Kimberley White	$9.95
Corporate Seduction	A.C. Arthur	$9.95
Crossing Paths, Tempting Memories	Dorothy Elizabeth Love	$9.95
Crush	Crystal Hubbard	$9.95
Cypress Whisperings	Phyllis Hamilton	$8.95
Dark Embrace	Crystal Wilson Harris	$8.95
Dark Storm Rising	Chinelu Moore	$10.95
Daughter of the Wind	Joan Xian	$8.95
Deadly Sacrifice	Jack Kean	$22.95
Designer Passion	Dar Tomlinson	$8.95
	Diana Richeaux	
Do Over	Celya Bowers	$9.95
Dreamtective	Liz Swados	$5.95

Other Genesis Press, Inc. Titles (continued)

Ebony Angel	Deatri King-Bey	$9.95
Ebony Butterfly II	Delilah Dawson	$14.95
Echoes of Yesterday	Beverly Clark	$9.95
Eden's Garden	Elizabeth Rose	$8.95
Eve's Prescription	Edwina Martin Arnold	$8.95
Everlastin' Love	Gay G. Gunn	$8.95
Everlasting Moments	Dorothy Elizabeth Love	$8.95
Everything and More	Sinclair Lebeau	$8.95
Everything but Love	Natalie Dunbar	$8.95
Falling	Natalie Dunbar	$9.95
Fate	Pamela Leigh Starr	$8.95
Finding Isabella	A.J. Garrotto	$8.95
Forbidden Quest	Dar Tomlinson	$10.95
Forever Love	Wanda Y. Thomas	$8.95
From the Ashes	Kathleen Suzanne	$8.95
	Jeanne Sumerix	
Gentle Yearning	Rochelle Alers	$10.95
Glory of Love	Sinclair LeBeau	$10.95
Go Gentle into that Good Night	Malcom Boyd	$12.95
Goldengroove	Mary Beth Craft	$16.95
Groove, Bang, and Jive	Steve Cannon	$8.99
Hand in Glove	Andrea Jackson	$9.95
Hard to Love	Kimberley White	$9.95
Hart & Soul	Angie Daniels	$8.95
Heart of the Phoenix	A.C. Arthur	$9.95
Heartbeat	Stephanie Bedwell-Grime	$8.95
Hearts Remember	M. Loui Quezada	$8.95
Hidden Memories	Robin Allen	$10.95
Higher Ground	Leah Latimer	$19.95
Hitler, the War, and the Pope	Ronald Rychiak	$26.95
How to Write a Romance	Kathryn Falk	$18.95

Other Genesis Press, Inc. Titles (continued)

I Married a Reclining Chair	Lisa M. Fuhs	$8.95
I'll Be Your Shelter	Giselle Carmichael	$8.95
I'll Paint a Sun	A.J. Garrotto	$9.95
Icie	Pamela Leigh Starr	$8.95
Illusions	Pamela Leigh Starr	$8.95
Indigo After Dark Vol. I	Nia Dixon/Angelique	$10.95
Indigo After Dark Vol. II	Dolores Bundy/ Cole Riley	$10.95
Indigo After Dark Vol. III	Montana Blue/ Coco Morena	$10.95
Indigo After Dark Vol. IV	Cassandra Colt/	$14.95
Indigo After Dark Vol. V	Delilah Dawson	$14.95
Indiscretions	Donna Hill	$8.95
Intentional Mistakes	Michele Sudler	$9.95
Interlude	Donna Hill	$8.95
Intimate Intentions	Angie Daniels	$8.95
It's Not Over Yet	J.J. Michael	$9.95
Jolie's Surrender	Edwina Martin-Arnold	$8.95
Kiss or Keep	Debra Phillips	$8.95
Lace	Giselle Carmichael	$9.95
Last Train to Memphis	Elsa Cook	$12.95
Lasting Valor	Ken Olsen	$24.95
Let Us Prey	Hunter Lundy	$25.95
Lies Too Long	Pamela Ridley	$13.95
Life Is Never As It Seems	J.J. Michael	$12.95
Lighter Shade of Brown	Vicki Andrews	$8.95
Love Always	Mildred E. Riley	$10.95
Love Doesn't Come Easy	Charlyne Dickerson	$8.95
Love Unveiled	Gloria Greene	$10.95
Love's Deception	Charlene Berry	$10.95
Love's Destiny	M. Loui Quezada	$8.95
Mae's Promise	Melody Walcott	$8.95

Other Genesis Press, Inc. Titles (continued)

Magnolia Sunset	Giselle Carmichael	$8.95
Many Shades of Gray	Dyanne Davis	$6.99
Matters of Life and Death	Lesego Malepe, Ph.D.	$15.95
Meant to Be	Jeanne Sumerix	$8.95
Midnight Clear	Leslie Esdaile	$10.95
(Anthology)	Gwynne Forster	
	Carmen Green	
	Monica Jackson	
Midnight Magic	Gwynne Forster	$8.95
Midnight Peril	Vicki Andrews	$10.95
Misconceptions	Pamela Leigh Starr	$9.95
Montgomery's Children	Richard Perry	$14.95
My Buffalo Soldier	Barbara B. K. Reeves	$8.95
Naked Soul	Gwynne Forster	$8.95
Next to Last Chance	Louisa Dixon	$24.95
No Apologies	Seressia Glass	$8.95
No Commitment Required	Seressia Glass	$8.95
No Regrets	Mildred E. Riley	$8.95
Not His Type	Chamein Canton	$6.99
Nowhere to Run	Gay G. Gunn	$10.95
O Bed! O Breakfast!	Rob Kuehnle	$14.95
Object of His Desire	A. C. Arthur	$8.95
Office Policy	A. C. Arthur	$9.95
Once in a Blue Moon	Dorianne Cole	$9.95
One Day at a Time	Bella McFarland	$8.95
One in A Million	Barbara Keaton	$6.99
One of These Days	Michele Sudler	$9.95
Outside Chance	Louisa Dixon	$24.95
Passion	T.T. Henderson	$10.95
Passion's Blood	Cherif Fortin	$22.95
Passion's Journey	Wanda Y. Thomas	$8.95
Past Promises	Jahmel West	$8.95

Other Genesis Press, Inc. Titles (continued)

Other Genesis Press, Inc. Titles (continued)

Soul to Soul	Donna Hill	$8.95
Southern Comfort	J.M. Jeffries	$8.95
Still the Storm	Sharon Robinson	$8.95
Still Waters Run Deep	Leslie Esdaile	$8.95
Stolen Kisses	Dominiqua Douglas	$9.95
Stories to Excite You	Anna Forrest/Divine	$14.95
Subtle Secrets	Wanda Y. Thomas	$8.95
Suddenly You	Crystal Hubbard	$9.95
Sweet Repercussions	Kimberley White	$9.95
Sweet Sensations	Gwendolyn Bolton	$9.95
Sweet Tomorrows	Kimberly White	$8.95
Taken by You	Dorothy Elizabeth Love	$9.95
Tattooed Tears	T. T. Henderson	$8.95
The Color Line	Lizzette Grayson Carter	$9.95
The Color of Trouble	Dyanne Davis	$8.95
The Disappearance of Allison Jones	Kayla Perrin	$5.95
The Fires Within	Beverly Clark	$9.95
The Foursome	Celya Bowers	$6.99
The Honey Dipper's Legacy	Pannell-Allen	$14.95
The Joker's Love Tune	Sidney Rickman	$15.95
The Little Pretender	Barbara Cartland	$10.95
The Love We Had	Natalie Dunbar	$8.95
The Man Who Could Fly	Bob & Milana Beamon	$18.95
The Missing Link	Charlyne Dickerson	$8.95
The Mission	Pamela Leigh Starr	$6.99
The Perfect Frame	Beverly Clark	$9.95
The Price of Love	Sinclair LeBeau	$8.95
The Smoking Life	Ilene Barth	$29.95
The Words of the Pitcher	Kei Swanson	$8.95
Three Wishes	Seressia Glass	$8.95
Ties That Bind	Kathleen Suzanne	$8.95

Other Genesis Press, Inc. Titles (continued)

Tiger Woods	Libby Hughes	$5.95
Time is of the Essence	Angie Daniels	$9.95
Timeless Devotion	Bella McFarland	$9.95
Tomorrow's Promise	Leslie Esdaile	$8.95
Truly Inseparable	Wanda Y. Thomas	$8.95
Two Sides to Every Story	Dyanne Davis	$9.95
Unbreak My Heart	Dar Tomlinson	$8.95
Uncommon Prayer	Kenneth Swanson	$9.95
Unconditional Love	Alicia Wiggins	$8.95
Unconditional	A.C. Arthur	$9.95
Until Death Do Us Part	Susan Paul	$8.95
Vows of Passion	Bella McFarland	$9.95
Wedding Gown	Dyanne Davis	$8.95
What's Under Benjamin's Bed	Sandra Schaffer	$8.95
When Dreams Float	Dorothy Elizabeth Love	$8.95
When I'm With You	LaConnie Taylor-Jones	$6.99
Whispers in the Night	Dorothy Elizabeth Love	$8.95
Whispers in the Sand	LaFlorya Gauthier	$10.95
Who's That Lady?	Andrea Jackson	$9.95
Wild Ravens	Altonya Washington	$9.95
Yesterday Is Gone	Beverly Clark	$10.95
Yesterday's Dreams, Tomorrow's Promises	Reon Laudat	$8.95
Your Precious Love	Sinclair LeBeau	$8.95